FRAMED

D0949101

OTHER BOOKS AND AUDIOBOOKS
BY CLAIR M. POULSON

I'll Find You
Relentless
Lost and Found
Conflict of Interest
Runaway
Coverup
Mirror Image
Blind Side
Evidence
Don't Cry Wolf
Dead Wrong
Deadline
Vengeance
Hunted
Switchback
Accidental Private Eye
Checking Out
In Plain Sight
Falling
Murder at TopHouse
Portrait of Lies
Silent Sting
Outlawered
Deadly Inheritance
The Search
Suspect
Short Investigations
Watch Your Back
Fool's Deadly Gold
Pitfall

FRAMED

A NOVEL

CLAIR M. POULSON

Covenant Communications, Inc.

Cover image *Confidential File* @ DNY59, iStockphotography.com

Cover design copyright © 2013 by Covenant Communications, Inc.

Published by Covenant Communications, Inc.
American Fork, Utah

Printed in the United States of America
First Printing: April 2013

14 13 12 11 10 9 8 7 6 5

ISBN: 978-1-62108-159-3

To Clay Yardley, who gave me the
idea and basic plot for this book.

CHAPTER ONE

A BEE WAS BUZZING AROUND Jerzy's head. The car swerved as he swatted at the bee, prompting the driver of an oncoming car to honk and shake a fist as he passed by. Jerzy muttered under his breath and drove on. The bee buzzed behind him for a moment, and then suddenly it attacked, stinging him right on the top of his bald head. The car hit the curb, and the front right tire exploded. He angrily pulled to a stop near the curb.

Gingerly rubbing his sore head, Jerzy looked around for the bee. He spotted it on the floor mat and angrily used his heel to merge the bee with the mat. With the bee dead, he got out of the car, walked around to the front, and surveyed the damage through his thick, gold-rimmed glasses. It looked to him like the curb had not only broken the seal between the tire and the rim, causing the tire to lose its air, but it had also bent the rim. It left him unable to drive anywhere until the spare was installed. He stared at it a moment longer and concluded that he was too close to the curb to change it, so he got back in the car, moved it forward a few feet, shifted into park, and got out. The sun was shining brightly and it was quite warm already. He glanced at his watch. It was almost ten o'clock in the morning.

Once again, he peered down at the damaged wheel over the end of his large, crooked nose and shook his shiny head. With the car now far enough removed from the offending curb to jack it up and change the tire, he unhappily set about that disagreeable activity.

Jerzy Grabowski was not fond of physical labor, and it had been many years since he'd changed a tire. Way too heavy for his five-foot-eight height, he was pudgy and soft. He prided himself on using his brains rather than his muscles for a living. Those brains, however, were not a lot of help right now. He wasn't even sure where to find the jack and lug wrench and no amount of thinking helped. He had to resort to looking. He finally succeeded in finding them.

His car, a light blue Buick, was of almost antique vintage, but it ran well and served his purposes just fine. He dragged out his jack. He was still trying to figure out where to put it in order to lift the front right end of the car when a snappy-looking red sports car, of some make he couldn't immediately identify, stopped across the street from him.

A pretty young woman in blue jeans and a light green blouse got out and started across the street toward him. "Hi," she greeted him with a bright smile. "Do you need some help?"

Was his blundering attempt at changing a tire that obvious? he wondered as he stared at the vision of loveliness that had stopped next to him. It was embarrassing to have a young lady offer to help him but not enough to cause him to turn down the offer. "I'm Adriana Chambers," she said with an air of confidence as she took the jack from Jerzy and expertly placed it beneath the frame.

"I'm Jerzy Grabowski," he said. "I appreciate the help."

"No problem," she replied, flashing him another bright smile. She knelt down to examine the tire and discovered that she had no way to get the old fashioned hubcap off. "Do you have a screwdriver?" she asked.

"I don't know," Jerzy said, feeling quite helpless. Together they looked in the trunk, and then Jerzy checked both the back and front seat areas of the car while Adriana watched. "Sorry, I don't," he said, looking sheepishly at the young woman.

"I know I don't have one in my car," she said with a frown, "but I have one at home. I just live a few blocks from here. I'll go get it and be right back."

"Thanks," he said as he watched her stride gracefully across the street to her sporty little car.

She hadn't been gone but a minute or so when a tall, thin fellow walked up to him on the sidewalk. He was carrying a briefcase and was dressed in a sports jacket and slacks. "It looks like you need my help," he said with a slight drawl. "What are you looking for?"

"I need something to get the hubcap off with," Jerzy said.

"Will this do?" the other fellow asked, popping open his briefcase and shuffling about for a moment before pulling a large flathead screwdriver from it.

When Jerzy nodded, the man handed it over and Jerzy popped off the hubcap. Together, they had the tire changed and the flat one back in the trunk with the jack before Miss Chambers had returned.

After a brief conversation, the two men got in Jerzy's old Buick. Jerzy rubbed his sore head and then said, "Where to?"

***

The brake lights of the old blue Buick came on briefly, then it turned right and disappeared down the street. It looked like there was someone in the passenger side of the car. Puzzled, Adriana shook her head. It had taken her a little while to find the screwdriver, then her mother had called and she'd had to run back in the house to find the address of a client her mother was supposed to be showing a house to at noon.

Adriana's mother was a wonderful woman and a very successful real estate agent. In fact, she owned her own agency, but since the devastating divorce from her husband a few months ago, she was absentminded at times. The divorce had caught her mother by surprise, and her father's unexpected and unexplained anger had taken an appalling emotional toll on mother and daughter. It had also hurt Adriana terribly, but she had moved home from her apartment at her mother's request to give her support. Neither of them could figure out what had come over Adriana's father. He had suddenly become a bitter stranger to both of them.

It had taken her three or four minutes to find the slip of paper her mother had written the address on. And it had taken another minute to call her back and give her the information. But it still hadn't been that long since she'd left the man with the flat tire. Oh, well. She guessed that Mr. Grabowski must have gotten the hubcap off and finished the job by himself, or maybe whoever was in the car with him—it sure looked like someone was in it—had come along on foot and somehow helped him get the hubcap off.

She shrugged and drove on, thinking about the homely man she'd stopped to help. He had such a strange name that she remembered it quite well. Jerzy Grabowski had not been more than two inches taller than her, and he was sort of flabby. The hair that rimmed his shiny bald pate was brown and quite long. She wondered what had caused the painful-looking red spot on the top of his head. She also had been left with the feeling that without the thick, gold-rimmed glasses, ones that made his brown eyes appear abnormally large, he would be unable to see much beyond the end of that large, crooked nose.

Adriana smiled to herself and then promptly put the strange man from her mind. Three blocks later, a police car, moving very fast, lights flashing, passed her going the way she had just come from. She looked in her rearview mirror and then glanced once more before it disappeared. This was an affluent neighborhood, and cops didn't often appear in it at such speeds with lights flashing like that. She hoped that there hadn't been a bad accident of some kind.

She dismissed the thought and found herself thinking about someone she was trying very hard to forget. Drew had given her the hurtful word just a couple nights ago after dating her steadily for so long. He was the reason she could so easily change a tire and perform other basic mechanical tasks. He'd not only taught her, but he'd also talked her into taking an auto mechanics class with him. They had a lot of other interests in common as well. It had never occurred to her, after all they'd done together, that he would so abruptly break up with her.

She had fought back tears as he told her that he wasn't going to be calling her again and he would appreciate it if she wouldn't call him. They were not right for each other, he'd further explained, baffling her. But that had been that—the breakup announced without preamble or even any evident regret. She'd cried herself to sleep two nights in a row wondering what was wrong with her. Was she not pretty enough? What was it? But she'd awoken this morning determined to get on with her life without dark, handsome Drew Parker. After all, if her mother could continue to function without her husband of twenty-two years, she could make it without her boyfriend of a year or so.

***

"I need you two to roll on this," Sergeant Lydia Tullock said urgently as she rushed up to a cubicle in the police department.

Brad Osborn looked up from his desk. "Do you mean me and Mike?" he asked.

"That's exactly who I mean, Detective. There's been a murder, and it's a high profile one," she said. "I'll come as soon as I can, but you two get up there and get started. A couple of uniformed officers are already on the scene. They've been told not to touch the body or anything else— just to seal off the murder scene."

Brad was already on his feet as the sergeant read out the address, but it was taking his partner a little longer. Everything always took Mike longer. Brad, the youngest detective on the force, felt the adrenaline flowing. This was the first homicide he'd been assigned to since being made a detective just a few weeks ago. "Come on, Mike," he said anxiously as their supervisor disappeared across the room.

"Calm down, kid," Mike said as he hoisted his bulk from his chair. "It's a murder. That means that the guy's already dead. He's not going anywhere." Mike then took a moment to pull his slacks up a little closer to his bulging belly, adjust his pistol in the shoulder holster beneath his right armpit, and shrug into a badly wrinkled and ill-fitting sports jacket.

Brad couldn't help but wonder why Mike didn't take better care of his body and of his general appearance. He believed that a police officer should be like his father, always spit shined, trim, and fit. From the time Brad came on the force, he'd tried to emulate that image, one he'd grown up with.

Mike finally followed him from the station, and with Brad behind the wheel, they headed for the scene of a murder. Brad knew the area, one where the rich and well-connected lived. Whoever had died in that part of the city had probably not died due to a drug deal gone bad or something similar. His gut twisted uncomfortably as he drove. He was determined not to mess up this high profile case in some way and in doing so tarnish the name of his retired father and the reputation of the department.

A second set of uniformed officers pulled up just ahead of Mike and Brad. A small crowd had already formed along the walk in front of the house, a sprawling two-story affair with a huge, perfectly manicured yard. Tan brick and brownstone framed the large front door. Brad got out of the car and waited while his partner did the same. Then together, they started up the walk, instructing the crowd to stand back.

At the door, Mike said to one of the officers standing there, "Would you mind taking the names, phone numbers, and addresses of anyone in that bunch back there who might have witnessed something? You never know. Someone might have observed something that would be helpful to us."

The officer nodded and moved toward the crowd as Brad and Mike stepped inside a large lobby with a gleaming hardwood floor. Brad glanced at the walls. The paintings hanging there were not copies, he saw at a glance; they were very good originals. A uniformed officer stepped outside of a room about twenty feet from the door. "The body is in here," he announced. "The victim is definitely dead."

Brad recognized the officer as Sergeant Deon Golen, a veteran officer that he'd worked with some as a rookie patrolman. Deon was about fifty, of medium height and build. He was well respected in the department, but unlike Mike, he had never desired to move from the ranks of the patrol division. Brad and Mike followed him into the room he'd indicated. The deceased lay on his back; blood pooled around him on the thick white carpet. His chest was also saturated with blood. At first blush, Brad thought the victim had been shot, as there was a single wound right over the area of the heart.

The detectives stood just inside the doorway for a moment. Brad surveyed the room. It was clearly a home office; a large oak desk was positioned toward the back of the room beyond the body. Behind the desk was a wall filled with books, many of them recognizable as law books. There were also a couple of file cabinets, not the normal metal variety but large oak ones, matching the desk. There were more original paintings on the walls. The desk had some papers scattered about the surface. A book lay open on one side, and beside it was a legal pad and pen. A pair of glasses lay on the pad.

"Who found him?" Mike asked.

"His wife and a neighbor lady," Sergeant Golen said. "They're upstairs in the bedroom. The wife is very distraught, as you can understand."

"Was she here when this happened?" Mike asked, swinging one hand in the direction of the dead man.

"No, she was at the neighbor's house, the same woman who is with her now," Deon responded. "But I think she must have come home shortly after it happened."

"Has anyone touched anything?" Mike asked.

"I checked for a pulse when I first got here," the sergeant responded. "There was none. His wife and the neighbor, who came in with her, also touched him. His wife says his wallet is missing."

"How does she know that?" Mike asked, a puzzled look on his face. "Did she check his pockets?"

"No, but she says he usually has it sitting on the edge of his desk where he can slip it into his pocket when he leaves the office. It's not there, as you can see."

"But it could already be in his pocket," Mike reasoned. "He may have been leaving when the killer came in."

"I don't think so," Deon said. "His wife told me that he wasn't going out today at all, that he was working here in his office."

"Who is the victim?" Mike asked.

Brad had been studying the pasty face on the floor in front of him. He knew the guy.

"Do you recognize him?" Sergeant Golan asked.

"Garrick Lenhardt," Brad said softly.

"Counsel for the defense," Mike added with a touch of bitterness as he too recognized the decedent. Garrick Lenhardt was not much loved by police officers. He was one of the most successful and ruthless defense attorneys in the entire state. Brad had only been cross-examined by him one time. Lenhardt had been very hard on him. But it had been a learning experience for Brad. After Lenhardt had torn him apart and humiliated him on the stand, Brad had come away from the experience determined to never be anything less than fully prepared when he was called to testify.

"I guess I won't have to endure any more cross-examinations by him," Mike said. He stared a moment longer at the victim, and then, all business, he turned to Brad. "Let's make sure that everyone knows that his wallet is missing. The killer, whoever it is, probably has it."

Brad pulled out his phone and made a call. The cops in the city didn't care for Lenhardt, but Brad knew that wouldn't stop him or anyone else from doing whatever they could to bring his killer to justice. At least that killer, whoever it turned out to be, wouldn't be able to hire Garrick Lenhardt to defend him, he thought wryly.

As soon as he'd completed his call, Brad turned to help Mike begin the laborious, meticulous task of investigating the murder of one of the best known attorneys in the state. Elsewhere, officers were checking every car they stopped. It would be a huge accomplishment to be the officer that found the wallet of the infamous lawyer and even more of an accomplishment to arrest his killer.

***

"Pull in here," the tall, thin man said, waving toward a 7-11 up ahead. "I need to go to the restroom."

Jerzy shrugged. "Don't be long, then," he said after pulling into the parking area and coming to a stop.

"Don't worry. I'll hustle. Do you want a drink?" his passenger asked.

"Yeah, a cold Pepsi," Jerzy said, closing his eyes and rubbing his head. The bee sting was hurting something awful. He wondered if he was allergic to the sting. He feared that he might get quite ill. He quietly cursed the bee.

The tall, thin man got out of the car, opened the back door for a moment, then it slammed, and Jerzy heard him walk away. Jerzy waited impatiently, wondering if he needed a doctor. After a few minutes, he began to squirm even though the sting didn't seem quite as bad. Maybe he wouldn't need a doctor after all. He was tired of sitting here in the hot car. His armpits were soaked, and sweat drained down his face. He couldn't imagine what was taking his passenger so long. He didn't want to just drive off and leave him, but he didn't want to sit here in the hot afternoon sun much longer either. It was getting almost unbearable.

He waited five more minutes, and then he got out of his car and walked into the 7-11. Once inside, he glanced around, expecting to see the tall, thin man shopping for goodies. But he couldn't see him at all. He cursed under his breath, then went over to one of the coolers, opened the door, and selected a large Pepsi. As he moved back toward the checkout stand, he stopped and picked up a bag of cookies. Feeling hungry, he decided to add a small pie and a bag of chips. When he came up to the check stand, his arms were full. He carefully put everything down and waited impatiently for the cashier to ring up his purchases.

He kept glancing in the direction of the restrooms, still expecting the tall, thin man to come out. After he'd pulled out his billfold and paid for his goodies and she was putting the stuff in a bag, he asked her, "Did you see the tall, skinny guy that came in here a few minutes ago?"

"Can't remember," the plump, middle-aged woman said.

He noticed a name tag on her shirt. "He's with me, Sue," he said, trying to sound friendly. "He's been awhile. He's tall and thin. Did I miss him when he went out?"

"I don't know. I don't remember seeing him. He didn't pay for nothing, I know that. I've been busy, and unless he bought something, I wouldn't have paid any attention," she said. Jerzy picked up his sack and turned away. But after taking only a single step toward the door, he turned back. "You're sure?"

"I'm not lying to you, mister," she said with a scowl.

"Okay," he responded, very puzzled.

He stepped out of the door and nearly dropped his sack when he saw a police car parked behind the old blue Buick. He stood for a moment, watching the cops as they approached his car and glanced inside it. Jerzy looked back, still hoping to see the tall, thin man. But the guy still hadn't reappeared. Finally, with his gut rolling—cops always made his gut roll—he strolled toward his car.

Both officers looked toward him and watched alertly as he approached the Buick. "Good morning, gentlemen," Jerzy said, trying to act nonchalant. "What's happening?"

"Is this your car?" the older of the officers asked.

"Sure is," he said. "It's getting old but it still runs good." He couldn't imagine why they were interested in his car.

"Do you mind if we have a look in the car?" the officer asked.

Jerzy hesitated, bringing sharp looks from both of the officers. "Yeah, sure, go ahead," he said. "I've not got much in there. What are you looking for?"

"You do it, Neal," the older officer said to the younger one.

Without a word, Neal pulled some clear latex gloves from his pocket and pulled them on. Then he opened the back, driver's-side door of the Buick and began rustling around. The first officer simply stood and watched Jerzy. Nervously, Jerzy rubbed his shiny head, wincing when his hand irritated the bee sting again. "Bump your head?" the officer asked. "It looks kind of sore."

"A bee stung me," Jerzy explained as he once again glanced back at the store. The tall, thin man seemed to have disappeared into thin air.

"Are you looking for someone?" the officer asked with narrowed eyes.

"No, just looking around," Jerzy said, becoming increasingly nervous. He unconsciously began shifting from foot to foot.

"Is there something you'd like to show us in your car?" the officer asked, advancing a step toward Jerzy.

Jerzy certainly couldn't think of anything. He just wanted to get in the car and leave—without the tall, thin man. But the officers seemed to be in no hurry at all. Neal, the younger officer, moved to the far side of the car. Again he stirred stuff around on the backseat. "Do you have some ID on you?" the older officer asked.

Jerzy pulled out his wallet and dug until he found his driver's license. After handing it to the officer, he rubbed the sweat from his face. The officer studied the license for a moment, and then he said, "What's your name?"

"It says it there," Jerzy responded irritably.

The officer's eyes narrowed. He said nothing. "Jerzy Grabowski," Jerzy finally said as sweat again formed on his face.

"Here, put this back in your wallet," the officer said as he held the license out to Jerzy.

As Jerzy took it, Neal called out to his partner, "Hey, Glen, you better come take a look here."

"Stay where you are," the officer named Glen said to Jerzy, and then he moved around the far side of the car. Jerzy began to feel slightly faint.

The officers spoke in hushed tones, and then Neal, the younger officer, moved back to the patrol car and slipped in behind the steering wheel. He spoke for a moment on his radio, and then he made a call on a cell phone. Glen, the older officer, moved back around the car and stepped over to Jerzy. "What were you using the screwdriver for?" he asked as he held it up with a gloved hand. Jerzy hadn't seen him put gloves on, but he had them now. That increased his nervousness.

"I had a flat tire," Jerzy said in a strained voice, his throat seeming to constrict. "I used it to get the hubcap off. I guess I forgot to put it in the trunk. Maybe I'll do that now."

He reached a fat hand for the screwdriver, but Glen pulled it back, shaking his head. "Was the hubcap bleeding?" the officer asked.

Jerzy shook his head. That was a stupid question. "'Course not," he said, his voice getting raspier each time he spoke. "Here, let me have it and I'll put it in the trunk." As he spoke, he took another step forward.

The officer held up the hand that was not holding the screwdriver and said, "Stay where you are, Mr. Grabowski," in a commanding voice.

Jerzy did what he was told. His stomach was really starting to roll now. He again glanced toward the convenience store entrance. "You said you weren't looking for anyone," Glen said mildly.

"I'm not," he said. "But I need to be going. What are you guys after, anyway?"

Before he could answer, Neal called out to Glen, "Come here a minute."

"Stay put, if you don't mind," Glen said and stepped back to the patrol car. The two of them conversed quietly for a moment, too softly for Jerzy to hear what they were saying. Finally, Glen stepped back to Jerzy and said, "Mr. Grabowski, you are under arrest."

"For what?" Jerzy croaked.

"Murder," the officer said and proceeded to read Jerzy his rights.

Jerzy found his voice again and protested loudly, "I didn't kill nobody. I don't know what you're talking about."

"We'll take care of your car," Glen said. "My partner is calling for a tow truck right now. As soon as it gets here, we'll take you down to the station with us."

It was all Jerzy could do to keep from throwing up. He couldn't imagine why they would be accusing him of murder. He'd never killed anyone in his life. He wasn't that kind of guy.

CHAPTER TWO

SERGEANT LYDIA TULLOCK ENTERED THE large front door of the spacious, expensive home of Garrick Lenhardt. Brad and Mike were conferring in the large entranceway. "Hey guys," she said. "Your suspect is in custody."

Mike grinned at her. "Boy, we got a break on this one," he said. "I can't believe the old boy was killed with a screwdriver."

"Watch what you say, Detective Silverman," Lydia said darkly. "We are in the victim's home, you know. And unless you failed to tell me that she left, his wife is still here somewhere."

"She's upstairs," Mike said, his face going red. "Her daughter is with her now. We let the neighbor leave. We'll get her full statement later."

Brad had been watching Lydia. She was an attractive woman in her midthirties. Her full figure nicely filled out the dark blue pantsuit she was wearing. She could be really pleasant at times, but she could also be nothing but business. This was apparently one of the latter times. She touched her perfectly combed short blonde hair as she turned her stern blue eyes on Brad. "The guys from the lab are with the body?" she asked.

"Yes, would you like to see the scene of the murder?" he asked in return.

She nodded and followed him. Mike stayed behind. Even though he was much older than the sergeant, she intimidated him. "If you don't need me," he called after them, "I'll go outside and see how things are going there."

Lydia turned and looked at him. "What's supposed to be happening out there?" she asked sharply.

"I asked the uniformed guys to get the identity of any witnesses," he said.

She nodded. "Good. Detective Osborn and I will check with the lab folks."

She only briefly looked at the body of the attorney, a man she had tangled with many times in her career. But her face showed nothing. She asked about the wound and was told that it could have been caused by a screwdriver, that it most certainly was not a gunshot wound.

Back in the hallway, a moment later, Brad said, "I understand the screwdriver that Officers Kellin and Warf found has traces of blood on it."

"That's what they reported to me on the phone as I was coming up. And as you know, they also found the wallet of Mr. Lenhardt on the backseat. It was lying beside a fedora hat and a small suitcase. The man they arrested claimed the hat and the suitcase. I'd like you and Mike to get down there and question the guy," she said. "He is proclaiming his innocence. But that's to be expected. I'd like you to see what you can get from him."

"I haven't had a chance to interview Mrs. Lenhardt yet," Brad said.

"I'll take care of that," Sergeant Tullock said. "And I have a couple more detectives coming here shortly. I'll have them canvas the neighborhood. Let's see if Mike and the officers have that list of people for us. Then the two of you can get down to the station. The chief and the mayor would both love to see us wrap this case up quickly. The entire defense bar will be all over them if we don't."

***

Krista Chambers walked with her daughter to the front door of the realty office. "Thanks for bringing those papers for me," she said. "Ever since your father abandoned us, I feel like I'm only about half here. I've got to get things together again, or this business will begin to slip, and I can't afford that. As it is, it will be hard to keep the house without your dad's income."

Adriana put an arm around her mother's shoulders and said, "It will all work out, Mom. Don't worry. The Lord will watch out for us."

As she was speaking, the phone began ringing. Krista's secretary poked her head out of her office and announced to Krista that there was a call for her. "I better go," Adriana said. "I'll see you at home tonight. And remember, it's my turn to fix dinner."

"You are such a dear," her mother said as she turned to reenter her office.

Adriana had barely started her car when she saw her mother running frantically from the realty building. Adriana rolled down her window as Krista ran up, her face gray and her hands shaking. "That was Zoe," she said, referring to one of their neighbors. "She called to tell me that Mr. Lenhardt has been killed."

"You mean Dad's friend—the attorney from up the street?" Adriana asked.

"Yes, he was murdered, stabbed to death right in his own house," Krista said, her voice breaking.

Adriana felt her knees begin to shake as she recalled the police car that had passed her earlier. "Murdered," she whispered faintly.

"That's what Zoe said. An officer came to the house to ask her if she had seen anything or anyone suspicious," Mrs. Chambers said. "And she told me that they want to talk to us. They want to talk to everyone in the neighborhood."

"Anyone or anything suspicious," Adriana said softly. The homely face of the man in the old Buick came to her mind. "It's probably nothing, but there was a guy I met near our place," she said when Krista looked at her inquiringly. "He had a flat tire. He looked like he needed help. I stopped to help him change his tire, but we couldn't get the hubcap off. He didn't have a screwdriver, so I went home to get one. That's what I was doing when you called. By the time I got back he was driving away. Someone else must have helped him."

"It's probably nothing," her mother said, laying a hand on Adriana's arm through the window of her bright red Jaguar XK, a present from her parents two years earlier.

"He was a strange man," Adriana said. "I can't imagine what he was doing in the area."

"Don't worry about it," her mother said. Her creased face gave away her own worry. "Just tell the police what you know when you see them. But be careful, honey. Whoever did this could still be in the area."

"Probably not," Adriana said as she continued to think about the guy with the strange name of Jerzy.

"This is just horrible. It's always been such a safe neighborhood," Krista said. "Why don't you come back inside? You can sit in on the meeting with my client. I would still like you to learn the business anyway."

"I'll be fine," Adriana said. "And you know I'll never make a good real-estate agent. That's your thing, not mine."

"Okay, honey, but be really watchful. And keep the house locked when you get home. I'll let myself in. And I'll try not to be too late."

Adriana watched her mother walk back to her building before steering her Jaguar out of the parking area. On a sudden impulse, she turned the opposite direction from what she'd planned. She knew where the police station was located. She thought she'd go there now and see if she could get her meeting with them over with before she went home. She had some studying to do and didn't want to be distracted by the thought of the police coming by to talk to her later.

**

Detectives Osborn and Silverman were taking turns questioning their suspect, Jerzy Grabowski. They were both frustrated with their lack of progress. The guy insisted that he was innocent, and even though he hadn't lawyered up yet, they were getting nowhere. Newly armed with some forensic evidence that had just come in from the guys at the lab, Brad entered the interrogation room to try once again.

He sat across a small wooden table from the suspect, started his small recorder again, and then sat and simply stared at the suspect for a moment. The man's gold-rimmed glasses had lenses so thick that they made his close-set brown eyes appear very large. The long brown hair that rimmed his shiny bald head added to a comic look that seemed to dominate his features. An unusually large nose didn't help his appearance. Neither did the large Band-Aid that covered the bee sting on the top of his shiny head.

Jerzy shifted his heavy body on the hard wooden chair, and perspiration covered his face and bald head. He pulled out a well-used, damp handkerchief and mopped at his head. "Do you need a drink of water?" Brad asked after continuing to watch the man squirm under his gaze. He didn't feel sorry for the guy—every indication was that he was a killer. But Brad was a humane person, and anyway, offering the man a drink of water might make him more comfortable and at ease, more willing to talk.

"Yeah, that would be great," Jerzy said.

Brad left the room and came back a moment later carrying a bottle of water, which he handed to the suspect. Jerzy opened it and took a large drink as Brad sat down across the table from him again. "Okay, let's go over some things one more time," Brad began. "First, you were in the neighborhood where the murder occurred, weren't you?"

"You guys seem to think I was," Jerzy said evasively. "I'm from out of state. I'm not familiar with the area, and I don't know where this so-called murder victim lived."

"But you did have a flat tire, and you told us where that happened," Brad reminded him.

"*About* where it happened," Jerzy corrected him.

Brad then said, "And you claim that a young woman stopped and offered to help you with the tire. That's unusual, isn't it? Isn't it usually men who stop to offer help to women?"

"Probably, but this girl was very capable. She didn't waste any time getting the jack under my car and jacking it up. I appreciated it. I'm clumsy about such things myself."

"I need to know some specific things about her," Brad said. "To begin with, did she tell you her name?"

"She did, but I don't remember it. It seems like it wasn't a real common name."

"In that case, I'll need to learn a few things about her. First, what was she driving?"

"It was a sports car, a bright red one," Jerzy answered. "She parked it right across the street from me."

"Did you notice the make?" Brad asked. Jerzy shook his head. "Did you happen to get the license number?"

"No, but I think it had Utah plates."

Brad then said, "Good. That helps. Was it a two- or four-door car?"

"I'm pretty sure it was only a two door. Really cute little car," Jerzy added.

"Okay, now, describe the young woman for me."

"She was a really good-looking girl," Jerzy said with a lopsided grin.

"I've got that," Brad said, smiling to himself. He didn't suppose that a guy like Jerzy had pretty girls pay much attention to him. "I'd like you to tell me more about her—you know, hair length and color, eye color, height, weight, clothing, and so on."

Jerzy was thoughtful for a moment. Finally he said, "Seems like she had long brown hair. It was very shiny. She kept flipping it out of her eyes as she worked." He stopped and thought again for a moment. "I don't know what color her eyes were, but they were nice." Brad waited. Jerzy went on. "Slender, nice figure."

Brad was beginning to think it would be nice to meet this girl. If nothing else, he thought, chuckling to himself, he might try faking a flat tire in that neighborhood. He brought himself back from his wandering thoughts. "How tall would you say she was?" he asked.

"I'm five eight," Jerzy said after a moment of scrunching his eyebrows. "She was probably a little shorter than me—maybe five six."

"Weight?"

"Perfect for her height," Jerzy said. "You ought to see her."

"I hope to," Brad said honestly, smiling at the suspect. "But I need more information about her. Can you describe what she was wearing?"

"Blue jeans and a green blouse," Jerzy responded. "She looked really good in them."

Brad shook his head. "I've got it that she's pretty. I'll be sure and not look for any homely girls when I attempt to locate her," he said. "Can you think of anything else about her that might help?"

"She had purple fingernails," Jerzy said with a chuckle. "That's all I can think of."

"Very good, Jerzy. Now, let's talk about your need for a screwdriver," Brad said, thinking about one of the most important pieces of evidence found in Jerzy's car.

"We couldn't find one in my car. I didn't have one, and she couldn't get the hubcap off," Jerzy explained. "She didn't have one either, so she said she'd go get one at her house."

"Meaning that she lived in that area," Brad said.

"Yeah, she said she lived just a little ways away. So I waited for her after she left," he said.

Brad was thoughtful for a moment. He and Mike had both disbelieved the story of the helpful young woman, but after Jerzy's description, Brad was inclined at this point to believe him. But he still didn't believe his story from that point on. It was time to go over that again.

"But someone else came along and offered to help?" Brad asked, trying to keep the disbelief he felt from coming through in his voice.

Jerzy mopped at his head again, took another sip of water, and shifted nervously on his chair. Brad kept his eyes on the suspect's face, leaning toward him, crowding him. Jerzy failed to meet his stern gaze. But he did say, "Yeah, a tall, thin guy, he come along and said it looked like I needed help."

"What did you say to him?" Brad asked.

"I said I needed a screwdriver. He said he had one in his briefcase."

"The briefcase that was not in your car when the officers checked it," Brad said flatly.

"Yeah, he had a briefcase. The screwdriver was in it. He used it to get the hubcap off, and then he put it back in," Jerzy said.

"Back in the briefcase?" Brad asked.

"I thought so, but I wasn't really watching him that close. I was trying to get the lug nuts loose. They were really tight," Jerzy said.

"So you didn't actually see him put the screwdriver in a briefcase?" Brad pressed him.

"Well, no, I guess not."

"What was the fellow's name?"

Once again, Jerzy mopped at his face, and his eyes shifted to the side. "He didn't mention his name," he responded.

"Had you ever seen him before?" Brad asked.

There was the slightest hesitation and then, "Don't think so."

"Describe him again," Brad said.

"Tall and thin," Jerzy said.

"Come on, you can do better than that," Brad said with a touch of anger. "You didn't have any trouble describing the girl. How old would you say he was? How tall? Eye and hair color. Help me here. If you saw him, you should remember something more."

Jerzy scrunched his eyebrows again and stared at the wall to his right. He seemed to be thinking, so Brad gave him time. Finally, without meeting Brad's eyes, the suspect said, "Over six feet tall. Black hair. I don't know his eye color."

"Think," Brad said. "If you want me to believe that this guy was the killer, like you said earlier, then you've got to first convince me that you even saw him, that you're not making him up."

Jerzy pushed his chair back from the little table and got to his feet. Brad also rose, watching the guy closely. Jerzy walked over to the wall, pressed his forehead against it, muttered something under his breath, and then turned back toward Brad, his face red and sweatier than ever. His eyes, magnified behind the thick lenses of his gold-rimmed glasses, were narrowed. He looked angry. Brad wasn't sure what to expect, so he braced himself.

But Jerzy just said, "Okay, now I remember."

"That's good, Mr. Grabowski. Why don't you sit down and tell me?" Brad asked, pointing at the wooden chair."

Jerzy took his seat, leaned his elbows on the table, rested his head in his plump, soft palms, and said, "His hair was quite short and neat—black, like I already told you. His eyes were gray, I think. He was wearing a suit, a dark gray one. He had a light gray shirt on and a blue tie with black spots. He looked like a salesman, one of them door-to-door kind.

He probably had pamphlets or some kind of samples or something like that in his briefcase."

"A salesman with a briefcase that contained a screwdriver but who had no car," Brad observed. Even though he had suddenly received a better description, he still figured that Jerzy had made it all up.

"That's right. He was walking," Jerzy said. He opened his mouth like he was about to say something else, but then he clamped it shut and stared at the wall again.

"Is there anything else you can tell me about him?" Brad asked. "You said something about gloves earlier."

"Yeah, he was wearing some thin black gloves."

He had to say that, Brad thought, if he had any chance at all of explaining what Brad had learned just before he came in for this session. The only prints that had been found were Jerzy's. And his prints had been on the wallet and the screwdriver, as well as the jack handle, the rim of the flat tire, the door handles, and so on. There had, however, been some other prints on the jack and the jack handle. If there was a Good Samaritan girl involved, and if she could be located, they could compare her prints to those on the jack.

"Oh, and I noticed that he had really long fingers," Jerzy said.

"But you don't know the man's name?" Brad asked.

"I told you I didn't!" Jerzy said angrily, pounding a plump fist on the little table, making it jump.

"Okay, then let's talk about what happened after the tire was changed. First, you never saw the girl again, is that right?"

"She didn't come back. I gave the tall, thin man a ride."

"Where were you taking him to?" Brad asked.

Again there was that hesitation that bothered Brad. "He said he needed a ride downtown was all. He said a partner had dropped him off, but he had finished early with whatever it was he was doing. He didn't give me any specific place though."

"Maybe the 7-11was close enough," Brad suggested.

"No, that's not downtown. You know that," Jerzy said, his brown eyes narrowed again behind the thick lenses. "He said he needed to go to the restroom and asked me to wait for him. That's why I stopped there."

"And you did wait, but he never came back out," Brad said, repeating what he'd been told in an earlier session.

"Yeah, that's what I said," Jerzy responded. He was looking angry again.

The door to the interview room opened. An officer poked his head in and informed Brad there was a potential witness here to talk to him. "Have Mike talk to him," he suggested, only to learn that it wasn't a *him* who was waiting and that Mike had gone home to get some lunch—he would be back shortly. "All right, get the witness's name and ask her to have a seat. I'll be just a few more minutes."

The officer left and Brad turned back to the suspect. "All right, Mr. Grabowski, let's talk about the wallet that was found in your car, the one with the name of the dead man on it. It has your fingerprints all over it. How do you explain that?"

"The thin man took it out of his briefcase when he was looking for the screwdriver," Jerzy said with confidence. "Like I told you, I thought he'd put it back in his briefcase. But he actually left the wallet on the front seat, on the passenger side. I knew it was his, so I picked it up and threw it in the backseat with his briefcase just before he got in the car with me. I told him not to forget it when he got out downtown," Jerzy explained. "When I stopped at the 7-11, he reached in the back for a minute. I thought he might have put it in the briefcase then. I heard him open it. But I guess he didn't put anything in it. Anyway, that's why my prints were on the wallet. He was wearing those thin black gloves. That's why his weren't." There was no hesitation as he told this little tale. Brad didn't believe a word of it.

"You didn't watch what he was doing in the backseat?" Brad asked.

"No, my head was hurting. I was afraid the bee sting was going to make me sick. And it was hurting really bad. I just sat there with my hands over my face, sort of resting," Jerzy said.

"So, you're telling me that the tall, thin man left the screwdriver and wallet but not his briefcase when he went into the 7-11," Brad said.

"He must have taken it in with him," Jerzy agreed, taking his glasses off and rubbing his eyes.

"But he left without the wallet or the screwdriver," Brad repeated as Jerzy replaced the glasses.

"I guess so. Like I told you, I didn't pay any attention when he got out of the car. That bee sting was hurting really bad, and I was hot. That old car of mine doesn't have any air-conditioning, and even though the windows were down, there wasn't much breeze. I was feeling awful. I told the guy to hurry."

"So other than apparently taking the briefcase, you don't know what the thin man did while he was messing in your backseat?"

"Yeah, that's what I told you already," Jerzy said impatiently. "He opened the back door. I thought he was putting the wallet back or maybe just putting it in his pocket. I knew he needed money when he went in because he asked if I wanted a drink and I told him to get me a Pepsi."

"Did you actually watch him walk into the 7-11?" Brad asked.

"I guess not, but that's where he was going. Like I told you, I wasn't feeling very well. I was resting my eyes."

Brad asked a few more questions, but he didn't learn anything new and finally said, "I guess that's all for now, Mr. Grabowski." He picked up his recorder, shut it off, and left the room. "You can put him back in the holding cell," he said to the officer standing outside the door. "I'm through with him for now."

CHAPTER THREE

By the time Brad had finished with the suspect it was well past lunch, and his stomach was growling. The fact that Mike had gone home for lunch irritated him, but it was not unusual. He asked where the witness was and was told that she was waiting in the lobby. "Send her to my cubicle," Brad said sharply and headed there himself.

He sat down at his desk and looked over his notes. He fingered the little recording device then put it in a desk drawer. Everything pointed to them having the right man, and yet he had been unable, so far, to get any kind of admission from the suspect. He'd hoped, in fact he'd even assumed, it would be easy when he talked to the guy earlier. He was disappointed that it hadn't turned out that way. Maybe it was his own inexperience that led to the failure, he thought gloomily.

He heard someone coming toward his cubicle and stood up. What he saw explained why Jerzy Grabowski had been so taken by the helpful young woman he'd described. What was filling Brad's eyes now was indeed a vision in tight blue jeans and a light green blouse, a vision with long brown hair and gorgeous hazel eyes—the color of the eyes had not been part of Jerzy's description. The rest was. The girl smiled, held out her hand, with long, light purple fingernails, and said, "I'm Adriana Chambers. You are Detective Osborn?"

Brad realized he hadn't been breathing, and he had to catch his breath before accepting the warm, smooth hand and saying, "Yes, I am."

"I didn't expect someone so young," she said with a smile that made him catch his breath again.

"Nor did I," he countered, and she laughed, seeming quite delighted.

Her laugh relaxed him a little, and he kicked his mind into gear, tore his eyes from her face, and said, "Why don't you sit down," gesturing to the chair between his and Mike's desks.

"Thank you," she said and very gracefully did as she was bidden.

Brad couldn't help himself. He'd never started an interview in such a strange way, but he looked into her hazel eyes and asked, "So, is it true that you change tires for men who don't seem to be able to do so themselves?"

The surprise that crossed Adriana's face answered his question even before she spoke. This was definitely the girl who had helped Jerzy Grabowski. She confirmed it when she asked, "Have you talked to a strange-looking guy named Jerzy?" she asked.

He nodded. "I have. He seems to have a hard time with the truth. But at least he wasn't lying about you," he said. "I think you and I have some things to talk about."

"When did you talk to him?" she asked, leaning toward Brad, the fragrance of her perfume doing nothing to ease the attraction he'd instantly felt toward this young woman, one who, he noted, was not wearing a wedding ring. He sure was glad that Mike had gone home for lunch. He looked forward to the next few minutes.

"I just finished interviewing him," he said. "Quite a guy, if I might say so."

"*Weird* is the word, but since you've talked to him I probably can't help you much," she said. "I only came in to make sure you guys knew about Jerzy—you know, that he'd been in the area where Mr. Lenhardt lives—I mean lived. Well, and I also came because a neighbor said the police wanted to talk to all of the people who live in the neighborhood."

"That's right. We'd have been knocking on your door at some point. But about Mr. Grabowski—you might be able to fill in a few details about your encounter with him," Brad suggested.

"I'd be glad to do that if it will help," she said. "Incidentally, why were you talking to him? Did he see something?"

"He is a suspect in the murder of Mr. Lenhardt," Brad told her.

Adriana gasped and her eyes grew wide. "You've got to be kidding," she said. "He is a strange-looking man, but he didn't seem like someone who would kill anyone, especially right in the middle of the day."

Brad smiled at her. "We've found over the years that not all murderers look the part. In fact, I don't think there is a look that can be made to fit a murderer. We do have some pretty strong evidence against him."

"Such as?" she asked.

"I'll get to that," he said. "Let me ask you a few things. First, what time did you stop to help Mr. Grabowski?"

"I didn't actually look at my watch, but it was around ten o'clock."

"That fits with what he told me," Brad said as he considered his next question. "Did you really change the tire for him?"

"I had planned to, and he seemed willing to let me. As it turned out, all I did was jack up the car and get his spare tire out of the trunk. But I couldn't get the hubcap off. It was an older model Buick that he was driving. I asked him for a screwdriver, but he couldn't find one. So I went home to get one for him."

"How is it that you know enough about how to change tires that you would feel comfortable helping a stranger?" Brad asked, hoping that it wasn't an improper question. But he did wonder.

She chuckled. "My boyfriend taught me to change tires and oil. And I took an auto mechanics class with him," she said.

A boyfriend. That figured. He nodded and then asked, "Did he actually look for a screwdriver?"

"Yes, we both looked in the trunk of his car, and then he looked in the back and front seat areas. He finally said he didn't have one, so I told him I'd go to my house and find one since I didn't have one in my car either. I live only a few blocks from where he had his flat."

"So you didn't actually look in the interior of the car for a screwdriver, just in the trunk?" he asked.

"I kind of glanced in, but I didn't look closely," she responded.

"So there could have been a screwdriver in there and you may not have seen it?"

"I suppose so," she said, scrunching her eyebrows. "But why would he have me go look for one if he had one? That wouldn't make sense."

"No it wouldn't," Brad agreed. "So you went home. Did you find one you could help him with?"

Adriana chuckled pleasantly. "Yes, but I was gone longer than I'd planned. My mother called me from her office and needed a favor. I ended up spending several minutes before I got back. He was leaving when I got there the second time. I guess he got it changed."

"You say he was leaving. Did you actually see him get in his car and drive off?"

"No. All I saw was his car a short distance ahead of me. He turned south and I kept going east."

"Was he alone?" Brad asked.

Adriana squinted thoughtfully and didn't answer for a moment. But finally she looked directly at Brad and said, "I thought it looked like there was someone in the passenger seat of the car."

"After you left him to go back to your house for a screwdriver, did you see anyone walking in the area?"

"No, I didn't see anyone," she said.

"Did you see any other cars in the area, someone else who might have stopped and helped him finish what you had started?"

"I might have passed a car or two near the house," she said. "But I definitely didn't see any cars in the block where he had been parked."

Brad thought for a moment before asking, "You think there might have been someone in the car with him?"

"It looked like it," she agreed.

"Are you positive?"

"Well, I guess not. But if there wasn't someone in there, then he'd stuck a hat on the headrest or maybe in the back window."

"Do you know what a fedora is?" he asked.

"Yes, it's a hat, kind of like you see gangsters wear in old movies," she said. "Was there one in the car?"

Brad nodded. "It was on the backseat, right by where the wallet was found, directly behind the front passenger seat. Could that have been what you saw?"

"I thought there was a person, but if the hat had been in the back window, it might have made it look like there was someone else in the car," she said thoughtfully. "But I don't remember seeing it when I was beside his car, and like I told you, I did sort of glance inside when we were looking for a screwdriver. You said it was on the seat, and maybe it was, but I didn't see it."

"That's where it was when the suspect was arrested. Maybe he put it in the back window after he finished changing the tire. And he might have moved it again when he stopped at the 7-11. Or it simply might have fallen onto the seat or something like that."

"Yeah, I guess," she said, shaking her head with uncertainty.

"Where do you think he got a screwdriver from?" Brad asked.

"I don't know if he got a screwdriver, but he must have found something to pry the hubcap off with. I couldn't get if off. The tire wrench was one of those four-way types: it didn't have a tapered end like standard issue lug wrenches do."

"And you didn't see a screwdriver in the car?"

"Like I told you, the only place I looked was in the trunk," she said, giving Brad an inquiring look. "You keep asking. Are you suggesting that there was one in his car?"

"Oh, there definitely was one. It was in the backseat on the floor behind the front passenger seat," Brad said. "Did he look there when you told him you needed one?"

"Yes," she said, nodding her head firmly. "He looked there; he even reached under the backseat and then under the front seat—at least it looked like he did. I didn't exactly follow him around the car while he searched. He also opened the jockey box. I know he did that."

"But you didn't look yourself?" Brad repeated.

"No. Except for in the trunk, I didn't look closely anywhere."

"So you can't say there wasn't a screwdriver in the car, in the backseat, or anyplace else that he looked?"

"No, I can't, but why would he tell me there wasn't one if there was? He seemed quite anxious to get the tire changed," Adriana said.

"Did you notice anything inside of the backseat of the car when you glanced in?" Brad asked.

"Like what?"

"Like anything. You tell me," Brad said.

Adriana flashed him one of her bright smiles. "I can't think of anything," she said. "I didn't see a hat, but it could have been there. Like I just told you, I really wasn't paying close attention to the inside of his car." She hesitated for a moment then said with a smile, "But I think there must have been something, something important like the screwdriver you say was there."

Brad decided to be more open with her about what they'd found. "There was a wallet on the backseat on the same side of the car where we found the screwdriver with blood on it. The wallet was right beside the fedora. There was a small suitcase on the other side."

Both of Adriana's hands flew up and her jaw dropped. "There was a bloody screwdriver?" she said in a shaky voice.

"Let's put it this way," Brad said slowly. "The screwdriver we found had some blood on it. It had been wiped off some, just not very thoroughly."

Adriana slowly shook her head, her long, wavy brown hair moving gracefully back and forth in front of her face. She wiped it away with a couple of swipes of her right hand. "He didn't want me to see the blood," she said thoughtfully. "That's why he said there wasn't a screwdriver."

Brad nodded. "That thought occurred to me."

"Whose wallet was back there? Surely it wasn't Garrick Lenhardt's," she said with a touch of fear in her eyes.

"It was Mr. Lenhardt's," Brad said and Adriana gave a faint mewing sound but said nothing. Brad went on. "Did Jerzy tell you what he was doing in the area?"

Adriana shook her head and again brushed those long, shiny locks back. "Had he just killed Mr. Lenhardt?" she asked without lifting her gaze from the surface of Brad's desk where it had settled a moment before.

"It's entirely possible," he said.

Adriana shivered visibly. "He might have killed me, too," she said, slowly moving her eyes upward until they met Brad's. "He didn't look dangerous, and he didn't act nervous," she said after a moment of looking into Brad's eyes. "He just seemed upset that he'd ruined his rim and flattened his tire. And he was in pain from the bee sting. It gave him a big welt on his head."

"Killers can be very cool," Brad said. "They can be pretty good actors when they want to."

"Will I have to go to court?" she asked, slowly shaking her head. "I don't want to go to court."

"I'm sorry, but it's very likely, Miss Chambers. Mr. Grabowski denies having anything to do with the murder," Brad responded.

"I don't think I want to see him again," she said plaintively, dropping her head.

Brad sat quietly for a moment, watching Adriana.

"I know a lot of people didn't like Mr. Lenhardt," she suddenly said, her head still bowed. "But he was a good neighbor. We live about a block from him. I go running every morning, and I always pass his house. I see him a lot. And my dad and he were really good friends. They often went golfing together."

She was silent for a moment, and Brad said nothing, just watched her. She finally looked up, shaking her head again. "Mr. Lenhardt was always friendly to me. He'd say hi or ask me how I was doing—that kind of thing. I guess I won't be seeing him anymore."

"I'm afraid not," Brad agreed. "Can you think of anything else that I should know?"

She was thoughtful for a moment. Then she said, "Yes. Well, no, but I have a question. Why would Jerzy have been driving the direction he was if he'd just killed Mr. Lenhardt?"

"What do you mean, Miss Chambers?" Brad asked.

"His car was facing west. We live west of where he had the flat tire. The Lenhardts live west of where he was, too. They live just up the street from us, to the north. Wouldn't he be going the other way if he'd just robbed and murdered Mr. Lenhardt? You know, wouldn't he have been driving away from our neighborhood, not toward it?"

"That's a good question," Brad said. "And I don't know the answer except to say that criminals often do strange things, things that don't make sense."

Adriana nodded her head. "Of course, he was driving east when I returned. He must have made a U-turn." She was thoughtful for a moment, and Brad simply watched her and waited. Finally, she said, "Can I ask another question about what Mr. Grabowski told you?"

Brad was not anxious for Adriana to leave. He was very much enjoying the bright spot she was creating in his day. So he said, "What would you like to know?"

"Well, I was just wondering if you asked him if he had anyone with him when he drove off."

Brad smiled at her and basked in the smile she returned. "He claims some guy carrying a briefcase came walking up the street from the west and asked if he needed help. He says it was just after you drove away to get a screwdriver for him."

"I didn't see anybody else," Adriana said. "Maybe he wasn't right on the street or something like that."

"Maybe, but that's why I asked you that question earlier. Anyway, he says the guy had a screwdriver in his briefcase and that he used it to get the hubcap off. The two of them changed the tire, and Grabowski claims that the guy asked him for a ride downtown."

"So there might have been someone with him?" she asked.

"Unless he's lying. But the only fingerprints on the wallet and the screwdriver are his," Brad said. "And there was no briefcase. No one else can confirm the fact that there was another man, a tall, thin guy; that's the way Mr. Grabowski described him. And he said he was wearing black gloves."

"Where did you arrest Mr. Grabowski?"

"He was arrested at a 7-11 by a couple of uniformed officers. He said the tall, thin man wanted to use the restroom, so he stopped and the guy got out and went in. Although Grabowski admitted he didn't exactly watch the man go inside, and no one else, including the cashier, can remember the other guy," Brad explained.

Adriana looked Brad right in the eye again and asked, "Why did the officers arrest him?"

"We had everyone looking for suspicious cars, and we had broadcast the fact that Mr. Lenhardt's wallet was missing. The officers were just going to talk to Jerzy when he came out of the 7-11, but he acted really nervous. So they asked if they could look in his car. When they did, they found the wallet and screwdriver. The lab has already confirmed blood on the screwdriver. And the victim's wound looks like it could have been made by a screwdriver. We'll have autopsy and DNA results later, but it looks pretty likely that the screwdriver was the murder weapon."

"So it was a robbery?" Adriana asked.

"Must have been," Brad said. "Nothing else makes sense. Of course, we have already made some calls to Mr. Lenhardt's firm. They've never heard of Mr. Grabowski."

"This is really weird," Adriana said, rising gracefully to her feet. "I guess I better go."

"Thanks for coming in. I would have met you eventually," Brad said as he also stood up.

"I guess so. Mr. Grabowski must have described me pretty well," she said.

"Yes, and your red sports car," Brad said with a grin. "I'm sure we'll be talking again."

"I hope so," she said as he shook her hand. "And when we do, please don't call me Miss Chambers. I'm Adriana."

"Got it. And I'm Brad. I'll need to talk to your parents and any siblings that live at home. We are talking to all the neighbors. I already know your mother wasn't at home. What about others?" he asked.

"I'm the youngest and the only one at home," she said. "I recently moved back. Mom needs me right now. It's been hard on her since Dad walked out."

"I'm sorry," Brad said, suddenly feeling very awkward.

"So am I," Adriana said, and for the first time, tears appeared in her eyes. She brushed them away and said, "Mom and I haven't had very good luck lately. First Dad leaves without so much as a warning—unless acting weird was a warning—and then my boyfriend tells me not to call him again." She shook her head quickly. "I'm sorry. That's more than you needed to hear. I'll go now. Thanks for listening to me, Detective."

Before he could respond about what a fool the boyfriend was, she spun and walked away; his eyes followed her. His partner passed by her as she left, and he came toward Brad, grinning broadly. "Taking a little time off from the case to talk to a cute girl?" Mike asked with a lazy smile.

"She's a witness," Brad said sharply. "After I get some lunch, I'll explain." He turned and left his partner, who had a puzzled look on his face.

***

The sun almost blinded her when Adriana left the police station. She pulled her dark glasses from her purse and slipped them on. When she reached her car, she fumbled farther in her purse for her keys. She couldn't find them. "Unbelievable," she said out loud. She peered into the car, and to her complete dismay, she could see them right where she'd left them, in the ignition.

Embarrassed, she headed back toward the front door of the station. Detective Osborn was just coming out. "Did you think of something else?" he asked when he saw her.

"No, I'm an idiot," she said with a frown.

"I think not," he countered.

"No, really, I am," she said. "I locked my keys in my car. I've never done that before."

"Well, it just so happens that I know a cop who has had some experience getting keys from cars. I have a tool for that purpose in my squad car. I'll go get it and help you," he said.

"But you're busy."

"Not too busy to help a maiden in distress," he said with a grin. "My car's around back. My partner just left it there."

"Why did you come out this door if you were going to your car?" she asked, puzzled.

"I wasn't going to my car. I was just going to walk down the street and grab some lunch. My partner went home for lunch, but since I live alone, I prefer to just grab a sandwich. There's a Burger King right over there," he said, pointing.

"I see. If you have time, I would appreciate the help, Detective," she said.

"Brad."

"Right, Brad," she said with a grin.

"I'll go get the unlocking tool, Adriana" he said. "I'll be right back."

"I'll walk with you," she said.

"Great, come on then."

When they had retrieved the unlocking bar and reached Adriana's red Jaguar XK, Brad whistled in admiration. "Wow, this is a nice car," he said.

She'd never been embarrassed about driving such an expensive car before, but she knew that cops didn't make a lot of money, and she suddenly felt very self-conscious. Not that it was her money that had bought it; it was her father who was wealthy. He and her mother had bought it for her. She explained that to Brad, who said, "You don't have to explain. All I ask is that you give me a ride once I get it unlocked."

"Of course," she said. "Maybe we could go to lunch together. I haven't eaten either. We could skip Burger King and go somewhere farther from your office."

"That would be great," he said with a grin as he began to work on her car. It appeared it would take him a while to get it unlocked. "Are you going to be able to get it?" she asked in concern.

"Oh yeah, eventually. These expensive new cars are tricky. They aren't meant to be broken into, even by well-meaning cops," he said.

She watched him as he worked, admiring the nice fit of his sport coat and slacks. After a couple of minutes, he began to perspire, and drops of sweat began to run down his face from beneath his curly, dark blond hair. He wiped the sweat away with the back of one hand. She couldn't tear her eyes from him as he worked.

Stop it, she scolded herself sharply. *You don't even know if he's a Mormon, and you know your standards,* she added to herself. But she couldn't help admiring him. Finally, with a grunt of satisfaction, he straightened up and pulled the long, thin tool out. "That's it," he said with a grin. "Let's go get some lunch."

He opened the door and helped her in, and then he hurried around to the passenger side and climbed in. After he'd fastened his seat belt, she started the car. "Thanks for helping me out of an embarrassing situation," she said as they pulled onto the street.

"Not a problem," he said. He looked over at her, and she glanced his way, their eyes meeting for a moment. With a very straight face, he added, "Now, remember, I'm a cop, so no speeding."

Adriana laughed. It was really hard not to be attracted to this handsome cop. She drove a couple of miles and turned into the parking lot of a Chinese restaurant. "I like Chinese, but if you don't, we can go someplace else," Adriana said as she suddenly realized that she should have given him a chance for input before turning in there.

"This will be great. It's one of my favorite places," he said with enough enthusiasm to relieve her concern.

***

The tall, thin man was sitting in a tan Ford Escort across the street from the restaurant holding a cell phone to his ear. "They're going in," he said into the phone.

"Follow them when they come out, Max," a voice on the other end of the phone said. Max Barclay didn't dare go against anything that Valentino Lombardi said. The man who had ordered the theft from the attorney wasn't someone to be trifled with. He had already expressed anger that the attorney had died. That hadn't been the plan. Now Max had to straighten out a few things because of what he'd been forced to do.

He pictured the boss in his mind as he continued to hold the phone to his ear. At seventy, Valentino appeared to be reasonably fit, although not as fit as he had been ten years ago when Max, at the age of twenty, had first gone to work for him. The man was always impeccably dressed, his gray hair perfectly combed. At only five eight, he weighed one hundred ninety pounds. Valentino was five or six inches shorter than Max but outweighed him by a good twenty-five pounds. But despite Valentino's increasing waistline, he was very bright—much brighter than Max, he admitted to himself.

Valentino had always paid Max well, but on the one occasion when he hadn't completed a certain assignment up to expectations, Max had thought for a few days that he was going to be killed. But the boss had given him another chance, and he had been doubly careful ever since. Today, however, was an exception. He feared for his future.

"But I've probably been described to the cops. If they see me, they'll come after me," he finally said, trying not to sound whiney but rubbing his short black hair nervously with long, slender fingers.

"I told you, I'll have someone there to take your place soon," Mr. Lombardi said. "But until then, you've got to keep track of the girl. Who knows what she might be saying to the cops. I don't want anything, and I do mean anything, to keep them from charging and convicting this Grabowski guy for murder. And more importantly, I also have to know how much she and her mother know about her father's dealings with

Mr. Lenhardt and a certain client of his. Actually, the mother apparently hasn't talked to her ex-husband much since the divorce, but I'm sure the girl has. She probably knows things that she shouldn't, and if so, at some point, she'll need to learn that it's very important that she keep her mouth shut about it. You went beyond what you were told to do today, but you can still redeem yourself. Just don't let it get messed up worse," Valentino concluded darkly.

"Yes, Mr. Lombardi," Max Barclay—tall, thin, dark skinned, and thoroughly evil—said to his even more evil and totally ruthless boss.

CHAPTER FOUR

ADRIANA AND BRAD ENTERED THE Chinese restaurant together, chatting quite comfortably for people who had so recently made each other's acquaintance. They waited for someone to seat them. As soon as the young man came with menus in his hand, his face lit up, and he said something, in what Adriana assumed was Chinese, to the detective. To her complete amazement, Brad spoke easily back to him, and the two of them carried on a conversation in that foreign language all the way to the table.

After they were seated, Adriana looked at Brad and asked, "What was that all about?"

Brad chuckled. "He's a friend. I met him while serving an LDS mission to Taiwan. He joined the Church and immigrated here. He and I attend the same singles ward."

"That's amazing," Adriana said. "I attend a family ward with my mother, but all I speak is English."

Brad laughed. "And you speak it very well."

In all the time she had dated Drew Parker, she had never felt as easy in his company as she did with this cop she barely knew. But she stifled her enthusiasm. This was just lunch, one she had suggested, she reminded herself. And yet, what were the chances that she would choose a place for lunch that turned out to be a favorite of Detective Osborn? *He probably has a girlfriend in that singles ward he attends*, she warned herself.

The slender Asian waitress beamed while Brad spoke in the strange, unfamiliar language to her. "You know her too?" she asked after the girl had taken their order.

"Oh yeah, I come here a lot. I've taken her out a few times," he revealed. "She's a good friend."

Despite her cautions to herself, Adriana felt disappointment flood over her. "She's very pretty," she said lamely.

Brad grinned. "She is, isn't she? She's nice too. They are brother and sister," he said.

"Who, you mean her and the guy who showed us to the table?" she asked.

"Yes, they came here together."

"So you met her in Taiwan too?"

"Yes. She accepted the gospel first. Her brother followed her. He was reluctant at first, but when she was baptized, he began to show some serious interest. They are both very strong—in the Church and as individuals," he said.

"What are their names?" she asked.

"She is Ling and he is Chang," he said. "I'm sorry; I should have introduced you to them. I'll do that when they come back."

When Ling brought their lunch a few minutes later, Brad said, "Ling, I'd like you to meet a new friend of mine. This is Adriana Chambers," he said. "Adriana, meet Ling Yu."

"It's nice to meet you," Adriana said.

"It is nice to meet you," Ling said in delightful broken English. "You are very pretty girl. Mr. Brad is lucky to find you."

"Yes, I am," Brad said politely, grinning at Adriana, who felt her face go red. "Would you ask Chang to come over here when he gets a minute? I'd like to introduce her to him."

"I'd be happy to, Elder Brad," she said.

"Just Brad, remember?"

Ling smiled and said, "Yes, just Brad. Would you two like anything else?"

"This is fine for now," Brad said.

After she had left their table, Brad laughed. "Sorry about that," he said. "She is a wonderful person, but she sometimes assumes things. I'm sorry if you were embarrassed."

"I can see why you like her so much," Adriana said. "She is really sweet."

"Yes, isn't she?" he said. "Let's eat. This smells wonderful."

A few minutes later, Detective Osborn introduced Adriana to Chang. He smiled charmingly and said, "It is a pleasure to meet a friend of Brad's."

"She loves the food here," Brad said. "It was her idea to come here for lunch."

"Yes, she has come in before. She was with tall, handsome man but not so handsome as Mr. Brad." He beamed at Brad, and the two of them broke easily into Mandarin Chinese again for a moment before Chang excused himself and walked away.

Adriana enjoyed her lunch very much, and even though they didn't speak a lot as they ate, she felt good just being with Brad. However, she couldn't help but wonder about the relationship between Brad and Ling Yu. She also found herself thinking about Jerzy Grabowski, accused murderer.

Adriana felt like she'd entered a whole new world. When they left the restaurant a few minutes later and re-entered the hot June afternoon, she felt deflated. When they reached her car and unlocked the door, Brad opened it for her, but instead of climbing in, she offered him the keys. "You drive."

"Are you sure?" he asked.

"Of course I'm sure," she replied with a grin.

"Then I think I will. It might be the only time I ever get to drive such a sporty car."

Adriana hoped not. But she feared it would be true. After all, what did she have in common with Brad? *The murder of Garrick Lenhardt.* That wasn't the connection she would have preferred.

Grinning most of the time, Brad took a long route back to the office. When he pulled in and parked, he looked over at her and said, "That was fun. Thanks."

"You're welcome," she said as she looked over at him and smiled.

"Well, I've got a murder case to work on," he said. "I imagine that my partner is wondering what has become of me."

"Brad," she said after he'd exited her car and come around to open the door for her.

He paused and looked at her, "Yes, Adriana?" he said, chuckling. "You have something on your mind?"

"Yeah," she said. "Don't forget to take your unlocking thing. You might meet another forgetful damsel in distress."

"Yeah, thanks," he said, taking it from her hand as she held it out. "I'm forgetful too."

He followed her as she circled the Jaguar and helped her into it. But before shutting the door, she said, "One more thing, Brad."

"Sure, what's that?" he asked.

"I don't think Jerzy killed Mr. Lenhardt."

***

"The girl in the Jaguar just let the detective off at the police station, boss," Max said into his phone.

"Follow her. I want to know exactly which house she lives in," Valentino said darkly.

***

Back in the police station, Brad couldn't get Adriana off of his mind. He sat at his desk and tried to think about the case. It seemed airtight against Jerzy Grabowski, and yet something nagged at him. He was pretty sure it was Adriana's last words as he left her in her Jaguar. She believed Jerzy was innocent. She was bothered, and so was Brad, about the direction the man was headed when the bee stung him. And it bothered him that she thought there was a second person in his car when she saw him leaving. Other than those two things, the evidence pointed strongly to the man's guilt.

Mike came into the cubicle and sat at his own desk, just a few feet from Brad's. He spun his chair around and, grinning broadly, said, "So, tell me about the witness. What did she have to say?"

"Not a lot," Brad said.

"It took a long time for her to say so little," Mike observed.

"Not really," Brad protested. "She gave me a statement, answered a few questions, and left."

Mike chuckled. "You both left," he said, "in a sporty little red car. I saw you ride off with her."

"So what?" Brad asked, irritated.

"Where did you go and what did you talk about?" Mike asked.

"And what business is that of yours?" Brad asked as he felt the heat rise up his neck.

"It's our case, Detective, not just yours. I need to know what you discussed with *our* witness."

"Fine, I'll go over it with you. But about me going somewhere with her, it was to lunch. She'd locked her keys in the car, and she offered to take me to repay me for unlocking it for her."

"That was nice of her," Mike said blandly. "And I'm sure you talked about the case while you were at lunch."

"Not much, but let me give you a rundown on what she told me," Brad said, changing the subject. "But before we get into that, let me fill you in on my last interview with our suspect." He proceeded to do just that in great detail. When he'd finished, he said, "Now, I'll tell you what Miss Chambers told me." He did so, and when he finished that account, he said, "So, as you can see, Mike, Grabowski was telling the truth about a young woman stopping to help him with the tire."

"Yep, looks like it. But it also looks like Mr. Grabowski lied about not having a screwdriver in the car. He also lied to the young woman about that. We've got a whale of a case against Mr. Gold-rimmed Glasses. There is no one, at least so far, that can corroborate the existence of the so-called tall, thin man."

"Actually, like I told you, Adriana says she thinks there might have been someone in the car with Jerzy when he was driving off," Brad reminded him. "That backs up his story, I'd say."

"I wouldn't count that as much, Brad. If she isn't absolutely positive, we can't use that as corroboration," Mike said stubbornly.

A few minutes later, Sergeant Tullock stepped up to the cubicle and said, "I'd like you two to go up and interview the neighbors. So far, the officers haven't turned up any actual witnesses, but I'd like you two to talk to everyone again."

"We can do that," Brad said eagerly. He was ready to get out of the office and get to work.

"Before you go, I'll need for you to bring me up to date on what you know so far," she said. "Both of you come into my office for a few minutes."

She turned and led the way to her glass-walled office, where they told her everything they had learned. When they had finished, she smiled and said, "Sounds like we got lucky on this one and got the perpetrator in short time. The chief will like that. But, as extra insurance, I'd like to find someone else besides Miss Chambers who saw our suspect in the neighborhood."

"We'll work on that," Mike promised.

"We have more than enough to hold him, but while you two are canvassing the neighborhood, I'll see what I can learn about the suspect—background, criminal record, and so on. But regardless of what I learn, it seems pretty clear that what we have here is a burglary gone sour, and tragically so. We should be ready by tomorrow morning to go to the district attorney and get formal murder charges drawn up."

***

Jerzy was brooding in his hot little cell. He was angry, but he also felt helpless. He had been framed for murder. And it had been a thorough job. The tall, thin man had done a number on him. He clenched his fist and pounded his bunk in frustration. The cops didn't believe a word he had told them. He cursed his rotten luck. He needed a good attorney, one who would believe him and go to work and find the dirty rotten man who had done this to him.

***

After leaving the police station, Adriana had driven home and tried to study for a little while. Then she'd gone to campus for her three o'clock class. When it was over, Adriana walked to the library to study some more. She'd missed half of what the professor had covered in his lecture. She'd had a hard time keeping her mind on what he was saying as her mind kept drifting to the two men she had met that day, two men who couldn't be more different and yet both of whom had already impacted her life and would probably impact it a lot more in the coming weeks.

Jerzy Grabowski was a strange man, and he was probably not a very good one, but she just couldn't imagine him taking a screwdriver from his pocket and violently stabbing Mr. Lenhardt in the heart. That horrible act would have taken physical strength, ambition, and courage of a sort. She didn't see him as having any of those. He was lazy enough that he was willing to let her do the work of changing his tire. The way he'd whined about the bee sting didn't exactly make him seem like a brave man. And he was certainly no specimen of physical strength. The cops had it wrong.

As she sat in the library, trying to read the chapter the professor had covered in his lecture, her mind still kept wandering. More and more she found herself thinking about the detective, Brad Osborn. She had never been attracted to a man as quickly as she had been to him. And the hour she'd spent with him had been more pleasant than any of the time she'd spent with Drew, as surprising as that was to her. There was just something about Brad that had grabbed her attention. Yes, he was a very good-looking man, but it was far more than that. She liked his personality, and she was drawn to his general goodness.

She shoved her thoughts into the background and began to read. For a couple of pages, she did okay, but then thoughts of Jerzy and Brad intruded once more. If Jerzy was innocent, and she couldn't help but believe he was, then Brad would have to prove it. Doubts of the man she had come to admire so quickly crept in. Would he dig deeper or would he, along with the other officers, take the path of least resistance and continue to build a case against an innocent man? That thought disturbed her—a lot. She tried to shove it from her mind. She needed to study. She tried to do so, but her mind simply wouldn't focus. After she'd finally made it through the chapter, she closed the textbook and got to her feet. She didn't know much more now than she had following the lecture. She was going to have to read it again, but she couldn't do it now. Maybe tonight at home she would be able to do better.

Feeling strangely heavyhearted, she walked back to her car and drove home. Her mother wasn't there yet, so Adriana began to prepare dinner. She loved this beautiful, spacious house, but without her father, it felt empty. Even when she and her mother were both at home, it didn't feel right here, not like it had when she'd been a teenager growing up with both of her parents and her two older brothers. Those days were gone and could never return. Her brothers seemed to blame her mother for the divorce, and they seldom came around anymore. Adriana had tried to tell them how it really was, but they simply couldn't believe it was their father's fault. So for all intents and purposes, she was estranged from her father and her brothers.

She heard the door open, and her mother called out, "Adriana, I'm home. Whatever you're fixing sure smells good."

Adriana rubbed her hands on a towel and walked out of the kitchen to greet her mother. "Hi, Mom," she said. "How did your appointment go?"

"It was great," Krista said, her eyes gleaming. "I made the sale! This will help ease the finances for a while. It was a big sale with a wonderful commission. I expected it to take months to sell, but the Lord saw our need."

"That's great, Mom," Adriana said, and she hugged her mother.

"How was your day, sweetheart?" her mother asked.

"It was, well, interesting but disturbing," Adriana said honestly.

Krista put her purse away and turned to Adriana. "I think that statement needs some explanation. You look troubled."

"I am," Adriana said truthfully, "but I better get back to the kitchen."

The two of them went in together. "Would you like to talk about it?" her mother asked as Adriana bustled around the kitchen. She loved to cook, and she was good at it, having been taught by one of the best—her mother.

"Maybe over dinner," Adriana said. "This is almost ready."

"I'll set the table while you finish up."

Ten minutes later, dinner was on the table. Krista had offered a blessing and was ready to begin when the doorbell rang. "I'll get it, Mom," Adriana said as she shoved back from the table.

Adriana opened the door, and her heart flopped mercilessly in her chest. It took her a moment to find her voice. Finally, she said, "Detective Osborn, please come in."

"Hi, Adriana. I'm Brad, remember?" he said with a grin that spread from ear to ear.

"I know," she said, flustered, and embarrassed that it showed. "Ah, would you like to come in?"

"Please, if you don't mind," he said. "I wanted to talk to you again, and to your mother, if she's home."

"Yes, of course," she said, her heart light. It might not be a social call, but seeing Brad again so soon just, well, did something to her, something pleasant and uplifting. "She's in the kitchen."

As soon as Brad saw that they were eating dinner, he said, "Adriana, I can come back later. I'm talking to folks in the neighborhood. My partner is doing the same. I'll be here late."

"No, now is fine. Brad, this is my mother, Krista Chambers. Mom, this is Detective Brad Osborn, who I was going to tell you about over dinner," she said.

Krista rose to her feet and said, "It is nice to meet you, Detective. Is this about the murder of Mr. Lenhardt?"

"I'm afraid it is," he said. "I'm sorry I caught you at a bad time. I'll come back in an hour, if that's okay."

Adriana was watching him as he spoke to her mother. Her heart was still fluttering. As much as she had liked Drew, he had never done this to her. What was the matter with her? she wondered. Suddenly, her mind cleared. "Brad, please, we have not even started eating. Why don't you join us? There is plenty."

"Oh, no, I don't mean to intrude," he said, looking like he was feeling awkward.

"Please," she said, reaching out and taking hold of his arm. "I'd appreciate it."

He slowly shook his head, but at the same time a mischievous smile crossed his face. "I'll join you on one condition."

"Anything," Adriana said, aware of the strange way her mother was looking at them.

Ignoring that look, he said, "You both have to promise not to tell my partner," he said.

Adriana laughed, and her mother smiled. "We promise, don't we, Mom?" Adriana said.

"Of course. I'll get you a plate," Krista said.

"May I take your coat?" Adriana offered.

Brad slipped it off, revealing a pistol tucked snugly under his left arm in a shoulder holster and a badge on his belt. It brought her back to reality. He was a real cop, not just a cute guy who'd come for dinner.

"My compliments to the chef," Brad said after he'd eaten several bites of chicken and potatoes. He was looking at Adriana's mother.

"That would be Adriana," Krista said, nodding toward her.

"Well, I am impressed," he said with feeling. "This is really good."

A moment later, Krista said, "Detective, Adriana was about to tell me about her day. Unless I'm wrong, you were a part of it."

"And what a pleasure it was," Brad said, his eyes meeting Adriana's briefly. She felt herself begin to blush, and she shyly dropped her eyes.

"You have a wonderful daughter," Brad said, and the blush became full blown. She didn't even dare look up at him. He went on. "She is quite amazing. How many young women would offer to help a man change a tire? Usually, it's the other way around."

Adriana took a bite of green salad, feeling her mother's eyes on her. "Did you help this officer with a flat tire?" Krista asked.

She chewed and swallowed before answering. "No, but he unlocked my car for me. I locked my keys in it," she confessed.

"Where was that?" her mother asked.

"At the police station," Adriana confessed.

Her mother's eyes grew wide, and with furrowed brows she asked, "What were you doing there?"

"It was about the guy with the flat tire," Adriana said. "I drove there after I left your office."

"Oh yes, I'd forgotten. You did mention that you had gone home to find a screwdriver for somebody," Krista said. "My, but my mind isn't functioning very well lately. I forget things too easily. Why did you need to talk to the police about the man with the flat tire?"

"Well, it's like this," Adriana began awkwardly. "It seems that he might have had something to do with . . ." She stopped and looked at the detective. He was watching her with twinkling eyes. "Detective," she began again, "would you mind explaining?"

"Only if you call me Brad," he said. "You keep forgetting."

She couldn't resist his grin, and she found herself relaxing. "Brad, will you explain to my mother?"

"I'd be glad to," he said, "but not until I have some more of your fantastic potatoes. I will tell your mother what happened, and then I have some questions for both of you."

Adriana handed him the bowl of mashed potatoes. He helped himself and added some gravy. She offered him more fried chicken and he took another piece. Then they all began eating again. A minute or two later, he said, "Is it okay if we finish eating first and talk about the murder after dinner? I don't want to spoil such a good meal with such a grisly subject."

After dinner, Brad offered to help clean up, but Adriana wasn't about to let him do that. "The dishes can wait," she said. "Let's go into the living room. And I'll get your coat for you. Then you can tell Mom all about what happened."

Brad told Krista what Adriana had done and seen that morning. She couldn't believe the accuracy of his memory. He didn't miss a single detail. When he'd finished, and Krista looked very worried, he turned to Adriana, who was sitting near him on a plush white sofa. "Did I miss anything?"

"No, you are as accurate as a digital recorder," she replied.

"It's my job to get things right," he said. "Now, Mrs. Chambers, I need to know if you saw anyone or anything this morning that might be suspicious."

"No, not that I can think of, and you can call me Krista, if you don't mind," she said.

"Not a problem," he said. "I guess what I really wondered is if you saw either the tall, thin man or if you saw the recipient of your daughter's generosity or his car, the old blue Buick."

"No. If I did, it didn't register. I can't remember seeing either one of them."

"How about earlier, like last evening or yesterday sometime?" he asked.

Krista shook her head, and Brad turned on the sofa and faced Adriana. "I'm sure you've been thinking about this a lot," he said. "Have you seen either of them before?"

"No, I'm sure I haven't."

Brad turned back to Krista. "This is a difficult case," he said. "My partner, my sergeant, and all the other officers involved think we have a slam-dunk case on this Jerzy Grabowski guy. But Adriana isn't so sure, and as I've been thinking about this all afternoon, I tend to agree with her."

"You do?" Adriana asked hopefully. "Really? So you will try to find the thin man?"

"I will do what I can," he promised. "However, I will be bucking my fellow officers, not to mention the district attorney. It will not be easy, but when you mentioned your concerns about the direction Jerzy's car was facing, it got me to thinking. It really doesn't make sense that he would be driving back toward the scene of the crime."

"That does seem strange," Krista said, shaking her head slowly. "I would think he'd be getting out of the area as quickly as he could."

Brad nodded in agreement. "And the fact that you think there was someone in the car with Jerzy when he left makes me think you really did see someone else," he added, his clear blue eyes gazing into hers. "You thought that even before you knew that Jerzy had told us that there was someone else involved, someone he claims framed him."

"But what can you do?" Adriana asked. "I don't know that Jerzy's a very good person, but I would hate to see him go to prison for something he didn't do."

"Honestly, I'm not sure what to do," Brad admitted. "But there is something that I've learned since I spoke to you. Mrs. Lenhardt says that her husband carried several credit cards in his wallet, the one we found in Jerzy's car. But even though there were a number of other things in it, including his driver's license, there were only two credit cards. His wife says that can't be. There should be at least five. I'm the only one who is concerned about that."

"But that's important," Adriana said urgently, brushing her hair out of her face. "They've got to realize that."

"My partner, Detective Silverman, says that Jerzy probably went through them and threw the ones away he didn't want," Brad said. "That is possible. Also, the wife says he always has four or five hundred dollars in cash in the wallet. There was less than a hundred."

"The tall, thin man took the rest," Adriana said firmly.

"Or his wife was wrong, Adriana. Again, Detective Silverman pointed out that Mr. Lenhardt might have spent it in the last day or two." Brad turned back to Krista, "I don't mean to get personal, but did you always know how much money your husband was carrying in his wallet?"

Krista's face fell, but she said, "Of course not."

"So even though Adriana and I might think that the tall, thin man took the cash, that might not be the case. I need more to go on or Jerzy will be convicted," Brad said as he rose to his feet. "Unless there's more that either of you can add, I better get going. I've still got to talk to more of your neighbors."

Both women shook their heads as they stood up. He fished in the pocket of his jacket and pulled out a couple of business cards. He handed one to each of the ladies and said, "If you think of anything, call me, please."

"He's an awfully nice man," Krista said after Brad was gone. "Did you notice the way he looks at you?"

"Oh, Mom, he's just a cop doing his job. He hardly knows I exist," Adriana said.

"I wouldn't say that. But before you get too involved with him, you need to learn more about him," Krista said.

"Mom, it's not like that at all. But I do know a little about him," she said.

"To me, it looks like you think he's okay," Krista said with a smile as she turned toward the kitchen. "And I don't ever remember you looking at Drew quite like you looked at Brad tonight."

Adriana followed her into the kitchen. "Is it that obvious?" she asked.

"Yes, dear, it's that obvious. Tell me more about him."

Adriana did just that.

CHAPTER FIVE

"I can't keep doing this," Max said to the boss.

"You're wearing a hat and false beard, aren't you?" Valentino asked on the phone.

"Yes, but I'm getting really nervous."

"No one knows the car you're driving. And you can switch the plates again in a few minutes. Quit worrying. Now, what's happening?"

"The detective, the young one she went to lunch with, just came out of the girl's house. He's going to the next house now, one to the west of hers," Max reported. "But he was in the girl's house for over half an hour. He hasn't been in any of the others for more than five minutes."

"We'll deal with her if we have to," Valentino said. "I just wish I knew what she's telling that young cop."

"I can't keep driving through the area. Someone will get suspicious," Max whined.

"Change cars then. By morning, I'll have your replacement there. Then you can bring me Mr. Lenhardt's credit cards."

"Okay," the tall, thin man said nervously. "You aren't going to make me go back in the lawyer's house, are you?"

"No, not if you're such a sissy. We'll use one of the other guys. But we have to find that file. You screwed up not getting it. You should have spent a few minutes searching his office after you killed him," the boss said.

"But his wife, she was just next door," Max said. "I was pushing it as it was. I'd been in there too long."

"You disappoint me, Max. You had already gone to plan B by killing Lenhardt. You should have finished your assignment and stolen the file even if it meant killing his wife, too. What's one more dead body? I swear, you need to get some guts about you again and learn to think on your feet or you might cease to be of worth to me. Call me if you see something important. Otherwise, I'll call you when your replacement arrives."

The line went dead, and Max looked blankly at the cell phone in his hand. Killing the lawyer had been easy, but this prowling around the neighborhood was getting to him. He suddenly decided to go now. What the boss didn't know wouldn't hurt him. He started the ignition.

***

Brad rang the doorbell again. He was still thinking about the visit next door. He'd known a lot of young women, and though Adriana wasn't the most gorgeous of them all, she was definitely an eye-catcher, and he'd never felt such an instant, strong attraction as he felt toward her. And her mother was a beautiful woman, slender and well-groomed like her daughter. They were about the same size, and they looked a lot alike. Mrs. Chambers, he judged, was probably in her late forties. He couldn't imagine why her husband had left her. It made him feel bad, and he barely knew her or Adriana.

A car engine started up, and Brad glanced away from the door where he was standing. A silver, late model sedan pulled away from the curb about a half a block to the west and drove in his direction. Just then, a woman answered the door; Brad turned and spoke to her, telling her who he was and why he was there. As the woman invited him in, he glanced back at the silver car, a Nissan, he thought, as it went by. The driver, he noted, looked tall and had a bushy beard and a small hat. Then Brad entered the house.

Something about the car bothered him. Had he seen it earlier? As he waited for the lady to close the door, he got one more glimpse of the Nissan. He quickly memorized the license plate just before the door closed. He was quite sure he'd seen the car earlier in the day.

The visit at this house, like all the rest but the Chambers', produced no helpful information at all. Leaving, Brad pulled out his small notebook, wrote down the license number of the Nissan before he forgot it, and made a call on his cell phone. The plate number he called in came back as stolen. He had the number of the plate and the description of the car broadcast citywide. Then he called Mike, who wasn't more than a block or two away. He had their squad car.

"Mike, there was a car parked near me. I'm sure I saw it earlier. I called in the plate number. The plates are stolen. I was wondering if you might have seen the car," he said.

"What did it look like?" Mike asked wearily.

"Silver Nissan, late model," Brad answered.

"Nope, haven't seen it," Mike said. "I don't know about you, but I'm about ready to quit for the day. Nobody has seen anything, and anyway, we've got our man."

"I haven't had any success either," Brad admitted. "But I'd like to keep at it for a few minutes more, maybe half an hour. Then you can pick me up."

Mike was through before that, and so fifteen minutes later when he pulled up beside the curb three or four houses away from the Chambers' house, Brad joined him.

The next morning, Sergeant Tullock asked for updates from the detectives. Brad reported the Nissan with the stolen plates. The other officers didn't think it was likely to have anything to do with the case, but the number was listed and sent over the air anyway.

Lydia had something to report to Brad and Mike. "Jerzy Grabowski has a record," she reported. "Nothing like this latest crime, but he does have a couple of breaking and entering convictions, a misdemeanor assault, two DUIs, and a few other minor things. None of them are recent, not even within the last ten years. And none of them occurred in this state. They are mostly in New Jersey."

"Well, he's made up for it now," Mike said with a chuckle. "When are we going to see the prosecutor?"

"As soon as we are organized. Let's go into my office and get prepared now," Sergeant Tullock said.

Brad followed the others, but he was still nursing the doubts he'd discussed with Adriana. He felt like they should be doing more, but he wasn't sure what. No one else agreed with him. It was a slam dunk as far as they were concerned. He had a sinking feeling that the prosecutor would agree.

In the sergeant's office, he again voiced his concerns. Lydia turned toward him, her eyes narrowed. "You're the only one who believes that, Brad," she said darkly. "You need to be a team player. So I expect you to keep those doubts to yourself when we visit with the prosecutor."

Brad took a deep breath and tried to control his sudden anger. After a moment, he said, "I thought it was our job to arrive at the truth, even if it isn't at first obvious. It seems to me like we should at least look into the possibility that Mr. Grabowski is telling the truth. Miss Chambers's testimony could very possibly cause members of a jury to have a reasonable doubt. Even if he *is* the killer, we need to make sure that we have all our bases covered or we could lose."

Sergeant Tullock stared at him for a moment, her face hard, but then it softened ever so slightly. "You do make a good point. We don't want to lose this case. Of course, I don't think it will ever go to a jury. Our defendant will fold long before it comes to that," she said confidently. "I think we might still get a confession from him."

Brad shook his head. "I don't agree, Sergeant. I can't shake him in even one aspect of his story. There are no inconsistencies."

"Then maybe I should try," the sergeant said. "I've had a lot of experience at this type of thing. So far he hasn't lawyered up, so after we get back from the DA's office, I'll have a try with him."

"Good idea," Brad said. "Maybe you can get somewhere with the guy." He didn't believe it for a moment, but he also didn't want to offend his sergeant.

"I wouldn't mind having another crack at him myself," Mike said.

Brad shrugged his shoulders. "Whatever you two think," he said. "But I still think we should try to find the tall, thin man or at least figure out if he exists."

"We'll see," Sergeant Tullock said. "But for now, let's put down what we've got and go meet with a prosecutor."

The prosecutor they were directed to was a tall, physically fit, forty-two-year-old lawyer by the name of Ross Harris. He was known as a hard-hitting, no-nonsense attorney with over a dozen years of prosecuting experience under his belt. Brad was encouraged. He'd worked with Ross before and knew the man didn't like to lose. The three officers were ushered into Harris's office and offered seats. Ross then sat behind his large desk and looked sternly at the three of them. "You are here about the murder of my worthy opponent, Garrick Lenhardt," he said after sitting silently for a few moments. "I hear you have a suspect in custody. We will be expected to be in top form on this case. Your evidence had better be good."

"It's airtight," Sergeant Tullock said. "You'll like this one."

"Does that mean you have a confession?" he asked.

"Not yet, but I think we'll get one," she said.

Brad groaned inwardly but tried to keep his feelings from showing on his face.

"If you were going to get one, I'd have thought you would already have it."

"I haven't talked to the suspect myself yet," Lydia said confidently. "When I do, I think he'll come around."

"Who's his lawyer?" Ross asked, lightly touching his dark, neatly combed hair.

"So far, he doesn't have one. He hasn't even asked," Detective Silverman answered.

Ross slowly nodded his head. "He will want one if we decide to charge him. Give me what you've got," he said. "Start with who the defendant is."

Sergeant Tullock took it from there. She outlined the case against Jerzy Grabowski very accurately, except in two ways; there was no mention of Adriana Chambers believing there were two people in Jerzy's car nor did she mention the direction in which it had been parked before that. Brad let it go. He knew his place. He hoped that it would eventually come up, and he couldn't see how it wouldn't—in court if not before. When it did, he didn't think Ross Harris would be happy, but that would not be his fault.

When the presentation was finished, Ross sat back in his chair, stroked his chin, and then said, "I'll get the charges drawn up and get copies to you so you can serve the defendant. At that point, he'll need to have an attorney if he doesn't have one before."

"I'll go talk to him again now," Lydia said. "I think I can tie this thing up by early afternoon."

"That would be nice, although, like you said earlier, this looks like a solid case with or without a confession. See what you can do. Once he gets a lawyer, I'm afraid it will be too late for more questioning," Ross said, rising to his feet, a signal that the meeting was over. "Let me know right away if you get the confession," he added as they left his office.

***

Lydia Tullock was an excellent interrogator, but she made no more progress with Jerzy Grabowski than Brad and Mike had. After two hours, she gave up. "He's a tough nut," she said in frustration. "And he's not nearly as dumb as he looks. He has his story figured out and he's sticking to it. Well, he can if he likes. He's going down for killing Mr. Lenhardt anyway."

Brad didn't argue with her. He just went on with his work. The murder of Garrick Lenhardt wasn't the only case he and Mike were working. They both stayed busy the next few days. On Friday morning, they elected not to go to the funeral of the attorney. However, Sergeant Tullock and a number of the senior officers did go. Brad and Mike stayed in the office working on reports.

***

The heat was almost overbearing early Friday afternoon, way above the normal for the middle of June. Adriana and her mother were standing in the large crowd that had gathered at the grave site of Garrick Lenhardt. Everyone was suffering from the heat. Adriana hadn't been thrilled about coming to the grave site after the funeral, but like others in the neighborhood, she felt like she owed it to Mrs. Lenhardt.

Garrick and his wife had not been active in the Church, but the sisters of the ward did what sisters do when tragedy strikes: they reached out in love, offering support, meals, sympathy, and offers of assistance in any way she could use it. A large meal was waiting for Garrick's family and friends at the church house when they were finished at the cemetery. Adriana had made a casserole and delivered it to the church before the funeral, as had many others. The Relief Society presidency and a few others had stayed at the chapel to finish the meal preparations while pretty much everyone else came out here.

The crowd was so large that Adriana couldn't hear what the bishop was saying, nor could she hear the words spoken by the deceased's brother as he dedicated the grave. Adriana wiped sweat from her face, hoping the ceremony would soon be finished. She looked over the large crowd and was startled to see her father standing on the far side of the grave. She didn't remember seeing him at the funeral although he might have been there.

When the ceremony was over, the crowd began to drift back toward their cars after many of them, including Adriana's mother, spoke some final words of sympathy to the widow. While she was doing that, Adriana worked her way around the crowd, hoping to talk for a minute with her father, but by the time she got to the other side of the grave, he was gone. She looked around, couldn't see him and, feeling bad, rejoined her mother. She didn't mention to her mother that she had seen him, and if Krista had noticed him, she also chose not to mention it.

When they finally arrived home a few minutes later, the first thing Adriana did was hurry to her bedroom to get out of her dress and into some shorts and a light, cool blouse. But when she entered the room, the first thing she saw were big words scribbled on her large mirror in pale pink, the color of her favorite lipstick. She gasped and grabbed the door for support as she read the message: *We're watching you. Lenhardt's death is none of your business. Stay out of it!*

The message filled the entire mirror, and her lipstick, or what was left of it, lay on the dresser with the cap off. Feeling faint, she finally pulled her eyes away from the mirror and glanced fearfully around her room. Other than the mirror, there was no outward sign of anyone having been in the room. She slowly backed into the hallway. Without shutting the door, she quickly went in search of her mother.

Krista's bedroom door was closed. Adriana tapped on it. "What is it, Adriana?" her mother called out.

"Mom," she said, her voice shaking with fear. "Someone's been in my room."

"What did you say?" Krista asked.

"Mom, come see! It's horrid."

Her mother emerged a moment later in a long white robe. She took one look at Adriana's face and said, "Adriana, you're white as a sheet."

"Mom, someone's been in my room," she said, her knees knocking and her hands shaking.

"Let's go have a look," Krista said. "You must be mistaken."

Adriana didn't argue. She knew her mother would know soon enough. The two of them hurried together to Adriana's room. Her mother did more than gasp when she spotted the sloppy pink message on the mirror of Adriana's dresser. She screamed, and Adriana grabbed hold of her, supporting her trembling body as she read the message.

She turned to Adriana, fear in her eyes, and said in a quavering voice, "We've got to call the police."

"How did someone get in the house?" Adriana asked as she and her mother clung to each other for support. "I know the doors were all locked." Since Mr. Lenhardt's murder, they had been doubly careful about locking the house, both when they were gone and when they were in the house.

"I wonder if anything was stolen," her mother said, clearly having no idea what the answer to Adriana's question was.

"I'll call Detective Osborn's cell phone," Adriana said. "His card is in my purse."

Her purse was on the floor, where she had apparently dropped it when she saw the message on the mirror. She picked it up, and she and her mother went to the family room, where she riffled through her purse until she found the business card Brad had given her. She entered the number into her cell phone and waited while it rang.

She was about to give up when the detective answered. "Hello, this is Detective Brad Osborn," he said.

She gripped the phone tightly and sank down onto the sofa where her mother had already seated herself. Both of them were still shaking, but the sound of Brad's confident voice gave her strength. "Brad, this is Adriana," she said. "Someone broke into our house while we were at Garrick Lenhardt's funeral."

For a moment, Brad didn't answer. When he did, his voice sounded deadly serious. "Are you at home now?"

"Yes," she said.

"Are you alone?"

"Mom's here too."

"Stay right where you are. I'm on my way," he said. "When I get there, I'll ring the bell and then knock three times. That way you'll know it's me. Don't let anyone else in."

"Thanks, Brad," she said. "Please hurry. We're so scared."

***

Brad grabbed his jacket from the back of his chair.

"Where are you going?" Mike asked.

"To the Chambers' house," he said. "It's been broken into."

"Whose house?" Mike asked, looking puzzled.

"Adriana's," Brad said.

"Oh, the girl with the red sports car. I better come with you," Mike said as he slowly got to his feet.

"Then you'll have to hurry because I'm not waiting," Brad said impatiently.

The urgency in his voice was all it took to get his partner moving because Mike matched him stride for stride all the way to their car. Brad drove, and he wasted no time. When they arrived, he pulled into the driveway, parked behind Adriana's red Jaguar, and jumped out. He rang the bell and then gave three hard knocks on the door.

Mike was beside him by the time Adriana opened the door. Her mother was standing right behind her, trembling visibly. Brad stepped through the door, and Adriana stumbled toward him. Her eyes were wide with fright, and she was pale and shaking. He held out his arms and she collapsed into them. He held her for a moment, wondering what he was going to find in the house that had frightened her so much. He was aware of Mike entering the house as well and of the door being shut behind him. "It's okay now, Adriana," he said. "I'm here now. You're safe."

"Thanks for coming," she said weakly. "We are so scared."

She had said that on the phone and he'd believed it then. He believed it even more now. He gently pushed back from her and said, "Okay now, tell me exactly what's going on. You said someone broke in. What did they do when they got in?" he asked.

"Come this way," her mother said, feeling much better now that the two officers were there. "We'll show you."

"This is Adriana's room," Krista said a moment later.

It was pretty clear what had frightened Adriana so badly. Brad glanced at Mike, whose eyes met his. Neither officer said a word, but Brad knew that Mike also saw the seriousness of the message scrawled on the mirror. When he spoke, it was to the girl looking over his shoulder. "What is it written with?" he asked

"My lipstick," she said. "I can still see it there on the dresser."

He glanced at her. "The lipstick you're wearing right now," he said. It wasn't a question.

"I left it on the dresser when Mom and I went to the funeral."

"Is anything missing from your room or anywhere else in the house?" Detective Silverman asked.

"We haven't looked. We haven't even gone any farther than this into Adriana's room," Krista said.

"That's good. Why don't you let us go in and have a look around the room? You two can come with us, but don't touch anything. Do look closely though. Tell me if you see anything that's been disturbed or if anything is missing."

The officers moved first to the large dresser. Adriana and Krista stayed back a few paces and watched them. Brad saw that Adriana was looking around the room. "Is everything in place?" he asked as he looked at the dresser in front of him.

"I think so," she said.

He picked up a single piece of stationary with small printed lettering on it. At first, he thought it must have been something Adriana had written. But when he saw that it was addressed to her, he knew it wasn't.

He glanced at her again. She was still looking around the room. He quietly showed the paper to his partner. The two of them read it together. "Wow!" Brad mouthed to Mike as they finished. Just then he heard Adriana squeal. He turned in her direction. She was staring wide-eyed at an oak and glass curio cabinet that sat against the wall near the window. It held several porcelain dolls.

"What is it, Adriana?" her mother asked.

"One of the dolls is gone," she said with a shiver. "It's the one with the pink and white dress with the red flowers on it. I didn't notice it until just now."

Brad watched as her mother also looked and then she said, "Yes, it is. Oh my." Both women looked quite faint.

"Adriana, Krista, why don't you two sit on that love seat over there," he said, gesturing toward a love seat near the curio cabinet.

They moved like a pair of robots, both of them staring, as they walked, at the curio cabinet. He would deal with the problem of the missing doll, but first he thought they should know about the note. It spelled out great danger to Adriana, and she had the right to know it. "Adriana, brace yourself. There's something you need to see here," he said after the two of them were seated.

She looked toward him. He was still holding the sheet of paper by one corner. "Is there something written on it?" she asked.

"Yes. It's addressed to you," Brad said. "I don't want you to touch it, so let me read it to you."

"Okay," she said shakily. Her mother put a supportive arm around her shoulder.

Brad said, "Okay, I'm going to read this now. It's only one page, typewritten in a large font. It says: *Miss Chambers, there are some things that are none of your business. You need to pretend you never met that bald, fat man that killed your neighbor. He is better off where he's at now—locked up! His bungling little attempt at burglary was beyond his ability. Killing the attorney was a stupid move on his part, but then I would guess that he is as stupid as he looks. His murderous act has interfered with something bigger than him, bigger than you can even imagine. I think you know what I'm talking about. If you do, keep your mouth shut. Mr. Lenhardt was an important man. He shouldn't have died. Don't let the same thing happen to you by being stupid like that bald fat man. Just forget all about him. And, Miss Chambers, whatever you do, don't call your friend Detective Osborn or any other cop. If you do, you'll regret it.*"

Adriana was shaking so hard that her teeth were chattering. Brad laid the note back down on the dresser where he'd found it. "That's what it says," he told her as he moved quickly across the room, past her king-sized bed, and knelt down in front of her and took her hand. "Please, Adriana, don't worry. We'll keep you safe."

"How?" she asked, her eyes wide with terror.

"Trust me, girl," he said. "I won't let anyone hurt you. We have done this kind of thing before."

"Okay," she said in a very small voice.

"What would you two have done if you had found this note before you called Detective Osborn?" Mike asked from where he was still standing beside the dresser.

Both women looked at him. Krista waved a hand feebly and said, "We would probably not have called you. Somebody is watching us. They knew we weren't here today. They probably know now that we're here and we called you. They could be anywhere."

Brad thought about the car he'd seen here four days before, the evening of the murder, the car with stolen plates. The driver, with his bushy beard and English-looking cap, had been watching this house. He was positive of it now. Brad had been here one other time in the past few days, and he guessed that whoever had left this note had known that. He shivered. "Okay, let's get on with looking around," he said, trying to sound brave and confident. "You say there's a doll missing."

"Yes, and I'm sure it was there this morning. I mean," she said, looking toward the curio doubtfully, "it had to have been. It's always there, and I didn't move it."

Mike called for the lab crew to come to the Chambers' house while Brad encouraged the women to look carefully around the house and see if there was anything else missing. In the process, they found the missing porcelain doll hanging by the neck from a towel rack in the bathroom attached to Adriana's large bedroom. That was the last straw for the distraught girl. She felt so rattled that Brad had to help her to her mother's room to lie down. Her mother wet a washcloth in cold water and gently placed it on Adriana's head.

The lab crew arrived, and Brad and Mike had them start taking prints. They photographed the mirror, the note, and the doll. Then they collected the doll, which was hanging by a shoelace taken from one of Adriana's sneakers that she kept in her expansive walk-in closet. They also took the note and the sneaker.

Adriana soon recovered enough to help her mother examine the rest of the house, but as near as they could tell, nothing else had been disturbed. Entry to the house had been by a back door, one that was out of sight of the street and shielded from the neighbors by large trees and thick shrubs growing just inside a tall privacy fence that enclosed the spacious backyard.

They were nearly finished up when Brad's cell phone rang. "Detective, where are you and Mike?"

"We're at the home of the young lady that helped Mr. Grabowski with his tire," he said. "Adriana Chambers."

"Well, I don't know why you're there, but I need you to get over to the Lenhardt house. Someone broke in while everyone was at the funeral," she said.

Brad groaned. "That's what happened here," he said. "And Miss Chambers has been threatened. A lab crew is here. We are nearly finished up. We'll go over there shortly, but first I've got to figure out what to do about Miss Chambers. She is in terrible danger."

"Surely there is no connection between that and Garrick Lenhardt," Sergeant Tullock said.

"Oh yes, there definitely is. More than you can imagine," Brad said.

"Okay, I tell you what," she said decisively. "We have some uniformed guys on the way to Lenhardts'. They can hold things down there for a few minutes. You stay there, and I'll meet you in a minute or two. Give me the address."

CHAPTER SIX

It was only four or five minutes after her call when Lydia knocked on the door. "You must have been close," Brad said when Krista let her in.

"I was on my way to Lenhardt's house," she said. "So tell me what's happening here."

"Just follow me," Brad said. "I'll show you."

The sergeant had but to see the mirror and Brad had her undivided attention. The note and the hanging doll had her shaking her head. "Oh my goodness," she said several times as she was led through the house.

A few minutes later, the three officers put their heads together out by their cars. "This is too much," Sergeant Tullock began. "However, it only confirms what we already believe, that we have the right killer. What we don't know is what else is going on. Maybe when we figure out what the burglary at the Lenhardt house is all about, then we'll have something to point us in the right direction here."

Brad's feelings didn't exactly mirror those of his sergeant, yet doubts had been sowed in his mind. He had to seriously consider that Jerzy Grabowski was the killer and that he had in fact stepped unknowingly into the middle of something else. But if so, what was that something else?

"What do we do about keeping Adriana safe?" Brad asked before they broke up to drive over to the Lenhardts' house.

"I'll have a car stationed here," Lydia promised. "The lab crew will be a few more minutes in there, and by the time they're done, there will be someone detailed to keep an eye on her. Later, we'll see what other arrangements we need to make. I will need to consult with the lieutenant before we decide that."

There were no notes of any kind left at the Lenhardt house. However, the lawyer's home office had been gone through very thoroughly. Even though most of the file cabinets had been locked, none of them had been spared the burglar's search. A pry bar appeared to have been used both on the oak file cabinets as well as one of the doors in the back of the large, rambling house. His wife had no idea what might be missing from the office, but she didn't think anything had been taken from anyplace else. She tearfully stated that she had always stayed out of Garrick's office. She explained that he spent a lot of time in there when he was at home, that he was always working, seldom taking time to relax. She seemed to have very little knowledge of his work.

At Mrs. Lenhardt's request, one of her husband's law partners came to the house. Like Garrick Lenhardt, Brian Bollinger was well known for his work as a defense attorney. Younger than Garrick, he was in his midfifties. He was a small man, barely five six, slender, well-groomed, with piercing blue eyes. His blond hair was thick and neatly combed. As he worked, his slender fingers occasionally stroked his large moustache. "You are welcome to watch," he warned the detectives, "but I have to look out for the interests of our law firm. I just need to take a look and see if anything is missing from Lenhardt's office," he said.

"That's fine, but if you find anything that might be useful to our case, I expect you to let me know," Sergeant Tullock said sternly.

"Hey, we want to know why Garrick was killed. We will cooperate fully," he said as he set to work.

Brad wasn't so sure he believed him. So as Mr. Bollinger carefully searched the desk, file cabinets, and bookshelves in Garrick's office, Brad stayed close and watched every move the little attorney made. It was over an hour later when Mr. Bollinger turned to Brad and said, "I think that's about it."

"What did you find?" Brad asked as his partner and supervisor looked on.

"Nothing," Bollinger said evasively.

"Maybe the better question is, what didn't you find that you expected to?" Brad asked astutely.

There was the slightest tic of one of Brian Bollinger's piercing blue eyes. Knowing that he'd hit a nerve, Brad pressed him. "What's missing, Mr. Bollinger?" he asked, moving close and towering over the smaller man.

Brian stepped back and started to go around Brad but stopped when Lydia stepped in his way. "Detective Osborn asked you a question. We would like an answer," she said, shaking a finger at him.

"Okay, it's almost certainly nothing, but there appears to be a file missing, one Garrick was working on at home," the attorney admitted. "But I don't see where that will help you."

"We will determine what helps and what doesn't," Lydia shot back sharply. "What is the file about?"

"Attorney-client privilege," Brian countered sharply.

"I'm not asking what's in the file," the sergeant said. "Just tell us who it's about. It certainly is a client, but what client?"

"I'll need to talk to the other partners about this," Mr. Bollinger said stubbornly. "I need to go now."

"You can tell us now, or we'll have Ross Harris subpoena the information," Brad said, trying to keep his anger in check.

"Okay, okay," the attorney said. "As you probably know, we are defending a man the prosecution calls a crime boss. We believe he's an innocent victim, a persecuted citizen."

Lydia smiled and said, "Gabriel Mancheski, charged with racketeering, money laundering, and assorted other felonies."

"Charged, but not guilty," Brian said stubbornly. "Now you know, and that's all I can say. I really do have to go now."

"Why was the Mancheski file here?" Lydia asked.

"Garrick was working on it, so he brought it home," he said. "We all do that from time to time. We are, as I'm sure you know, a very busy firm."

"Did he bring the entire file?" Brad asked.

"Of course," Brian said, giving him a superior look. "And it was a thick file, as you can imagine."

"Yes, I suppose it would be," Lydia said. "Why would someone be interested in stealing that file?"

"I don't know," Brian insisted, finally pushing his way past the officers and leaving the house without another word.

Brad was thinking about Lydia's question, one that Brian claimed not to know the answer to, but he had a feeling that that wasn't necessarily true. To his colleagues, he said, "Maybe this murder isn't a simple home burglary gone sour."

Mike and Lydia both looked at him with raised eyebrows. Shaking his head, Mike said, "Don't tell me you think that Jerzy Grabowski was a hired killer."

"I think we should at least consider that. But I also think that we need to consider the fact that someone else could be the killer." Brad asked, "What if someone else actually did it and that person was a hired killer?"

"Not likely, Brad. We have our man," Mike said with a touch of anger. "And we have our motive—robbery."

Brad dropped the subject—for now.

Later, when the officers were all back at the station, there was some discussion over who should be assigned to the two burglary cases. Lydia and her supervisor maintained that it was not something that her squad should be saddled with, that they had the murder to work, and that they couldn't see any firm connection. Some sided with them and others didn't. The other side of debate held that the reference to Jerzy Grabowski in the threatening note addressed to Adriana Chambers was plenty of connection and that the same team should be working on all of it. And the further fact that the two break-ins had both occurred during the funeral of Mr. Lenhardt illustrated that everything was tied to the murder. The debate was taken all the way to the chief of police. The chief responded decisively, clearly directing that both break-ins be handled by Lydia's squad since there were, in his mind, clear ties to the murder of Garrick Lenhardt.

Had they been a bigger department, they would have had separate homicide detectives, but that was not the case here. There was simply one investigation division, and since Lydia Tullock's squad had been the ones assigned to the murder, they would take the other cases as well. The chief left no room for debate.

"I'm sorry to load you two down even more," Sergeant Tullock told Brad and Mike that afternoon, "but you will be handling the investigations of the burglaries at the Chambers and Lenhardt homes."

"That's nonsense," Mike argued. "We have enough to do without worrying about those burglaries."

"There is no point in arguing, Detective," Lydia said. "I agree with you, but the chief doesn't, so we'll do what he says. Is that clear?"

"It's clear," Mike agreed, "but it doesn't mean we have to like it."

"On the other hand, it does mean that we will do our best to solve both crimes," Lydia said. She turned to Brad, "Are you with us on this, Detective Osborn?"

"All the way," he said, attempting not to appear too eager, just supportive of his superiors. He didn't add the fact that he wanted very much to work on the burglaries because he believed that if they could solve them they would find the proof he sought that Jerzy was not the killer. It would also mean he would be in close contact with Adriana Chambers, and that idea was appealing. Even if he hadn't been assigned the case, keeping Adriana safe would have continued to be an important priority to him.

"If you need help, all you have to do is ask and I'll assign some of the others. These cases are on the chief's radar screen, so they have got to be handled quickly and thoroughly," Sergeant Tullock said. She smiled at Brad and added, "And that means that you might want to explore the possibility that Jerzy Grabowski was a contract killer, silly as that seems to me."

It seemed silly to Brad as well, but he didn't comment on it. What didn't seem silly was that the tall, thin man, whoever he was, might be a contract killer. Poor Jerzy Grabowski was just an innocent man who was in the wrong place at the wrong time.

CHAPTER SEVEN

ADRIANA WAS BESIDE HERSELF WITH worry. She couldn't understand why she had been threatened. After dinner that evening, she parted the blinds and looked out the window for the hundredth time to make sure that there was a cop car parked out there. Her mother joined her and said, "We've got to do something, Adriana. The police can't keep someone outside our house forever. I can't bear to think that someone might actually hurt you." She wiped tears from her eyes and put an arm around Adriana, pulling her close. "It's up to me and you to keep you safe."

"I love you, Mom," Adriana said as she let the blinds fall back into place. "I don't know what we can do."

"You'll need to go somewhere else, someplace safe," Krista said.

"I have classes," Adriana said. "I can't just pick up and leave. Anyway, what have I done? Yes, I probably shouldn't have stopped to help that guy, but even though I did, I can't see how that makes me a danger to anyone."

"The note said that this was something bigger than you understood. Maybe there's something that we don't know about," Krista suggested as the two of them moved back into the family room and sat down in front of a blank TV screen.

"But what does that mean? I don't know anything that could hurt anybody," she said as the doorbell rang. She stiffened. "Who could that be?"

"I don't know, but let's make sure it's someone we know before we open the door," Krista said.

Together, they walked toward the door. Once again, Adriana stepped into their large living room and parted the blinds. The cop car was still there. The doorbell rang again. "I'll answer the door, Adriana," Krista said. "You go back in the family room and stay out of sight."

Adriana did as her mother asked, but she didn't sit down. She waited just inside the room and listened as her mother called out, "Who is it?"

Adriana couldn't hear the response from the other side, but she let out a sigh of relief when she heard her mother unbolt the door. It had to be someone they knew. Even then she didn't move until she heard her mother say, "Brad, it's good to see you. Please come in."

Overwhelming relief came over Adriana, and she stepped into the hallway and practically ran toward the detective. His face lit up when he saw her. She wanted to fall into his arms, but she restrained herself and instead stopped near him as Krista shut the door. "Brad, we don't know what to do," she said. "I've never had anything like this happen before." Tears moistened her eyes.

Brad did what Adriana hadn't dared to. He stepped closer, reached out, surrounding her with his strong arms, and pulled her close. When he did that, her eyes filled with tears. "We'll get through this, Adriana," he said.

His words, especially when he used the term *we*, gave her almost as much comfort as the arms that were holding her tight. "Thanks for coming by," she said as she wiped her eyes before the tears started running.

"I'm working," he said as he released her from his firm embrace and stepped back, "and I have a lot of questions for you two."

"We'll answer the best we can," Krista assured Brad. "Let's go in the family room." She led the way while Adriana and Brad followed, side by side.

After they were all seated, Brad said, "I'm sorry for the rough day you've had. I'd like to have gotten back to you sooner, but I've been very busy."

"I can imagine," Krista said.

"My partner and I will be working both the break-in at your house and the one at Lenhardts' since there seems to be a connection to the murder and the break-ins," he explained.

"We were just talking about this when you came," Krista said. "We can't figure out what the person who broke in here meant in the note by this thing being bigger than we think."

"That's what we've got to figure out," Brad said. "By the way, Detective Silverman had to go home, so he's off for the night, but I thought that it would be best if I talked to you ladies now. That's why I'm here alone."

"I'm just glad you're here," Adriana said from her position next to him on the sofa. "I have been thinking about that note and the other . . . stuff, all afternoon. What did I do?"

Brad patted her arm and said, "Nothing, I'm sure, but apparently someone doesn't think like I do. Now, let's talk. First, let me explain what we found at the Lenhardts' house earlier today."

"Yeah, we've been wondering about that," Adriana said. "Did Mrs. Lenhardt get threatened too?"

"No, it looks like the burglar was after something," Brad explained. "Mr. Lenhardt, as you probably know, has an office in his home. Apparently he brings work home and spends time on it there. His home office was worked over pretty good. The burglar used a bar of some kind to break into every file cabinet. He appeared to go through things pretty thoroughly. He left quite a mess. We had one of Garrick's law partners come to see if anything was missing."

"Was there?" Adriana asked, watching Brad closely.

He nodded and said, "Yes, as a matter of fact, there was. It was a file, a thick one, on one of the cases that Lenhardt was working on. Does the name Gabriel Mancheski mean anything to either of you?"

Krista gasped and her eyes grew wide.

"I take it that means it does," Brad said.

"Yes," Krista said softly. "He came here once. He didn't seem like a very good man."

"Mom, do you mean that guy who came looking for Dad that one Saturday when I'd come home for the weekend?" Adriana asked. "The old white-haired guy that walked with a cane and used a lot of profanity?"

"Yes, that's Mr. Mancheski," Krista said. "Brad, is he in some kind of trouble?"

"Lots," Brad responded. "Although the lawyer from Mr. Lenhardt's office says the guy is innocent, we don't believe that for a second. What did he come to see your husband about?"

"I don't know. That was after my husband and I started having trouble. He wouldn't say anything about the guy. They talked privately for an hour or so, but I could hear their voices, especially Mancheski's when he swore. He was quite loud. I was relieved when he left, but Carson, that's my ex-husband's name, got pretty angry when I asked what the man wanted."

"Dad was acting really weird for two or three months before he walked out on Mom," Adriana revealed. "I wonder if this man had anything to do with whatever it was that changed Dad."

"Your father changed before he left?" Brad asked, looking intently at Adriana. "In what way did he change?"

Adriana looked at her mother, whose face was filled with anguish. "I'm sorry, Mom. This might be important," she said.

"Yes, it might," Krista agreed, wringing her hands as she rose to her feet. "Carson grew distant. Like most married couples, we argued from time to time, but we didn't have what I'd call big fights, not until those last few months."

Krista crossed the room and stood by a large entertainment center that filled much of one wall. With her arms folded in front of her and her back to Adriana and Brad, she went on, "He quit going to church. He'd never been as strong in Church activity as I would have liked, but he usually had some kind of calling, and he usually attended meetings with me and the kids. He stopped all of a sudden and refused to talk about it. He just made it clear that he didn't want to go anymore."

She sniffed and wiped her eyes. Brad and Adriana sat quietly and watched her. "We had a pretty big fight one day. It started when I asked him why he wouldn't go to church anymore. Adriana was living on campus at the time," Krista said. She turned and faced them. "I'm sorry, Adriana, but I never told you about this."

"It's okay, Mom," Adriana said. "I never expected you to tell me everything. It wasn't my business."

Krista didn't comment about that. She went on speaking, her eyes drifting aimlessly around the room, "I asked him if he'd quit going to church because he was doing things that he was ashamed of. He exploded at me. He told me I was nuts. I assumed that I'd hit a nerve. I had an idea what it was; so many men have similar problems. I asked him if he was into pornography." She shuddered and was silent for a minute. The young people on the sofa waited. Finally she said, "I thought he was going to strike me. Never in our married life had I been afraid of Carson, but he scared me that day."

Adriana got up from the sofa and walked over to her mother. "I'm sorry, Mom," she said. "So was that why he left?"

"That was a while before he walked out, several weeks before then. He didn't hit me, and for a little while he didn't speak. When he did, all he said was, 'No, Krista, I am not into pornography. And before you ask, I can tell you honestly that I have always been faithful to you, so don't accuse me of that, too,' or words to that effect. We never talked about that again. But honestly, dear, I'm certain that he was telling the truth about that."

"Oh, I hope so," Adriana said as she put an arm around her mother's shoulders.

"But there is something else," Krista said. "He never gave me any specifics, but he did say something about the fact that business wasn't like it used to be, that there were men he had to work with who gave him a lot of trouble." Krista shook her head sadly. "He wouldn't say any more about it. He just left the room. I never said anything to him about not going to church after that. Things got worse over the next few weeks, and then one day, without any warning, he came home after work and informed me that he had filed for divorce that day and that I'd be served with the papers."

Krista began to sob. Brad joined the two of them by the entertainment center and said, "Why don't you sit down again."

Krista nodded at him, and with Adriana's arm still around her, she returned to the chair near the sofa where she'd been sitting earlier. After she was seated, Adriana sat down on the arm of the chair and Brad returned to the sofa.

"Is that the night he left?" Adriana asked.

"Yes, he packed up a bunch of things and told me that he'd be back for the rest. He was but it was the next day while I was at work. I don't know where he went that night. He never even told me where he was living for a long time. We've hardly spoken since then. Our attorneys carried messages back and forth. I saw him in court, and then, well, like you know, Adriana, he hasn't been part of my life since then."

"Do you get alimony?" Brad asked.

"Not much. I got the house, but I also got the remainder of the mortgage. I'm not sure how much longer Adriana and I can continue living here." She sighed. Suddenly, Krista straightened her shoulders, looked squarely at Brad, and said, "I'm sorry. I didn't mean to burden you with my problems. Go ahead and ask whatever else you need to."

Adriana rejoined Brad on the sofa. "Do you think that my troubles are because of Mr. Mancheski?" she asked Brad.

"Unless you two can figure out any other connection between you and the Lenhardts, I'd have to say that it might be," Brad said.

"Dad and Garrick were friends," Adriana said. "They golfed together a little and that kind of thing."

"Did Garrick or anyone in his firm ever represent your dad on any legal matters?" Brad asked.

"Not that I know of," Krista answered. "But Carson never talked much about his business life in those last few months before he left, so I can't say he didn't."

"What kind of work does Carson do?" Brad asked next.

"He works for a large corporation that does business all over the country. They deal in a lot of things, mostly the service industry. He is a vice president of some sort, or at least he was when we got divorced. I suppose he still is. He always made really good money. But he didn't like to talk about his work," Krista said. "Especially the last year or so we were together."

"Is there any chance that his connection with Gabriel Mancheski could have something to do with the threats that were made today?" Brad asked.

"I can't imagine what it would be," Krista said.

Brad turned to Adriana and asked, "Do you ever see or talk to your father?"

"Once in a while. He's tried to get me to turn on Mom, like he got my older brothers to do, but I always tell him that I love her and nothing he can say will change that. But he still calls me occasionally to ask how I'm doing in school and that kind of thing."

Brad was thoughtful for a moment. Adriana watched him, wondering what he was thinking. Finally, he asked, "Do you ever go to his house or go out to eat with him or anything like that?"

"Yes, he has taken me to dinner a few times, and I have been to his home. He lives in a condominium now. It's surprisingly small, not what I would think he could afford," she said. "He calls it a condo, but it's really just an apartment. But I haven't been there a lot, only four or five times."

"Has he ever mentioned either Garrick Lenhardt or Gabriel Mancheski when you've been with him?" Brad asked.

Adriana thought for a minute. "Not that I recall," she answered.

"When was the last time you saw him?" Brad asked.

"That's easy," Adriana said. "He was at the funeral today. At least, he was at the grave site. I saw him there on the far side of the crowd. I tried to go around and talk to him, but I couldn't get there before he left."

"What about before today?" Brad asked.

"A couple of weeks ago," she responded. "He met me at a restaurant, the same one where you and I ate the other day."

"How did he seem that day?" Brad asked.

"Funny you should ask that," Adriana said. "He was distracted. We didn't talk much. He seemed troubled over something. But I know better than to ask him about such things. So I didn't. When we left the restaurant he didn't ask when we could meet again. He usually does that. He just got in his car and drove away."

"Can you give me his address?" Brad asked. "I'm going to need to talk to him."

"It'll make him angry," Krista warned. "But I certainly understand why you need to see him."

After writing down Mr. Chambers's address and cell phone number, Brad visited for a few more minutes. As he left, he said, "Call me if you need me, either one of you—day or night."

***

Brad spoke briefly with the officer on duty outside the Chambers' house. He wanted to make sure that he kept a close eye on Adriana and her mother. He gave the officer his cell phone number and asked him to call if he saw any suspicious vehicles or people in the area. "The young lady who lives here is a witness in the murder case of Garrick Lenhardt. She has been threatened. Make sure nothing happens to her."

The officer promised to keep a close eye on things. Then, before he walked to his own car, Brad said, "And make sure the officer that relieves you has my number and understands the seriousness of this situation here."

As he drove away from Adriana's house, he looked at the clock on his dash. It was a little before eight. He thought about going home, showering, fixing himself a sandwich, and sitting down in front of his TV to watch a baseball game and begin the new book he'd recently purchased.

He abandoned those thoughts, pulled to the side of the road, and placed a call to the number Adriana had given him for her father. It rang several times before it was answered. "Hello," a man's voice said.

"Is this Carson Chambers?" he asked.

"Yes, and who are you?" Carson asked.

"I'm Detective Brad Osborn. I just spoke with your daughter, Adriana," Brad said, deciding not to mention Carson's ex-wife, "and I think that you and I need to meet."

"Is she okay?" Carson asked, concern suddenly evident in his voice.

"Not really," Brad said. "She is in danger. She gave me your address. Do you mind if I swing by? We need to talk."

There was hesitation, but then Carson said, "Okay, for her I will give you a few minutes."

Adriana had been right, Brad thought as Carson Chambers invited him in; her father certainly didn't live in the luxury to which he had been accustomed before his divorce. In fact, the *condo* wasn't any nicer than Brad's apartment. He stepped in and said, "I'm Detective Brad Osborn. Thanks for agreeing to meet with me."

"What's this all about?" he asked. "Why is Adriana in danger?"

"That's what I'm trying to figure out," Brad said. "Can we sit down and I'll tell you what's going on?"

Carson clearly wasn't a good housekeeper. He had to clear a spot for the two of them to sit in his living room. Once seated, Carson asked, "Does this have anything to do with the murder of Garrick Lenhardt?"

"As a matter of fact, it does," Brad said.

"But why?" Carson asked. "Adriana didn't witness anything, did she? If so, she hasn't called me to tell me about it."

"She is a witness of sorts," Brad said.

"What did she see?" Carson asked with a frown.

Brad spent the next couple of minutes explaining about Jerzy Grabowski. "Mr. Grabowski has been arrested and charged with the murder, but frankly, Adriana thinks he's innocent, and I'm leaning toward agreement with her."

"Whether he is or isn't, I can't see why my daughter would be in danger," Carson said. "And, anyway, what makes you think she's in danger?"

"I was getting to that," Brad said. "Let me tell you what happened today during the funeral for your friend, Garrick Lenhardt." He watched Carson's face closely to see if there was any kind of reaction to the mention of the word *friend*. There wasn't even as much as a tic of an eye.

"Okay, so tell me what happened. I was at the funeral and at the cemetery too. I didn't see or hear anything that would indicate she was in danger," Carson said.

"The problem wasn't at the funeral or the cemetery," Brad said. "During the funeral, two houses were broken into—your ex-wife's and Mrs. Lenhardt's."

That announcement brought Carson angrily to his feet. He clenched his fists, turned away, muttering something unintelligible under his breath, and finally turned back. "What did the burglar do at the house?" he asked, almost as if he still had some kind of claim to the place.

The anger that Carson had shown a moment before was nothing compared to the explosion when Brad informed him about the messages on the mirror and the sheet of computer paper. He had to wait for Carson to quit slamming his fist against the wall and quit spewing words he hoped he'd never subjected his wife or daughter to. When he finally calmed down, Carson turned to Brad and asked, "Did you find anything else?"

Brad was on his feet now too. He thought it just might be possible that the mention of the hanging doll would cause Carson to strike out at him. He wanted to be ready. "Yes," Brad began, watching Carson closely. "One of her porcelain dolls had been removed from her curio cabinet and hanged by a shoelace in the bathroom."

To Brad's relief, there was no explosion at that point. But Carson's eyes were wide and his skin was white. He began to shake his head and again turned away, muttering something that Brad couldn't hear. When he finally turned and faced Brad again, he said, "I'm sorry. This is very upsetting. I hope you can catch the person that did this."

"I plan to," Brad stated.

"Then you better get at it," he said, clenching one fist and twisting his mouth. Then, in a lowered and very dangerous sounding voice, he said, "Detective, you better hope I don't catch him first."

"Let me and my colleagues work on finding him. Don't go out on your own. Please, Mr. Chambers, tell me whatever you can that will help us catch him."

"I wish I could," he said without meeting Brad's eyes. Then, after only a brief pause, he asked, "What was done in Garrick's house? Surely there weren't threats against his wife."

"No, there were no threats there. His home office was searched and damaged a bit, and a file was stolen," Brad said.

Carson shook his head. "That's all?"

"All that we could tell for sure," Brad responded. "One of Garrick's partners, Brian Bollinger, gave us a hand in trying to determine what, if anything, was taken. He was the one who found out that a file, a thick file, had been stolen."

Carson looked at him and Brad finally asked, "What can you tell me about a man by the name of Gabriel Mancheski?"

Carson was not good at keeping his features under control. The mention of the man brought red to his face and fire to his eyes. "Why do you ask?" he finally asked.

"Lenhardt was defending him on federal crimes. It was his file that was stolen," Brad said. "I know you know the man, but what I need to know is if you have any idea who might have stolen the file and why."

"I don't have any idea, and I barely know him," Carson said sharply. "Now, if that's all, I'll show you to the door."

Brad didn't need to be shown to the door. It was only a few feet away. "First, can you answer a couple more questions?" he asked.

"No, you better go now, Detective. And you better get busy and find out who is threatening my daughter," Adriana's father said with a dark face as he walked over and opened the door.

"If you think of anything else, please call me," Brad said as he handed Carson a card. He didn't want to go yet, but it was pretty clear that he was no longer welcome. He headed for his car.

CHAPTER EIGHT

ALONE IN HER ROOM, ADRIANA sat on her love seat, head in her hands, tears in her eyes, and frightening thoughts in her head. At this moment, she was mentally connecting dots. But she couldn't make the dots connect smoothly. At the beginning was her decision to stop and offer to help Jerzy Grabowski. That completed the first line, one from her to Jerzy. From Jerzy she mentally drew a line to her murdered neighbor, Garrick Lenhardt. But as she thought about it, she decided that it should only be a dotted line. She was no more convinced now, after the terrifying threats, that Jerzy was a murderer than she had been before.

She mentally went back to Jerzy, and this time she drew a line from Jerzy to the shadowy, tall, thin man. Then from him it went to Mr. Lenhardt's dead body. She thought about it for a minute. Then she again replaced the lines in her mind with dotted ones. That made two dotted lines, but between them, she was quite sure, a solid line existed.

Sitting up and rubbing her aching head with one hand, Adriana considered where the next line should go. The confusion of a mental dot-to-dot prompted her to put it on paper. She got up and crossed the room to the desk that sat against a far wall in her spacious bedroom. Her computer sat there, a lavender laptop, connected to her printer. She took a sheet of paper from the printer then sat down at the desk, pulled a pencil from the drawer, and began to draw her mental chart on the computer paper.

She put her own name at the top of the paper, but after thinking for a minute, she erased it and wrote it instead in the lower right-hand corner. She was at the end of the dot-to-dot exercise, she thought grimly, not the beginning. Next she wrote *Jerzy Grabowski* a couple of inches above her name and drew a solid line between her name and his. Next, she wrote the words *tall, thin man* two inches to the left of Jerzy's name and connected the two with a dotted line. Then she wrote *Garrick Lenhardt* two inches above but centered between *Jerzy Grabowski* and *tall, thin man*. Dotted lines soon went diagonally from each of those two names to the name of the dead attorney.

She sat back and studied her little chart, chewing thoughtfully on her pencil. Finally, she once again put the pencil to work on the paper. This time she drew a question mark and the words *thief/burglar* two inches above and two inches to the left of *Garrick Lenhardt,* drawing a solid line between them. After another few moments of chewing on the pencil, Adriana wrote once more. This time her pencil left the words *Gabriel Mancheski* two inches above *Garrick Lenhardt.* A straight, solid line soon connected the two.

After studying the chart for a few moments, Adriana drew another dotted line. This one looped from *thief/burglar* to the right side of the paper and then down to *Adriana.* It was only dotted because she had no way of knowing if the same person had broken into her home and Garrick Lenhardt's. It seemed logical, but then it could have been two different people acting on behalf of one unknown person. There could be almost no doubt that the two break-ins were closely connected.

Adriana laid the pencil on her desk and rose to her feet, shoving the chair back. She walked over to her dresser, opened her purse, dug around in it for a moment, and finally withdrew a pack of gum between her thumb and forefinger. A minute later, she again sat down at the desk, chomping nervously on a stick of gum, sparing the end of her pencil.

Taking the slightly damaged pencil up again, she poised it over the paper and held it there while she chewed and considered things. Finally, she wrote another name on the left side of the page about four inches from the top. To it, she drew a line up and across the page from *Garrick Lenhardt.* Then she drew another line, a dotted one this time, from *Gabriel Mancheski* to that other name, one that made her tremble and sob. The name she had last written was *Carson Chambers,* her own father.

Putting the pencil back on the desk she wiped at her wet eyes and studied what she had drawn. Sometime, in the past hour, Adriana had reached a conclusion. She prayed that she was wrong, but somehow, she couldn't shake the feeling that her father was somehow connected to this unholy jumble that now held her hostage. She had also made a decision, for better or for worse, that she wasn't going to sit around fearing for her safety while Brad and the other officers tried to sort it all out. She was going to try to figure it out herself.

The thought made her shudder, but she shook off the trepidation and braced herself. For her sake and for her mother's, she was determined to find some answers. She left the incomplete dot-to-dot chart on her desk, fully intending to get back to it later, and picked up her cell phone. She dialed a number she knew by heart and waited, her heart thumping, while it rang.

Finally, a voice she both loved and despised answered. "Dad," she began, trying to keep her voice steady and her nerves strong, "we need to talk."

"I was going to call you," Carson said. "I had a disturbing visit from a young detective."

"Was it Detective Osborn?" Adriana asked, her heart suddenly lighter. Brad must be thinking along the same lines she was. "What did he want?"

"He asked me if I had any idea who might be making threats against you," Carson said. "You need to be careful, sweetheart. I have no idea who might do such a thing, but I'm worried sick about you."

"The police are protecting me," Adriana responded. "And I will be careful. Did the officer ask you about—?"

Her father cut her off. "I'm coming over," he said. "We can talk in person."

"I don't think that's such a good idea—I mean you coming here. I want to talk to you, but Mom wouldn't like it if you came here," Adriana said.

"Oh, I wouldn't come inside. You could come out and meet me. We could just drive around for a while, or we could even come here to my apartment," he suggested.

"What will I tell Mom?" she asked, beginning to tremble. After her thoughts of the last hour, she didn't have a lot of faith in her father. She couldn't imagine that he would ever hurt her, but she was still bothered by his request.

"Do you need to tell her?" Carson asked.

"Maybe not. She went to bed early. She's very upset, as you can imagine," Adriana said.

"No more than I am. Why don't you meet me out on the street?"

Adriana almost said yes, but then she remembered the officer out there and said, "There's a cop parked out front."

"Adriana, I really want to talk to you. I'm terribly worried about you. Can you get away without the officer seeing you?"

"I guess I could," she said hesitantly. Then she thought about her determination to try to figure things out, and she steeled herself. Meeting with her father was a good first step. "I'll slip out the back door and sneak a couple of houses down around the corner. You could pick me up in front of the Turners' house."

"That's a good idea," Carson said. "Meet me there in twenty minutes."

While she waited, Adriana went over to her desk and studied her chart. Then she had an idea. She dialed Brad's cell phone. He answered almost instantly. "Adriana, are you okay?" he asked urgently.

"Of course, I just wondered if you have a fax machine at home. If you do," she said, "there's something I'd like to send you."

"Yes, I have one," he said and gave her the number. "What do you need to send me?"

"Oh, nothing much; just a little doodling I've been doing. I'll send it right away. If you'd look at it and call me back, I'd appreciate it. Thanks Brad."

She faxed the chart without any explanation on it. She just hoped to get his reaction to it, to see if he was indeed thinking like she was.

She looked at her watch. She was down to fifteen minutes. She hoped he'd call before she had to go meet her father. She needn't have worried about that. Her phone rang a couple of minutes later, and Brad's voice was urgent. "Adriana," he said without preamble, "don't do anything except take care of yourself. You aren't thinking of trying to talk to anyone on your own about this, are you?"

"What would I say and who would I talk to?" she asked deceptively and quickly tried to steer his thinking away from where he was headed. "I've just been sitting here thinking, and I wondered if you had sort of, you know, made the same connections that I have?"

"To a degree," he said. "But surely you don't think your father is involved in any of this?"

She thought about his question but didn't answer right away. Brad must have sensed her hesitance, for he spoke again. "I hope that your father isn't involved in any way, and I don't think he is, but like you, I can't help but wonder what his connection with Gabriel Mancheski is—how he knows him."

His assessment made it easy for Adriana. "Yeah, that's what I was thinking. It's probably not even important that Dad knows that guy."

"You're almost certainly right," Brad agreed. "Are you doing okay tonight?"

"Yes. I'm scared, but with that officer right outside, I feel secure for the night. Mom's already gone to bed," she said. She looked at her watch again. She needed to get going. "Thanks for looking at that. It's probably stupid. But I can't help thinking about things."

"I'll keep you informed of my progress," Brad promised. "I'll let you go now. You take care."

As soon as the call was over, Adriana put on her shoes and a light jacket, shut off her bedroom light, and slipped silently through the dark house. She left by one of the back doors and, by keeping close to the neighbors' houses, was able to get to the end of the street without ever being in sight of the cop in front of her house. She stopped in the shadow of a pair of large trees that stood beside the long, curved driveway of the Turners' house. She didn't have to wait long before her father's silver Mercedes pulled up. She quickly ran to it and got in the passenger side, and her father drove away without a word.

After a block or two, he looked over at her and smiled in the dim light of the Mercedes' interior. "Are you okay?" he asked.

"I'm fine, just a little shook up," she said.

There was nothing but light conversation, things like how her university classes were going and what she and her friends had been doing the past few days, all the way to Carson's condo. But once they were inside, Carson was all business. "Tell me about the guy you stopped to help," he said in his sternest voice, one he used to use on her when she was a small girl and slightly out of favor with him. "You need to stop doing things like that."

"Things like what?" she asked defensively.

"Like stopping to help strange men along the road. You're a pretty girl, Adriana, and you never know who might try to take advantage of you, even hurt you," he said. "You know better."

She didn't argue. After the past few days, he didn't need to tell her about dangerous people. "Sorry, Dad," she said meekly.

"Okay, now tell me about the guy."

She spent the next few minutes explaining what had happened and why she didn't think Jerzy was involved. He made it clear that he didn't agree. "It sounds to me like someone doesn't want you interfering with the police on the case they have against Mr. Grabowski. He's almost certainly the killer. Just leave it alone and let the police make their case."

Again, she didn't argue, but it disturbed her that her father couldn't see why it was so unlikely that Jerzy was the murderer. She hoped that wasn't because he didn't want the police looking beyond that strange man for the killer, although she couldn't imagine, after all that had happened, that they wouldn't be investigating a lot of people. Then again, she thought as her father lectured her about the dangers of getting involved, there may not be a big investigation since Brad was the only one who believed that Jerzy might be an innocent man.

Her father asked if she'd like some ice cream. She remembered that ice cream was almost a vice with her father. And she wasn't far behind him in that respect. "Yes, that would be great, Dad," she said.

He got up and went into his kitchen. She also stood up and walked nervously around his living room. She noticed his checkbook lying on a desk in the corner of the room. On an impulse, she tore out a deposit slip. She folded it and put it in her pocket, not at all sure why. She put the checkbook back where she'd found it and stared at the desk. She opened the top middle drawer, listening to make sure her dad was still busy in the kitchen. She looked through the drawer for a moment and was about to shut it when she disturbed a handwritten paper addressed to her father. She picked it up and began to scan through it, alarmed by what she was seeing. Before she had a chance to read it all, she heard her father returning. She shoved the note in her pocket with the deposit slip and hustled back to her seat on the sofa. When her father came back into the room, she was seated again where she'd been when he left.

She ate the ice cream slowly, relishing every bite. She and her mother didn't eat a lot of ice cream. They both constantly worked at keeping themselves healthy. It wasn't until they'd finished that she finally asked her father the question that she'd wanted to ask him ever since calling him. "Dad, what do you know about Gabriel Mancheski? I know you've met him, and I know that Mr. Lenhardt was his lawyer."

Carson's eyebrows lowered, and he looked at Adriana through narrowed eyes. "Very little," he said gruffly. "I talked to Garrick about him, just in passing, while we were golfing. Mr. Mancheski has some serious legal problems and, as I guess you already know, Garrick was defending him. The day Mr. Mancheski came to the house to see me, he was actually looking for Garrick and couldn't remember which house was his. He'd golfed with us one day, and Garrick had mentioned that we were neighbors. He found our house that day, and all I did was tell him where to find Garrick's."

Adriana hated the very thought, but she was almost certain her father was lying—it couldn't have taken him an hour to give directions to Mr. Lenhardt's house. She wondered what dark secrets he was keeping from her, why he would lie to her. She tried not to let her disbelief show, and she asked him if he had any idea who had threatened her. "I don't," he said. "But believe me, I intend to find out. You're my little girl, and whoever is behind this is going to answer to me."

He sounded tough, but when he spoke, his eyes shifted to one side and didn't meet hers. That bothered her—a lot. Her dad was definitely not being truthful, and it did nothing but deepen her fear. Even though he sounded sincere about the threats made against her, she didn't believe that he had no idea what was motivating them. It was time to have him take her home.

She yawned and said, "I'm getting really tired, Dad. I better go home."

"Yes, you've had a terrible day," he agreed. "Grab your jacket and let's go."

They talked very little on the way home. Adriana pretended to be nodding off. Her dad seemed distant and deep in thought. She felt something on that ride that she had never felt in his presence until this night—fear of him. She didn't like that feeling.

***

Brad's phone rang shortly after he'd gotten to bed, his mind preoccupied with Adriana and her problems. He'd left it plugged in, charging, on his bed stand. He reached for it, hoping it wasn't Adriana in some kind of trouble. He answered it and was surprised to hear the officer who had been left to watch Adriana's house on the other end.

What he was told brought him upright in bed. Then he spun his feet over the edge and asked the officer a couple of questions. "Thanks for the information," he said, "and keep me posted if you observe anything else."

He put his phone back on the bed stand, turned on his light, and wrote down the license plate number the officer had given him. Then he thought about what he'd just been told. It might be nothing, but it had piqued the interest of the officer on duty in front of Adriana's house. He sat on the edge of his bed, deep in thought. The officer had noticed a silver Mercedes drive by quite slowly, but until he passed by a second time, he had ignored it. After all, he'd explained to Brad, a Mercedes in that neighborhood was not out of place. But the guy had seemed to be looking awfully closely at the Chambers' house, and that had bothered the young patrolman. It also bothered Brad.

He called the dispatcher and asked them to run the license plate number that the officer had given him. He shivered when he got his response. The number came back to a Mercedes owned by Carson Chambers. He hadn't been entirely open with Adriana when he'd told her he didn't think her father was involved when she'd listed her father on the chart she'd made. He had come away from his short interview with Carson Chambers with a deep feeling of unrest, even suspicion. He didn't think the man had been even close to open with him. Brad was certain he was hiding something important.

He looked at the luminous alarm clock beside his bed. It was almost midnight. He tried to tell himself that Adriana's father was only doing what any conscientious father would do under similar circumstances. Surely he was just out trying to do what little he could to keep her safe. But then again, maybe he had other motives.

Despite the lateness of the hour, he picked up his phone again and hesitated only briefly before dialing Adriana's number.

***

Adriana was still thinking about the note she had just read, the note she'd taken from her father's desk. It haunted her. Her father had lied, just as she'd thought. She paced her bedroom, worrying, feeling nauseated and dizzy. She jumped when her cell phone began ringing across the room. She rushed over and picked it up with shaking hands. Who would be calling her this late? The very question made her shake with fright.

She opened the phone, and tears of relief threatened when she saw the number of Detective Brad Osborn on it. She took the call almost frantically. "Brad, thank goodness it's you," she said.

"Adriana, are you all right?" he asked in concern.

"Yes, I'm okay, but I've had a scary night," she said. "I hope it isn't about to get worse," she added as she fought to maintain control of her emotions.

"I just called to check on you," he said. "I'm sorry it's so late."

"That's okay. I haven't even gotten ready for bed yet," she admitted. "I've been busy."

For a moment, Brad didn't say anything. Adriana wondered anxiously what he was thinking. Finally, he said, "Adriana, did you see your father tonight after you talked to me?"

Now it was her turn to hesitate. But this was Brad she was talking to, a man she trusted and liked. "Yes," she said softly. "He picked me up and we went over to his place to talk. He lied to me, Brad. He lied to me." She shook her fist in frustration.

"I'm coming over," he said. "Is that okay?"

"Yes, Brad, please do. There's something I've got to show you. But when you get here, just knock lightly on the door. The doorbell might wake Mom up, and I'd rather she not be disturbed."

CHAPTER NINE

THERE WAS A DIFFERENT OFFICER on duty when Brad pulled up in front of the Chambers' house. Brad spoke to him for a moment, telling him Miss Chambers had called and asking the officer to watch diligently and to call him if he had any concerns at all. Then he approached the house. Adriana must have been waiting just inside the door because she opened it almost before he'd finished knocking. She silently signaled for him to enter and led him into the family room.

"Mom won't hear us here," she said. "Her bedroom is upstairs on the far end of the house."

They talked for a minute or two with Brad reminding her how important it was that she exercise caution in all that she did. She listened with her head slightly bowed. She responded with an apology for leaving without letting the officer know. "I'm sorry. I'll be more careful," she promised.

"You said you had something you wanted to show me," Brad prompted her.

Adriana picked up a paper from an end table and handed it to him. Brad read it through before he said, "Where did you get this?"

"From Dad's apartment," she said.

"Does he know you have it?"

"No, of course not. He went into the kitchen to get us some ice cream; while he was gone I snooped in his desk. It was in a drawer. It looked important."

"It is that," Brad agreed somberly. "Your dad apparently has something to hide, something important enough that someone is blackmailing him over it."

Adriana nodded and Brad looked again at the handwritten note: *Mr. Chambers, I know what you did. Unless you want this information given to* *certain individuals you'd rather have kept in the dark about your activities, you will need to send me some money. Those certain individuals will include your ex-wife, your daughter, your sons, your friend GL, and the cops. An initial installment of $100,000 will be expected on October fifth at nine in the evening. A courier will knock on your door at that time. The money is to be in the form of a cashier's check with the payee left blank. It is to be in a sealed envelope addressed to EP. You know who I am, so that is sufficient. This initial payment is to be followed up on the fifth of each month after that at a rate of $10,000 per month, payment and delivery in the same fashion. Don't disappoint GM. Also, if you let anyone know of our arrangement, what I have will be appropriately disseminated. EP.*

Brad looked up again. Adriana's worried eyes were on his face. He shook his head. "Do you have any idea who GL, GM, and EP are?" he asked.

"I know who two of them are," Adriana's mother said as she strode into the room in her robe. "What is going on here, Adriana?'

Adriana looked helplessly at Brad. He said nothing. She looked at her mother and said in a small voice, "I didn't want to bother you with this," she said.

"Adriana, we are in this together," she said. "Please, don't keep me in the dark about anything."

"I thought you were sleeping," Adriana said, sounding embarrassed.

"I was trying but without much success," Krista said. "I came down to get some milk and toast, and I saw the light on in here."

"Okay, Mom, I guess you might as well know. But it will only worry you more," Adriana warned.

"Then we'll worry together," she said as she sat on the other side of the sofa Adriana was sharing with Brad. She put her arm around her daughter's shoulder and said, "Okay, what is this about a bunch of initials?"

"Mom, there's something I need to tell you first, and please, don't get mad," Adriana pleaded. "Brad already scolded me and I promised not to do it again."

"We'll see," her mother said noncommittally.

"I went with Dad for a little while tonight after you went up to bed," she confessed.

"Adriana, that's—" Krista began.

"Mom, it was stupid, I know, but I'm glad I did it," Adriana interrupted quickly. "I won't do it again. But you need to see this. It was in

Dad's desk. I . . . I guess I stole it." As she spoke, she took the note from Brad and handed it to her mother.

Adriana and Brad glanced briefly at each other as Krista took the note, and they watched her face closely while she read. When she finished, she said with a trembling voice, "Something bad happened; that's why he changed so dramatically. This . . . this blackmail letter confirms that, except it must be much worse than I imagined."

"So, after reading it, do you still think that you know who the initials refer to?" Brad asked as he reached for and retrieved the note from Krista.

"Just two of them. I'm surer than ever that GL is Garrick Lenhardt and GM is Gabriel Mancheski. I have no idea who EP is, but it's clearly someone Carson knows," Krista said, a touch of anger in her voice.

Brad had another question for Adriana, but her mother asked it. "Did you take anything else from your father's place?"

Adriana had a guilty look on her face. "What is it?" Brad asked. "I've got to know everything you do if I am to get to the bottom of this."

"I took this," she said. She stood to pull the deposit slip from her pocket and, handing it to Brad, sat back down.

"Is this from his checkbook?" Brad asked.

She nodded. "I don't know what good it is, but I thought it would be nice to know what Dad is doing with his money." She glanced back at her mother and then said, "Mom, he makes so much money. It's not fair that you might not even be able to keep the house."

"Maybe not so much now," Krista said as she rose from the couch and strolled across the room. With her back to Brad and Adriana, she said, "Didn't you say he moved into a small condo a few months ago, Adriana?"

"I wouldn't even call it a condo. It's more of an apartment," Adriana said, looking at Brad, who nodded in agreement. "He moved into it in November," she added. "Until then, he had a very nice place. I guess now we know why he moved."

"Blackmail," Krista said as she turned and faced Brad and Adriana. "Blackmail, murder, threats against my daughter—these things are related, and Carson's hands are not clean."

***

Four lawyers sat around a table in a small conference room. They were all former law partners of the late Garrick Lenhardt. The meeting had been called by the firm's new senior partner, Brian Bollinger. Over the past hour he had led a discussion about the problem created by the theft of the file on their biggest, wealthiest, and most dangerous criminal defendant, Gabriel Mancheski. Some of the material had been duplicated, but most of it was lost to them and in someone else's hands—not a comforting thought for Brian and his partners.

Gabriel Mancheski was an old man, seventy-five on his last birthday, but he was also a powerful man. He would not be happy to hear that his defense team had allowed someone, presumably his opposition, to be in possession of some very sensitive information. The other three partners questioned Bollinger regarding how the file had come to be in the home of Garrick Lenhardt. Brian had explained that it had been Lenhardt's decision, and as the senior and founding member of the firm, that had certainly been his right.

The discussion was more of an argument at times, and Brian finally had to remind the others that it was too late to lament what had happened, both to Lenhardt and to the file. Brian began to speak. "We have no choice but to have Mr. Mancheski come in and meet with us. He'll be angry, he'll threaten us, he'll punish us financially, but he won't drop us. Right now, I don't think there is another firm in the county who would take over his defense. I know that you would like for me to tell Mr. Mancheski to find someone else, that we already lost our top man, but he won't take kindly to a show of weakness, and that's what it would be."

He paused and entertained a couple of questions. To one question, he responded, "It's true that we have lost a lot of important information, much in the form of notes that Lenhardt made regarding things Mancheski had told him. We have no choice but to ask Mr. Mancheski to fill in everything he can. That's how we will get part of the information back."

When asked how they would get the rest, Brian's face darkened. He leaned forward, slammed one of his fists on the table, and said, "We will find out who took it and take it back."

How would they do that? His answer was direct and firm. "I've done a little checking, and I've heard of a man by the name of Earnest Pyatt. He's ruthless, crooked, and expensive. We'll hire him."

***

Adriana had promised Brad Osborn that she would not meet her father again without someone who could guarantee her safety. She didn't want to anyway. She now knew that he was deeply involved in something both illegal and dangerous. She looked at the deposit slip she had taken from his checkbook. She looked at her computer. She thought about the promise she'd made. She thought about what she hadn't promised. Determined, she booted up her computer.

It was Saturday morning. An officer in a marked car was parked outside. She felt trapped in her own home. She didn't have anything to do except some studying. It could wait. Adriana was a whiz on the computer; she was majoring in computer science at the university. She learned quickly and didn't forget what she'd learned. She had never tried her hand at serious hacking before, but she was about to do so. She could only hope that she would be successful.

Thirty minutes later, she had succeeded in gaining access to her father's bank accounts. She soon found evidence of money that had disappeared in the exact amounts and at the exact times the blackmailer had specified. She also learned that his personal finances were lean. She reasoned that he could have money in other banks, but she had a feeling that if there was, it wouldn't be much. He was being bled dry financially.

However, this revelation didn't solve the question of what he'd done that had led to his dilemma. It didn't help her understand what it was that Gabriel Mancheski and her father had in common. She didn't know how to learn that unless . . . An idea formed in her head. It might get her nothing, but it was worth a try, she decided firmly. She had promised to stay away from her father. But she hadn't promised not to call him.

She dialed his cell phone number, hoping that he'd answer but not betting on it. It was good she hadn't bet on it because she'd have lost. Her father answered after four or five rings. "Adriana," he began. "Are you okay this morning?"

"Is anyone about to kill me? Is that what you mean? I don't know, Dad," she said darkly. "What I want to know is why anyone thinks I'm a threat. I can't and don't want to hurt anyone."

"Sweetheart," he said, with what seemed like sickly sweetness in his voice. "It's because of that man you tried to help."

"Maybe partly," she agreed, but she was convinced there was a lot more to it than that. "But frankly, I think it's because of whatever you did that is causing you to be blackmailed."

The silence from her father's end of the phone was palpable. She let him stew over what she'd said. The silent period stretched to over a minute. It was her father who finally filled the void. "Adriana, what are you talking about?" The anger in his voice was masked but not well.

"Dad, I think your actions have put my life in jeopardy," she said boldly. "If something happens to me, I hope you can live with your guilt."

"Adriana, do you have any idea what you are saying?" he demanded. "Who put such terrible, traitorous thoughts in your head?"

"You did, Dad," she replied coldly, even as her stomach churned with discomfort. So far he hadn't denied anything. "I know it's about Gabriel Mancheski. I want to know why, and I want to know what you're going to do about it."

"Adriana, what are you talking about?" Carson demanded. "Why are you talking to me like this?"

She wasn't going to let him put her on the defensive. He was her father, and despite all he'd done—breaking their family apart and who knew what else—she still loved him. She wanted to make that clear. "Dad, I love you." She went on, unbending in her newly found determination. "But I also know that you have done some terrible things. There's no use denying it, and don't ask me how I know because I won't tell you and I won't be put off. Please, Dad, if you care about me at all, you will tell me what you've done, who's blackmailing you, and why I am in danger."

She waited to see if he would give her any response. When all he did was clear his throat, she said angrily, "Dad, I'm your daughter, your own flesh and blood. You can't let them kill me. You're the only one who can stop this. Please, please, do something." Then she simply clicked off her phone.

A minute later, Adriana went one step further and shut the phone off. She wanted her father to stew over her allegations. Maybe he'd decide to come clean, but she figured he'd need some time to think about it before he did. She looked out the window to the front of the house. There was still a cop parked outside, but he looked very bored. She wasn't sure how he would keep her safe if anybody seriously wanted her dead. She shivered and went up to her bedroom, shut the door, and stretched out on her bed, her mind in turmoil.

Adriana was alone. Her mother had gone to her office earlier, saying that she needed to show some property to a serious buyer. She had left with a stern warning for Adriana to stay home and let the cops do their work. So far, she'd stayed home, and other than hacking into her father's bank account and making the call to him, she'd let the cops do their work without any interference. But as she lay on her bed, trying to ease the turmoil in her mind, she began to consider what else she could do.

The house phone rang from time to time, but she ignored it. She wanted to think. Anyway, she figured it was probably her father, and she wasn't going to talk to him yet. She wanted him to stew longer. She fell asleep for a few minutes, but when she awoke, she was so nervous that she began pacing through the house. She snacked on some cheese and crackers. She peeked out a window again and watched the obviously drowsy cop out front. Suddenly, feeling like a prisoner in her own home, she decided she needed to do something. It was time she took charge of her life. She could do that. She *would* do that. She made some plans as to how she would begin that process.

She turned on her phone, looked up a number in the phone book, and made a call. She dressed in comfortable blue jeans and a loose-fitting blue blouse. With her favorite running shoes on her feet, she once again looked out the window at the police car. The officer never looked around. His head was leaning back against the headrest. He appeared to be dozing. A lot of good he was doing her, she thought, but with what she was planning, it didn't matter anyway. She looked at her watch. In five minutes, it would be time to go and meet the cab she had called.

***

An average-sized man dressed in a brown sports jacket over a tan shirt and tan slacks approached the police car parked in front of the Chambers' house. He came from the rear, stepped up to the open window, and stopped. The officer appeared to be dozing. The man chuckled to himself as he reached through the open window, thrust a syringe toward the officer's neck, depressed the plunger, and withdrew it. The officer woke up, struggled for a moment, and then slumped forward onto the steering wheel.

The man put the used syringe back in his pocket and walked quickly toward the front door. He rang the bell and waited.

***

Adriana jumped when she heard the bell. She scrambled to a window and looked out. The cop was no longer leaning back against the headrest. Instead, he was leaning against the steering wheel. That looked wrong to her. It was an awkward position, even for a sleeping man. She felt a wave of panic sweep over her. The doorbell rang again. She suppressed the panic and didn't waste another moment. She sprinted through the house and slipped out the back door. She shut it quietly behind her then ran as fast as she could across the large backyard and scrambled over the high fence into the neighbor's backyard.

With great heaving breaths, she stopped in the shrubs on the far side of the fence and peeked through a small crack. Someone she didn't recognize came around the house, stopped at the door she'd just exited, bent down for a moment doing something she couldn't see, and a moment later opened the door. He looked around, ran his hand over his dark, slicked-back hair, and then stepped inside her house.

Adriana gasped, took a deep breath, and offered a prayer of thanks for helping her get out. She turned and hurried through the Winkles' yard, around the house, and to the street in front. There was no taxi there. She looked at her watch. It was almost time for it to appear, and this was where she'd told the dispatcher she'd be waiting. Of course, she'd left the house quicker than she'd planned.

She began to tremble and forced herself to regain control. If she was going to be in charge of her own life, her own safety, she had to be strong. She considered the possibility that the man she'd just seen break into the house was not alone. She looked around. Could someone be watching her at this moment? She didn't see anyone, but she had to consider the possibility. She had to consider every possibility.

The taxi was late. She looked back at the front door of the Winkles' house. If there was anyone at home, maybe they would let her wait there until the cab came. She started decisively up the long walk when she heard a car coming down the street. She looked and heaved a sigh of relief when she saw the cab approaching. She ran back to the street and jumped in the second the cab stopped. "Go," she said urgently. "There's someone after me. He might try to follow us."

The cabby looked over his shoulder, saw her face, nodded in grim assent, and pulled rapidly into the street, speeding away. Adriana reached in her pocket for her phone, intending to try to reach Detective Osborn, but the phone, to her horror, was gone. She looked back. Would the guy try to follow her? She leaned up and spoke to the cabby again. "Make sure we aren't followed, please. Just take me to a mall—any shopping mall. Just don't let anyone follow you."

He grunted and made a hard right turn then a short time later, a hard left. He grinned back at her. She felt better, but she kept a sharp lookout anyway.

***

Even though it was Saturday, both Brad and Mike were hard at work. Unfortunately, they were making very little headway. They were not working on the murder of Garrick Lenhardt; everyone but Brad was still quite confident that they had their man, Jerzy Grabowski, and that it would be a waste of time to try to find the shadowy, likely nonexistent man he claimed he had given a ride.

Their efforts were centered on the break-ins at the Chambers and Lenhardt homes. Brad was frustrated with their lack of success. And he was constantly worried about Adriana Chambers. He had tried several times to call her, but her phone was off. He finally tried the home phone, but it went to voice mail after several rings.

Frustrated, he attempted to make contact with the officer outside Adriana's home. The officer's cell phone also went to voice mail. The last time they'd talked, over an hour earlier, the officer had assured him that all was quiet there. Adriana was at home, but her mother was not. Brad and his partner were currently trying to identify possible suspects in the theft of the file on Gabriel Mancheski. They had met with no success so far. Finally, Mike proposed that they go visit Mr. Mancheski. He was currently out on bond, and he lived in a neighboring city in a home that was larger than the Chambers and Lenhardt houses combined.

Brad argued that before they drove out of town that they should stop and check on Adriana. "Remember," Brad said, "she's right in the middle of this thing, and it bothers me that the officer on duty there isn't answering his phone."

"And she's pretty," Mike said with a grin. Brad gave him an irritated look. Mike threw his hands in the air in mock surrender, still grinning. "Okay, let's go up there. Then we can look for Mr. Mancheski."

"I'm also worried that she isn't answering her phone. I just want to make sure she's okay," Brad said.

They pulled up behind the patrol car parked in front of Adriana's house. "Mike, something's wrong," Brad said as he noticed the unnatural way the officer was leaning against the steering wheel.

Both men jumped from their car and sprinted up to the officer. "Hey, wake up," Brad shouted. There was no movement. With a twist in his gut he put his fingers against the man's carotid artery. To his relief there was a strong heartbeat. "He's alive but out cold," he said to his partner as he straightened up and looked anxiously toward the house.

Mike, who was standing beside him, said, "We need to get medical help for him before we go in the house."

"You get help and call us some backup; I'm going in," Brad said. "Watch in case I scare someone out." Without waiting for Mike's almost certain argument, Brad pulled his gun from his shoulder holster and rushed to the door. It was locked. He didn't touch the doorbell for fear of alerting a possible intruder to his presence. He ran around to the back, sick with worry.

The back door nearest to him was hanging open. He slowed down and approached cautiously. He slipped through and began a careful inspection of the house. He had only covered a few rooms on the main floor when he heard sirens. Before going upstairs to the bedrooms, he opened the front door and shouted for assistance. Mike and a pair of uniformed officers joined him. He sent one of the uniformed officers out to the backyard to keep an eye out for anyone who might try to escape. He shouted to the officers attending to the unconscious officer, "Watch in case someone tries to come out."

The three officers continued the search Brad had started. Brad was most anxious to get to Adriana's bedroom, fearful that he might find tragedy there. What they found was an empty room and, after more searching, an equally empty house. There was no evidence of anyone hiding anywhere, even though they searched long and hard. At one point, Brad began again trying to call Adriana's cell phone, but he got no answer.

Later, while he directed a search of the backyard and the outbuildings, he again called Adriana's cell phone. One of the dozen officers now swarming through the yard shouted and signaled for Brad to join him. Brad ran over and picked up a ringing phone from the grass where the officer was pointing. He clicked his own phone off, and the one he'd just retrieved quit ringing.

It was Adriana's phone. He felt like he'd been hit by a truck. There was almost no doubt in his mind that something terrible had happened. Someone had gotten to her.

CHAPTER TEN

SITTING IN THE LITTLE JAIL cell feeling sorry for himself was getting to Jerzy Grabowski. Other than his newly assigned lawyer, Gloria Metz, he hadn't had any visitors. Surprisingly, the correctional officers were relatively nice to him. None of them spoke highly of the man he was accused of killing. If he'd been guilty, he might have taken some pride in it, but he was not guilty. He'd been framed, and if he could get out, he'd go looking for the tall, thin man and, if he ever found him, set things straight.

Unfortunately for him, getting out wasn't looking too good. He liked his new lawyer. She was only in her midthirties, but she struck him as a fighter. She was the only chance he had, and even though she talked tough, it was hard to believe he'd be found not guilty by a jury. He'd been set up very effectively. It angered him beyond words.

It was early Saturday afternoon when a corrections officer told him that he had a visitor. He couldn't imagine who would be coming to see him. He was escorted to the visiting room and placed in a tiny room, open behind him, where he was watched by an officer. He sat in the chair that was offered to him and faced the glass partition. He was told that when his visitor appeared, he was to pick up the telephone receiver and use it to communicate.

He couldn't imagine who would be coming to visit him. When his visitor appeared on the other side of the glass and picked up his phone, Jerzy still had no idea who he was. The man was about average in size, with dark, beady eyes, slicked-back black hair, and he was wearing a brown sports coat over a tan shirt and tan slacks. He introduced himself as Cedric Brewer. "I work for a man by the name of Valentino Lombardi. He has a message for you."

"What are you talking about?" Jerzy asked as he began to tremble.

"Mr. Lombardi says you've gotten yourself into a bit of a spot, but he also says that you would be a fool to fight the charges. Just admit to killing Mr. Lenhardt; that's all you have to do, and if you'll do that, you won't get hurt."

"What, I'm supposed to take the fall for something I didn't do?" Jerzy asked, his eyes wide with surprise.

"That's exactly right. It's the healthy thing to do, healthy for you."

"But I don't even know this Lenhardt guy. I didn't kill him. I can't admit to killing him when I didn't do it," Jerzy pleaded.

The man who called himself Cedric Brewer narrowed his eyes and glared through the glass at Jerzy. "Just do as you're told," Cedric said in a quiet, threatening voice, "and you will get out of prison much sooner than you will by fighting the charges."

"But there's a witness, a girl who knows I didn't do it," Jerzy said in an attempt to defend himself against this man and the person he claimed to be working for.

"She won't be testifying," Cedric said darkly. "She's not going to be available to say anything. I've got to be going now."

"Don't do anything to her," Jerzy pleaded. "She's a good girl."

"That has nothing to do with anything," Cedric told him. He paused and glared at Jerzy a moment longer. "Just confess and maybe she'll be allowed to live," he concluded darkly. He put the phone down, got up from his seat, signaled to the guard that he was ready to leave, and left Jerzy staring at him.

Jerzy was shaking and sweating like he was sitting in the hot sunlight instead of the comfortably air-conditioned jail. The correctional officer, when he escorted him back to his cell, asked Jerzy if he'd had a good visit. Jerzy asked, "Do they record each visit here?"

"Not always," the officer replied. "Why?"

"Oh, nothing," Jerzy mumbled, and the officer, thankfully, didn't press the matter.

Back in his cell, he sat on the edge of his steel bunk and pressed his fingers to his temples. The thing that worried him the most was the pretty girl who had stopped to help him. He didn't want her to get hurt, and he had a feeling that, whoever this guy really was, hurting her was the least he'd do if Jerzy didn't confess. He thought his head would explode. He didn't know what to do. He'd been framed. He was innocent. But so was she, and he'd never had someone so sweet and beautiful be so nice to him.

He swung his legs up and stretched out on the bunk. He felt big tears coming into his eyes. He turned his face toward the wall, away from his cellmate. He'd never been so miserable in his life. He didn't have any idea what to do. But at some point, he knew that he had to figure something out.

***

As she had requested, the taxi dropped Adriana off at a mall after the driver had taken her on a crazy ride and finally assured her, with a big grin, that they hadn't been followed. She had to go somewhere and do something. Going home was not an option. She was pretty sure the officer out front of the house was dead, and she was equally convinced that if she hadn't left the house when she did, she'd be dead too.

She fought the impulse to run for the nearest entrance to the mall, forcing herself to simply approach at a brisk walk. Once inside, she relaxed a little. For the next few minutes, she strolled the long hallways, blending with hundreds of other people while trying to decide what to do next. She knew what she'd planned to do when she'd first decided to leave, but she wasn't so sure of that now. And without a phone she felt especially vulnerable.

She remedied that situation quickly by stopping at one of the mall's electronics stores where she bought a cheap cell phone with enough minutes on it to get her by for a while. Then she shopped for some clothes and personal items, thinking that it might be a while before she could go back to the house. Finally, she bought a small duffle bag to put her purchases in. With the duffle bag slung over her shoulder, she began roaming the long hallways of the mall once more as she tried to decide what to do next. Suddenly, it struck her that the officer, the one she thought was dead, might still be in front of the house. She had to make a call and get someone there right now. If he *was* alive, he would need help.

The decision made, she took out her new phone and punched in a number she had memorized earlier.

***

When his phone began to vibrate, Brad quickly pulled it out and looked at the screen. There was no number listed. He wondered for a moment if he should ignore it but decided not to. As soon as he heard the voice on the other end he was glad he'd answered. "Adriana," he said, trying to ignore the twisting and bucking that was occurring in his gut. "Where are you?"

"Brad, I'm okay. I'm safe, but I don't dare tell anyone where I am right now. I barely escaped from my house before a man went inside. You guys better go there right away. I think he killed the officer who was watching the house."

"No, the officer is okay. The man injected him in the neck with something that caused him to lose consciousness. He'll be okay except that he might be in a little trouble for not keeping a sharper lookout," Brad said.

"I'm so relieved. He looked dead," Adriana said.

"What about you?" Brad asked. "I was afraid someone had taken you. We've got to protect you."

"Your department tried," she said, "and they failed. I think I'll take care of myself now."

"No, Adriana, please, let me take care of you. I promise I'll keep you safe," Brad pleaded.

"I know you'd try, Brad, but you have crimes to solve. I'll be all right. I'll call you if I need to. I lost my other phone, but I'll have this one on me," she said.

"I found your old one," he said. "It was lying in the grass in your backyard. What did you do? Climb the fence to get away?"

"Yes," she said.

"Adriana, please reconsider," he begged. "I don't think you realize how serious this is."

"I think I do. I like you Brad, but I'm afraid that I've got to protect myself now the best way I can. The most important thing you can do for me is find whoever is doing this and stop them."

"We're trying, Adriana, believe me," he said. "Did you see the guy who came to your house today?"

"I saw him through the neighbor's fence," she said.

"Describe him to me."

"Average size, I'd say," she told him. "He was quite far away and we have a big yard, but I did notice a couple of things. His hair was black and combed straight back like mobsters you see in the movies. And he was wearing tan pants and a brown jacket."

"That does help," he agreed. "It helps a lot."

"I've got to go now. I need to let my mother know I'm okay," she said suddenly, and she cut the phone call off.

Brad stood looking at the phone in his hand, stunned at her sudden departure. Mike said, "I assume that was Adriana."

"Yeah, and she won't let us help her," he said morosely. "She got away safely, and she thinks she can take better care of herself than we can."

"Can't say I blame her," Mike said. "We certainly let her down."

"Yeah, I'll say."

***

According to Adriana's watch, it was almost two o'clock. She decided there was one more thing she wanted to do before she left the mall to go . . . wherever she decided to go. She also wanted to do what she'd told Brad she was going to do, but she knew her mother was busy and a few more minutes wouldn't hurt. She found a beauty salon and asked if she could make an appointment. "It needs to be this afternoon," she said.

There was a cancellation, and she was told that one of the girls could get to her in about fifteen minutes. She thanked them, said she'd be back, and once more strolled into the mass of shoppers in the hallway. She decided that she better make the call to her mother now. Once she was in the salon, she might not be able to use her phone.

The phone rang several times before her mother answered. "Mom, it's Adriana," she said.

"It didn't show a number," Krista said suspiciously. "Whose phone are you using?"

"I lost my other one, and I bought a new one," she said. "Before you start worrying, Mom, I—"

Her mother cut her off. "I'm already worrying," she said. "If you bought a new phone that means you aren't at home. It isn't safe to leave. You know that."

"It wasn't safe to stay," Adriana argued.

"But Adriana, there's a cop outside the house."

"Yeah, sleeping," Adriana said. "He let some guy walk right up on him and poke a needle in him and, well, put him clear out, I guess you could say. Then the guy came to the house. I ran out the back and over the fence into the Winkles' yard. I caught a glimpse of him through the fence before I left. I must have lost my phone when I climbed the fence. I called Detective Osborn. He found it in the backyard."

"Adriana, this is terrible," Krista moaned. "I'm almost finished here. Where are you now? I'll come pick you up."

"I'm not going home, Mom," she said firmly. "And I don't think you should either. I've decided to look out for myself. You should do the same."

"Then we'll find a place to stay together," Krista said urgently.

"No, I think it will be safer if neither of us knows where the other one's at," she said. She knew that was a lame excuse, but she had things she had to do and she couldn't do them with her mother watching over her shoulder. But she couldn't tell her that. "I'll keep in touch, Mom," she said lamely. "And try not to worry too much. I'll take care of myself, I promise."

"Adriana, please tell me where you are right now."

Adriana shook her head as she said, "I can't, Mom. I'll call you later. Love you." She clicked off and headed back for the salon.

***

It was quiet in the office, as it often was on a Saturday. "Detective Osborn," Sergeant Tullock said urgently as she strode up to his cubicle, where he and Mike had been making some phone calls. "You need to go to the jail immediately."

"What for?" he asked.

"Something's going on with our suspect," she revealed. "They say he wants to talk to you, but only to you."

"About what?" Brad asked as he got to his feet.

"I don't know. That's why you need to get over there. The officer who called me said that he was pacing, pounding his head on the wall, and moaning. They're worried about him," she said. "I'll help Mike finish these calls while you go. Let me know what you learn."

***

The girl staring back at her from the mirror scarcely resembled Adriana Chambers. With her hair bleached blonde and cut shorter, about shoulder length, she looked like a whole new person. She had also bought a pair of glasses with clear glass in them and had added more makeup than she'd ever worn in her life. She examined herself carefully. *This should do*, she told herself. Now, it was time to decide what to do next, where to go, and how to keep herself safe from her enemies, whoever they were.

The *keep herself safe* task required her to find a sporting goods store in the mall. There she bought a small can of pepper spray and a large folding knife with a sharp serrated blade. She shoved the knife into one of the front pockets of her jeans. She added a small flashlight a few minutes later, but she put that in her purse, which she in turn stuffed in her duffle bag. One bag was enough to carry, and it was easy enough carrying the duffle bag because she could keep it slung over her shoulder.

Adriana decided to kill more time by getting something to eat. All the walking had made her hungry. She checked her supply of cash, the handful she'd taken when she was preparing to leave the house. She still had enough for a few more purchases, but she'd need to get to an ATM before she left the mall. She knew it was dangerous to use her card, but once she left here she wouldn't be coming back, so if anyone tried to trace her, it would only lead them to the ATM she'd used, and by then she'd be long gone. She shoved the cash back in her purse as she left the sporting goods store. Moments later she sat down in a restaurant and placed an order. She wasn't anxious to leave the mall. She felt safe here, but she couldn't stay forever. Eventually the mall would close. She could, however, eat a slow, nourishing meal while keeping a sharp eye out for danger.

***

By the time a corrections officer escorted Brad to the visiting area of the jail, Jerzy was already sitting across the glass from the chair he was told to sit on. "This won't do," Brad said to the corrections officer who was escorting him. "I need a private interview room. I'll need to record my interview with him."

The officer shrugged, spoke on his radio for a moment, and then told Brad to follow him. He and Jerzy were soon sitting face-to-face across a small table in a tiny room that was most frequently used for attorneys to meet with their prisoner clients. Jerzy looked dreadful. He'd lost weight, his eyes were slightly glazed behind the thick lenses of his glasses, and he seemed extremely nervous.

"Jerzy, do you mind if I record this conversation?" Brad asked as he prepared to set up his small digital recorder. The murder suspect shrugged, offering no objection. As soon as Brad was ready, he made the introductions on the recording, date, time, identities, and purpose of the interview. Then he said, "Okay, Mr. Grabowski, you asked me to come and speak with you. However, I am not comfortable doing this without your attorney present. I can wait or come back later if you'd like to call her." He assumed Jerzy didn't want his attorney, but to be on the safe side, he wanted a record of his having offered.

"I don't want my attorney right now. I know I have the right, but I don't want her here. I want to talk to you alone."

"You are giving up your right to be silent?" Brad asked.

"Yes. I wanna talk to you, to tell you the truth."

"I think we should get your attorney here first," Brad said, suddenly concerned with where this might be going.

"No, let me talk now," Jerzy said, half coming to his feet. "I mean it. I have the right to talk if I want to, and I want to. If you get my attorney, I won't say a word. I swear it."

Brad was thoughtful for a moment, and then he said, "What exactly do you have to say?"

The man sat back down, lowered his head, kept it that way for a moment, and then he slowly lifted it again. His glazed eyes finally met Brad's. For a moment, Brad thought that the man was not going to say anything more. However, after a minute, Jerzy said in a low, sluggish voice, "I did it." That was all. He dropped his eyes again.

"You did what?" Brad asked.

The close-set brown eyes never made the trek upward again, but after a moment, in the same sluggish voice, Jerzy said, "I killed Mr. Lenhardt."

Brad froze. He couldn't believe what he was hearing. It wasn't possible. He waited while he collected his thoughts before he suggested, "Let's get your attorney over here."

"No!" Jerzy shouted, his voice suddenly very loud and angry. "Let me talk."

"Why didn't you tell me when we spoke before?" Brad asked after giving the agitated defendant a moment to calm down.

"I didn't want to," Jerzy said.

"What made you change your mind?" Brad asked.

"I'm feeling guilty," was the response.

Brad didn't believe him. He decided to fire some questions at him quickly, to see if the man maintained his new confession and if it was consistent with the facts. "How did you kill him?"

"I stabbed him."

"What did you stab him with?"

"A screwdriver. You already know that, Detective Osborn."

"Why did you kill him?"

This time there was no ready response. Brad waited. Jerzy began to massage his temples again. "Have you said all you want to say?" Brad finally asked.

"No, I'm just thinking," Jerzy said, sluggish again. "He didn't want me to take his wallet."

"Did you take it?"

"You guys have got it now, don't you? You took it from my car, didn't you?"

Brad didn't respond to those questions. "What did you do with the credit cards and cash that were in it?" he asked.

Jerzy looked blank. He rubbed his chin. Finally, he said, "I threw them away, the cards, that is. There wasn't much cash."

Despite what Mrs. Lenhardt had said, he knew that it was possible that Garrick hadn't been carrying a lot of cash. "Where did you throw the credit cards?"

"Just along the road somewhere."

"Why didn't you throw all of them away?"

Again, the suspect had to think for a minute, but he finally responded. "I thought I might need some," Jerzy said.

Brad fired a question he thought might throw him off. "Who asked you to kill him?"

Again, Jerzy's response was slow, but he finally said, "Nobody. I did it on my own. I decided to rob the guy and had to kill him."

"You robbed him and then threw his credit cards away?" Brad asked skeptically.

"Yeah, I didn't think I could use them all."

Brad abruptly threw a different question at him, still hoping to get him to make a mistake. "Where was your car parked when you killed him?"

Once more, Jerzy had to think about his answer. He eventually said, "On the street."

"Where on the street? I need you to be more specific."

"Just on the street," Jerzy said stubbornly.

"Who is the tall, thin man?" Brad asked in an attempt to throw another curve.

Jerzy spoke quicker this time. "He don't exist."

"Then where did you get the screwdriver?"

"I had it with me when I went into the guy's house."

"No, you sent Miss Chambers to get one to get your hubcap off. But when she came back, you'd finished changing the tire without her help and were driving away. Where did you get the screwdriver that time?"

Once again, his response was far too deliberate. He seemed to be trying to think, to get his story figured out as he spoke. He continually pressed his temples. He refused to meet Brad's eyes. "It was in my suitcase where I put it after I killed the guy," he finally offered.

"Why didn't you get it out earlier instead of letting Miss Chambers think you didn't have one?" Brad asked.

Brad was convinced this confession wasn't genuine, that it was totally bogus. There were too many times that the guy stalled in giving his answers. It was like he was making them up as he spoke. The same was true in his response to this latest question. "It had blood on it. I didn't want her to see the blood," Jerzy responded.

That was a reasonable response, and had it not been for the length of time it had taken him to come up with the answer, it might have been believable. But Brad didn't believe it. Something had happened to get this pathetic man to make a confession he knew wasn't true. "Jerzy, Miss Chambers is prepared to testify that she saw someone in the car with you as you were driving away."

"Not true," Jerzy said, suddenly meeting Brad's steady gaze. "She can't testify." There was another long pause. Brad kept silent himself, waiting to see if Jerzy would go on. He finally did. "She would be lying for me. I don't want her to lie." Another long pause followed. Then he said, "She's a good girl. How many good girls would stop to help out an ugly guy like me? I don't want her to be h—" He cut himself off.

"You don't want her to be what?" Brad prompted.

"Nothing. I want to plead guilty. I'll tell my lawyer to let me plead guilty. I'm through talking. I want to go back to my cell now."

Brad tried in vain to get the man to speak again, but Jerzy was apparently quite serious. He kept his mouth closed tightly. Brad finally spoke into the recorder, closing the interview, and in a few minutes he was on his way out of the jail. But he suddenly stopped and went back inside. He asked the officer at the window if Jerzy had had any visitors that day. When told that he had indeed had one, the officer shoved a sign-in sheet toward him and poked his finger at a name written there.

Brad pulled out a small notebook and wrote down the name of Sam Brown, thinking that, whoever this Sam Brown was, he probably hadn't used his own name but had instead written down a simple, generic one. Brad asked if the officer could remember what Sam Brown looked like. He wrote down the description and left, mentally noting that it was the same description Adriana had given him of the man who had broken into her house. There was definitely something going on here and it wasn't good.

CHAPTER ELEVEN

In an attempt to make himself feel normal, Carson Chambers spent Saturday afternoon on the golf course. He went there by himself, and it was one of the worst rounds he'd ever played. The men he'd golfed with, all total strangers, looked at him like they wondered what he was even doing on a golf course. He tried to do better as the afternoon went on, and he did make some improvements in his game, but not anywhere near what he was capable of. He was too distracted. All he could think about were the threats against his daughter.

As he left the clubhouse and walked back to his Mercedes, he was alarmed to see someone leaning against it. He was a slightly smaller man than Carson, wearing tan pants and a brown jacket over a tan shirt. His black hair was slicked back on his head. The look on his face and in his beady black eyes made Carson shudder. Carson was quite certain that he'd never seen the man before.

He tried to ignore him by simply walking to the trunk while clicking it unlocked. He put his clubs in and shut the lid. Then he walked around to the driver's side of the car and reached for the door handle even as he watched his visitor in his peripheral vision. The other guy had finally pushed himself away from the car and was moving deliberately around it. By the time Carson had the door open, the man was beside him. "Carson Chambers?" the fellow asked.

"Who wants to know?" Carson asked as he faced the black-haired man.

"My name's Cedric Brewer," the fellow said as an evil grin spread across his face. His eyes remained hard and focused on Carson. "Who inherits the car when you're dead?" he asked.

"I don't plan to die until long after this car is worn out," Carson said, trying to show a bravado he didn't feel.

"I have news for you," Cedric said coldly. "Unless you convince your daughter to recant her story of helping Jerzy Grabowski and you convince her to keep her mouth shut about the payments you are making to keep certain information private, you will die and so will she."

"She doesn't know anything about the blackmail," Carson said with an angry hiss.

"My boss and I don't happen to believe that," Cedric said. "So you make sure she keeps her mouth shut. I would recommend that you move her far away from here, to another state. Otherwise, she will be dead too."

"Listen, Mr. Brewer—" Carson began.

"I don't have to listen to anything," the man broke in angrily. "You are doing the listening. I'll be going now, and if you know what's good for you and your daughter, you will do as you are told. Believe me, you don't want to see me again, because if you do I can assure you that I will be the last person you ever see."

With that, Cedric Brewer strode quickly away. Carson got in his car, his hands shaking so badly he had a hard time getting the key in the ignition. When he succeeded, he looked over his shoulder in time to see Mr. Brewer get in a black Escalade. He didn't even attempt to start his own car until the Escalade was out of sight.

As Carson drove toward his apartment, he examined his sorry life, something he had not done in any kind of honest depth since he had first contemplated leaving Krista. It was a hard admission to make, even to himself, but he did finally confess that he had made a shambles of both his life and the lives of his family. Most of what he'd caused with his actions was beyond repair. But there was one thing he could do, and that was to save the life of his daughter.

He drove straight to his condo, or rather his apartment. He was fooling no one by calling it a condo. Once he was inside, he dialed Adriana's cell phone number. It was time to help her get someplace safe, for he was certain that the hoodlum with the slicked-back hair was a cold-blooded killer and he wouldn't care who he killed, even an innocent girl. The phone began to ring and as he waited impatiently for Adriana to answer it, Carson's heart began to pound.

***

A cheeseburger was placed in front of Brad, along with fries and a glass of milk. He slowly picked up a fry and began to nibble at it. It wasn't so much that Brad was hungry as that he didn't want to present what he'd learned from Jerzy to his partner and his sergeant any sooner than he had to. Not that a delay would make it any easier; it wouldn't. He knew how they would react. They would consider this a capstone on the case against Jerzy in the murder of Garrick Lenhardt, a murder Brad was convinced he had not committed. But no one else would believe that. And even if they did, he had a feeling that Jerzy would do exactly what he'd said he would—plead guilty to the bogus charge. In the meantime, the real killer was still out there somewhere, free to kill again if he so chose.

He heard a phone begin to ring, an unfamiliar tone. It startled him from his anxious thoughts. It was coming from the pocket of his sports jacket. It was Adriana's phone, the one he'd picked up from the lawn behind her house—the one he'd hoped to get back to her and which it didn't appear he was going to be able to do, at least not anytime soon.

Brad pulled out the phone and glanced at the number. The name of the caller was displayed right there on the screen; this was a number she had entered in her phone's memory. Her father was trying to call her. On an impulse, Brad clicked a button and put the phone to his ear. "Mr. Chambers, you have reached Adriana's phone, but this is Detective Brad Osborn speaking. It is critically important that you and I talk."

For a moment, there was no response from the other end. When someone finally spoke, Brad recognized the voice of Carson Chambers. "What are you doing with my daughter's phone?" he demanded. "Is she all right?"

"No, she is not all right, Mr. Chambers. I didn't steal her phone. I found it where she dropped it as she was fleeing from someone I'm sure you know. Where can we meet?"

Carson ignored Brad's question and asked, "Where is she?"

"I wish I knew that," Brad said honestly. "Unfortunately, she won't tell anyone. Please, I need your help. Your daughter's life is at risk."

Brad thought he heard a sniffle, then Carson spoke, his voice broken. "Not at my apartment," he said. "It would be dangerous for your car to be seen here. And not at the police station either. I can't let my car be seen there."

"I'm having a bite to eat," Brad said. "I'll eat slowly and you can hurry over here."

"Okay, where are you?" Carson asked.

Brad told him, and then he said, "I'll order you something if you like."

"Thanks, but I don't think I can eat. I'll order a coke or something when I get there."

Brad was a little surprised at how quickly Adriana's father made it from his apartment to the small café where Brad was sitting alone in a corner booth. He spotted Carson the moment he walked through the door. From the way he was dressed, he guessed that he'd come from a golf course. But the look on his face didn't seem like that of a man who had recreation and relaxation on his mind. He looked haunted. His eyes were sunken, and he walked toward Brad with his shoulders slumped forward. He took a seat without a word and then looked back as if to see if there was someone pursuing him.

Brad was the first to speak. "Thanks for coming, Mr. Chambers."

"Call me Carson, and it's the least I could do," Adriana's father said, his voice sounding as dejected as the look on his face. "Are you sure you don't know where Adriana is?"

"I wish I did, but I don't. However, I have reason to believe she's safe for now."

Carson heaved a sigh, and then he dropped his eyes and said, "We've got to save her, Detective. My life is over. But if I can save Adriana before they kill me, at least I will have done something good for a change. I have made a mess of my life and hurt a lot of people in the process. I'm prepared now to do what I can to help my daughter. Then I don't care what they do to me."

Brad studied the bleak face and the downcast eyes for a moment. Convinced that Carson was sincere, he said, "Why don't we start at the beginning? We seem to have privacy here; the place is nearly deserted."

"Which beginning?" Carson asked as he finally lifted his eyes and looked at Brad. "The beginning of my destroying my life and my family or the beginning of the trouble Adriana is currently in?"

"I want to hear it all, if you are willing," Brad said. "But my first priority is Adriana and her safety."

"I'll speak fast," Carson said just as a waitress stepped up and offered him a menu. "No thanks," he said, waving the menu away. "Just bring me a cola."

After she'd walked away, Brad said, "Do you mind if I record this? I have a small recorder in the pocket of my jacket."

At first, a look of alarm crossed Carson's face. But the haunted look came back quickly, and he shrugged his slumping shoulders and said,

"No, go ahead. Just talking to you will assure my death if they find out, and they will. But it doesn't matter; I no longer have anything worth living for anyway."

"Maybe it seems that way now, but things do have a way of getting better if we try hard enough," Brad said as he pulled the little digital recorder out and turned it on.

Carson looked at him and shook his head. "You have no idea," he said.

Brad suspected Carson might be right. He made some introductions into the recorder and then said, "Okay, why don't you start by telling me what you're being blackmailed over."

Carson looked shocked. "How did you know about that?"

"I know more than you think," Brad said. "Who is blackmailing you and why?"

Carson took a deep breath, held it for a moment, and then exhaled. "There is a man by the name of Valentino Lombardi. He seemed like a successful businessman when I first met him. Have you heard of him?"

Brad shook his head, and for the sake of the recording, he said, "I don't think so."

"Well, I met him when I was at a convention in New York. We did a business deal," Carson said, shaking his head. "At least I thought it was a business deal. It looked like I'd make a lot of money, and that's what my life had become about. All I wanted was to make a lot of money, as if money will buy anything a person wants. I can tell you, Detective, it won't."

He paused for a moment, slowly shaking his head, and then he said, "Anyway, we completed the deal, and it was only later that I learned that the deal had hurt of lot of innocent people, bankrupting many of them. I should have known that Valentino's deal was too good to be true, that someone else would suffer by the work I had agreed to do for him. Anyway, I shut my eyes to all of that. I think some people may have committed suicide when they learned they were financially ruined. At least that's what I was told. It turns out that two of them were killed by Valentino's men, murdered. I don't know what they did to incur Valentino's wrath, but Valentino has evidence that implicates me. If I do what I'm doing right now, talking to the police, I was told that the information and evidence would be given to the authorities and I would be charged with the murder of those two men."

"Where are these people from?" Brad asked, keeping his face as expressionless as he could despite what he was hearing. "The ones who have died, I mean. Both those who committed suicide and those you say were murdered."

"Again, I don't know for sure who committed suicide, if anyone did. Anyway, the people who invested in our deal were from all over the country, but one of them was from here in the state. He was killed in a hit-and-run accident. I'd let one of Valentino's men borrow my car. He'd claimed his was broken down and he needed a ride. I never got my car back. I was initially told that it was stolen, but then when I learned that this man had been killed, I contacted Valentino and asked him what happened. He told me that I had killed him, hit him with my car and fled. You can imagine how shocked I was. When I told him that I wouldn't stand for an accusation like that, he just laughed."

"Where is the car now?" Brad asked.

"Valentino has it hidden somewhere. If I talk, like I am," he said bitterly, "then it will turn up."

"What about the other murder victim?" Brad asked.

"I suppose that someone else is being blamed for his death."

"Who are you accused of killing?"

"A guy by the name of J. T. Vogler."

Brad rocked back in his seat. "That was listed as a hit-and-run," Brad said. "I remember the case."

"That's right, and my little Toyota Corolla, if it turns up, will implicate me. And the dealings I had with Vogler, along with ones that Valentino and his henchmen made up, will put me behind bars for life," Carson said. "Frankly, I'd rather be dead—and I will be."

"What did Vogler do that would make Valentino want to kill him?" Brad asked.

"I helped him invest some money, over a million dollars. Vogler got cold feet and told me he wanted his money back. I couldn't have done that if I'd wanted to. I told Valentino, and he said he'd take care of it. Now I know how he takes care of problems. And now I'm one of his problems."

Brad thought about Adriana. "Does any of this have anything to do with your daughter?"

"I didn't think so at first, but now I do." Carson rubbed his eyes for a moment as they began to mist up. He took a couple of deep breaths. "Valentino and his men apparently think that I said something I shouldn't have to Adriana. It's not true, but they think that she could somehow implicate them by what they think she knows. They shut me up with blackmail. They seem to think they can shut her up with threats."

Brad shook his head. "How do you know they think you've told her?"

"Why else would she be threatened?" Carson asked. His face became cloudy, and he looked up as a waitress appeared with his cola. She put it down in front of him, and he picked it up and took a sip. His hands were shaking so badly that some of the drink spilled onto the table. He put the drink down and sopped the spilled drink up with a napkin. "A guy was waiting by my car when I left the golf course today. He told me that he had a message from Mr. Lombardi."

"What was the message?"

"He said that unless I convince my daughter to change her story about helping Jerzy Grabowski, and also unless I convince her to keep her mouth shut about the payments I'm making to keep *certain information* private, she would die and so would I. And now you know what that *certain information* is."

"Yes, but Adriana doesn't?" Brad asked.

"She doesn't know anything about why I'm in trouble," Carson said sadly. "I told the guy that, but he said he and his boss don't believe it. The guy told me to make sure she doesn't say anything or they would kill both of us. He said I should make her move out of state. We've got to find her and we've got to get her someplace safe."

"Adriana knows that you're being blackmailed," Brad said, watching Carson's face closely for a reaction.

All he did was shut his eyes for a moment. When he opened them he said, "She told me. I don't know how she figured it out, but she knows. I didn't tell Mr. Brewer that."

"Who is Mr. Brewer?" Brad asked.

"He's the guy that confronted me today. He says his name is Cedric Brewer and that he works for Valentino Lombardi."

"Have you met him before?"

"Today was the first time."

"Can you describe him to me?" Brad asked.

Carson did so and Brad shook his head angrily. He pulled the notebook out of his shirt pocket and read his latest entry, the one he'd made when he'd looked at the visitor's log at the jail. He'd written the name

Sam Brown, followed by *tan pants, brown coat, tan shirt, and black hair, combed straight back.*

Now he knew why Jerzy had changed his story. Sam Brown or Cedric Brewer or whoever the man was had threatened him, and he'd also threatened Carson. Brad was pretty sure that he'd also been the man who broke into Adriana's house that morning. Cedric Brewer had had a busy morning.

Carson had been watching as Brad consulted his notebook. "What is it, Detective?" he asked.

"Are you sure you don't know this man?"

"Positive," Carson said.

"Does the name Sam Brown ring a bell?"

"No, why?"

Brad held up the notebook and shook it. "Someone wearing tan pants and a brown sports coat with slicked-back black hair visited Jerzy Grabowski at the jail."

"Did Jerzy tell you that?"

"No, but someone did go there. And then Jerzy called for me and when I met with him he confessed to killing Garrick Lenhardt," Brad revealed. "But his confession was weak."

"He was threatened, wasn't he?" Carson asked.

"I think so, but Jerzy doesn't admit any such thing," Brad responded. "Are you sure you don't know Jerzy?"

"I'm sure," Carson said. "I'm also sure that he didn't have anything to do with Garrick's murder. He was just in the wrong place at the wrong time. He's another innocent victim of Valentino Lombardi."

"Jerzy claimed, before today, that a man finished helping him change his tire. Jerzy described him as tall and thin," Brad said. "Does that description, broad as it is, fit anyone you met in Mr. Lombardi's organization?"

"Not really," Carson said.

"Okay, now let's talk about someone else," he said. "Tell me about Gabriel Mancheski."

"A thoroughly bad man," Carson responded. "Garrick was defending him on a number of serious charges."

"In your opinion, is he guilty of the charges?" Brad asked.

"I don't know, but I suspect that he is. He and Valentino Lombardi have had some kind of dealings. He came to me, asking questions about Valentino and what I'd done to help him. I denied everything, but he didn't believe me. He even came to my house one Saturday. I told him that I didn't ever want to see him again or even talk to him," Carson said.

"Would Mr. Lombardi have any reason, as far as you know, to either make sure Mancheski went to prison or, for that matter, to make sure he didn't?" Brad asked.

Carson shook his head. "I have no idea. The two of them, if my guess is right, are birds of a feather. They are both rotten to the core. I'm pretty sure that Valentino once worked for or with Mancheski. Whether they are still somehow involved with each other I don't know, but if I had to guess, I'd say they are more likely enemies now."

"Okay, thanks Carson," Brad said. "Do you have any idea who would want to have Mr. Lenhardt killed?"

"Honestly, I don't. If he'd done something to offend Valentino, he would certainly be capable of it, but I don't know that there's any connection at all," Carson said, shaking his head. "Well, that might not be true. If there is bad blood between them, as I think there might be, then the fact that Garrick was defending Mancheski might be some motivation,"

"That would make sense," Brad agreed.

Carson was thoughtful for a moment, and then he said, "I suppose you've considered this, but Garrick defended a lot of people and got them out of pretty serious stuff, but he wasn't always successful. Someone he failed to win for might be behind it."

"Thanks, I've thought about that," Brad admitted.

"You should think about it more," Carson said. "Now, what about my daughter? What can you do to help her?"

"First I've got to find her. Then, believe me, Carson, I'll do whatever it takes to keep her safe. You have my word on that. I'll also help you," Brad said.

Carson shook his head. "No, I'm on my own. They'll find out we've talked, and when they do they'll kill me," he said morosely. "I just don't want my little girl hurt."

"Where are you going now?" Brad asked.

"Home to get some things," Carson said. "Then, if no one kills me, I'm going to just drive. I don't know where, but I'll go somewhere." He turned to Brad, his eyes misty again. "If you hear from my daughter, please let me know."

Brad promised, and picking up the check, he went to pay while Carson left the café.

CHAPTER TWELVE

THE MALL WAS AS CROWDED as ever, but Adriana felt like the place was closing in on her. She'd wasted all the time she could stand. She'd visited dozens of stores, made no further purchases, and worried until she felt like she was going to explode. And yet, despite the feeling of the mall growing too small for her, she was scared to leave. She didn't know where to go or what to do. She had to make some plans—either that or call Brad and ask him to come get her.

She didn't want to do that. Well, she did want to do that, but she couldn't. She wasn't sure he could keep her safe. She wanted to prove that she could take care of herself. She didn't want Brad to think of her as a timid, fearful girl. She was determined to depend on herself. All through the long day, her thoughts kept coming back to her father. She was angry with him for all the things he'd done that had hurt her and her mother. And she was angrier than ever that he'd put her in her current situation. She was sure that it was mostly because of him that she was in such terrible danger. Finally, she decided to confront him again. She didn't think it would do any good, but at least it would be doing something. She pulled out the new, cheap phone and punched in his number.

When he answered, he said sharply, "Who is it and what do you want?" Wow, but he did sound stressed.

"Dad, it's Adriana," she said, trying to keep her anger in check. "I'm going to be killed if you don't help me. Please, Dad, tell me what you've done."

"I'm so relieved that you called," her father said in a much softer voice. "I've been worried sick."

"Over what?" she asked coldly. She wasn't in the mood to feel sorry for her father.

"Over you, sweetheart," he said. "I know you're on your own and in danger, and you're right: it's my fault."

"What have you done?" she asked again.

"Let me meet you somewhere. I'll do everything in my power to keep you safe," he said, sounding urgent. "And I promise I'll tell you everything."

"Tell me now, on the phone. I'm listening," she said abruptly.

"No, we have to sit down together."

"Dad, I promised Detective Osborn that I wouldn't meet with you alone again," she said. "So it's on the phone, now, please."

"I have a better idea. Call Detective Osborn. He can tell you everything," her father said.

"How can he do that?" she asked doubtfully.

"I just met with him. He recorded our entire conversation. He knows it all now," he answered. "He also knows what danger we are in, both of us. But I don't care about me anymore. I deserve whatever they do to me, but you are innocent."

"Dad, what is going on?" she asked as icy fingers began to tear at her stomach. She shivered.

"Watch out for a guy who goes by two names, Sam Brown and Cedric Brewer," he said. "He visited Jerzy Grabowski in the jail as Sam Brown. He visited me as Cedric Brewer. Among other things, he said that if you don't recant your statement about helping Mr. Grabowski, he'll kill us both. I think, at least Detective Osborn thinks, that he has coerced Jerzy into changing his testimony. He spoke with the detective and confessed to the murder of Garrick Lenhardt. He plans to plead guilty. But even that isn't enough to save you, Adriana. There is more. Either meet with me or call Detective Osborn. Please. And do it now."

"Okay, Dad. I'll call you back," she said as she felt her knees go weak. She disconnected and found a place to sit. Once she had managed to calm herself down, she planned her next move. She wanted to call Brad, but that would have to wait. There was someone she had to see first. It was risky, but she would try it anyway. She was determined to not let fear rule her. There was too much at stake. She went to an ATM, withdrew as much as she could, and prepared to leave the mall.

A taxi dropped her off at the jail almost an hour later. She had already booked herself into a hotel room, paying with some of the cash she'd withdrawn and using a false name. She'd left her newly purchased belongings there, including her knife and pepper spray. There was no way she could get inside the jail with those. She stood outside for a moment, looking at the imposing structure. Finally, she took a deep breath and walked resolutely inside.

When she asked to visit with Jerzy, the officer said that he'd already had two visits that day, one from a friend and the other from a detective. He asked what her relationship to the prisoner was. She told him that she was his niece and that she really wanted to see him. He shoved the visitor log through the slot at the bottom of the window and told her to sign in. She wrote down, *Sarah White*, not even thinking of how suspicious that might seem to anyone who looked closely, considering that Jerzy had already been visited by a person using the name of Brown. Color seemed to be in today when it came to phony names.

A few minutes later, she was escorted into a small booth. Across the window from her, Jerzy Grabowski looked at her with puzzlement on his face. "They said my niece was here to see me. I didn't know that I had a niece. I have a sister, but I haven't seen her in many years," he said. "Are you her daughter?"

She smiled. At least her disguise worked. "You don't recognize me, do you?" she asked.

He adjusted his thick, gold-rimmed glasses, squinting as he leaned closer to the glass that separated them and studied her closely. "There is something familiar about you, but you certainly don't look like my slob of a sister. You're actually pretty."

"Thank you, Jerzy," she said. "I had to change my looks so I wouldn't be recognized. Picture me with longer, dark brown hair," she said as she pulled off her glasses.

He looked closely for a minute, then he gasped, and his ruddy face went white. "It's you!" he gasped. "You helped me with my tire."

"That's right. I'm Adriana Chambers. But I've been told that you deny ever meeting me. And that you say that a tall, thin man didn't also help you," she said sternly. "You are innocent, Jerzy. I know you are. You can't confess. It would be a lie."

Jerzy stared at her for at least thirty seconds, his mouth opening and shutting. He rubbed his bald head, and sweat beaded on his face. Finally, he spoke. "You never saw me, miss. You can't say you did. Please, forget about me."

"I can't do that," Adriana said. "I saw what I saw, and you know it. I want to help you."

"They'll kill—"

He shut his mouth and pulled the phone away from it.

"Who threatened you?" she asked. "Was it a guy with slicked-back black hair in a brown sports jacket?"

From the way his mouth dropped open and his eyes grew wide, she knew she'd scored. He lifted the phone again and spoke into it. "How did you know?" he asked, his voice low and his eyes shifting back and forth as if watching for that evil man to appear.

"He threatened me, too, Jerzy."

"He's dangerous," he said, his voice getting shaky now.

"I know that," she said. "He came after me at my home this morning. I narrowly escaped."

"Oh, Miss Chambers, that's horrible. But now you know that you can't say you saw me. Let me just plead guilty. It will keep us both alive," he begged.

"It won't help me," she said. "You're not the only reason they want to kill me. They are also after me because of something my dad did." She glanced at her watch, "I can't stay longer. But please, say you'll reconsider. Say you'll fight this terrible thing they say you've done and that both of us know that you didn't do."

"I don't know, Miss Chambers," he said, rubbing his bald head nervously.

"At least think about it. Will you do that?" she pleaded.

"Okay," he agreed after another brief period of silence. "I'll think about it. But you be careful. You're a good girl, the best one I've ever known. Don't let them hurt you."

As he said that, big tears started running down his chubby cheeks. He took off the thick-lensed glasses, making his eyes look small. He rubbed at them, then looked up, put the glasses back on, and said into the phone, "I'll always remember you, Miss Chambers. No matter what happens to me, I'll never forget what you are trying to do for me. Thank you."

Adriana left a minute later. She hurried away from the jail, using her cell phone to call for a taxi as she walked. She kept a close lookout around her, and it was with a great deal of relief that she finally saw a taxi coming. She went right back to her hotel. She needed to relax for a little while and decide what her next move would be.

***

The past ninety minutes in the office of Sergeant Lydia Tullock had been tense. Brad, Mike, and Sergeant Tullock had all listened to the recording of his interview with Jerzy twice, from beginning to end. Then they had discussed it, argued about it, and finally looked at each other with anger on all three faces. Lydia and Mike were angry with Brad, and he was angry with them. Lydia finally said in her sternest command voice, "Listen, Detective Osborn. This is exactly what Assistant District Attorney Harris asked us to get. We've got it now and I have no intention of wasting it. We'll take it to ADA Harris on Monday, and he'll share it with Grabowski's attorney. We'll let them take it from there. You will stay out of it. Do I make myself clear?"

"It isn't right, Sergeant, and both of you know it."

"You either act like a team player, or we'll pull you off this case and the related ones," she threatened, her blue eyes shooting fire.

Brad glared at her, but he knew he was beat, at least for now. He needed to keep on working this group of cases, for Adriana's sake if nothing else. He softened his look, forced a smile, and said, "You've got it. Now, I told you before we began this discussion that I was delayed by another interview. I have another recording you need to listen to."

"Does it move us forward in the matter of the break-ins?" Sergeant Tullock asked. "I don't have time to waste."

"It's a huge break," Brad said nodding. "This is really big."

"Then let's hear it," she said, looking at her watch. "And it better be good."

Brad fiddled with the small digital recorder for a moment, and then he said, "Okay, here goes. I'll let it speak for itself."

It did just that. Both of his fellow officers couldn't keep the astonishment from their faces. Nor could they hide their concern over what they were hearing. A few minutes into the recording, Brad's phone vibrated. He pulled it out and looked at it. There was no number listed. His stomach twisted, and he said, "I need to take this."

The others just grunted, and he opened Lydia's office door and stepped quickly through it as he put the phone to his ear and said, "Hello."

"Hi," came a voice he was becoming way too fond of.

"Adriana?"

"Yes. Hi, Brad. And before you ask, I'm safe and I'm fine, and I'm not telling you where I am," she said.

"Okay," he said. "I mean, it's not okay, but I guess it is what it is. What can I do for you?"

"My dad said that you—" Adriana began.

"Adriana, you promised that you'd stay away from him," Brad interrupted urgently.

"I haven't seen him," she said. "But I called him. He said that you have a recording of him telling you why he's being blackmailed. He said you'd tell me all about it. He didn't want to tell me over the phone, and I told him that I promised you that I wouldn't meet with him alone. So it's up to you to fill me in."

"Thanks for keeping your promise," he said, feeling bad about doubting her but wishing with all his heart that she'd meet with him. "I can't play it for you right now," he said. "It's in use. Detective Silverman and Sergeant Tullock are listening to it right now. I'll call you back as soon as we are through."

"Okay," she said. "But please, don't be long. I want to know what's going on," she said.

"I'll need the number of your new phone," Brad said. She gave it to him. "Thank you, Adriana. Be careful. I couldn't stand it if anything happened to you."

"Why?" she asked.

"Work it out," he said softly and disconnected.

He stepped back into Lydia's office. The recording was still going, and both officers still listened intently. When it finally came to the end, Brad clicked his recorder off and looked at the other two. Lydia was slowly shaking her head. She said, "Wow! Brad, that's dynamite. Good work."

"Thank you, Sergeant," he said evenly. "The question now is what to do with what we've learned."

"And how do we keep our witness alive?" Mike asked. "The murder and the break-ins are all connected to this or my name ain't Silverman."

"Oh, it's connected all right," Lydia said. "We've got our work cut out figuring what those connections are. It looks like we'll be working late today and all day tomorrow. I think it's time to get the lieutenant in here."

"I'm glad you get to call him," Mike said smugly. "Rank does have its privileges. I know he didn't want to be disturbed today unless it was absolutely necessary."

"And that's what it is," Lydia said. "I guess I'll call him. And I think that while we're waiting for him, I'll see if I can get another pair of detectives in here. There is a lot of work to be done. Why don't you two go get some dinner," she suggested. She looked at her watch. "Let's meet back here at seven sharp. And have that recording with you, Brad."

Mike headed home for dinner with his family. Brad went back to his cubicle, glad that he had already eaten since he didn't have time now. He intended to call Adriana back, but he felt uncomfortable doing so without being someplace private, or at least with walls. So he carried his recorder to a small conference room, shut the door, and made his call.

"It took you a long time," Adriana said when she answered.

"Sorry, and I have to be back in another meeting at seven. So let's get this recording going," he said. "I actually want to play two of them for you. The first one is of your dad and me. The other one is my meeting with Jerzy Grabowski at the jail. Your dad probably told you about Jerzy's confession."

"Yes, but Jerzy didn't do it, Brad. I know he didn't," she said.

"And I agree with you. Okay, pay attention now. This is the one with your dad. As we listen, if you have questions or comments, just interrupt me. Are you ready?"

"Yes, I guess so. Play it," she said.

Brad started the recording. He had his phone on speaker so that he could let the recorder do its thing and still be able to hear or speak to Adriana when he needed to. He could picture her with her phone to her ear as her father's voice began the explanation and confession to Brad on the recording. She interrupted when mention was made of his dealings with Valentino Lombardi. "Who is that guy?" she asked Brad.

He paused the recorder and said, "We don't know that yet. But it appears that he's a crime boss of some kind. Your dad didn't know that when he first got involved with him."

"Dad was just too greedy," she said with a touch of anger in her voice. "Go ahead; start it again."

The recording played on. Once again Adriana asked him to pause it when her father's voice mentioned the accusation of murder that had been made against him. "He's not a murderer, Brad," she said, the anger was replaced with what Brad was sure were sobs. "He might have done a lot of horrible things, but I can't believe he'd ever kill anyone. I also can't believe he's just going to let them kill him."

"He's more concerned about his gorgeous daughter than he is about himself," Brad said seriously.

His statement struck a chord with Adriana, and for a moment she was silent. Finally, she said softly, "Dad's not all bad. I don't want him to get hurt. You can start it again."

She listened to the rest of the recording without interruption. He could hear her breathing quietly as they listened to her father's description of how he was framed for murder and then blackmailed to keep the evidence from being taken to the authorities.

"We've got to find these guys and stop them from destroying Dad," she said fiercely. "This is horrible."

"Not *we*, Adriana, *me*. The other police officers and I have to do it. Don't forget that they're after you too," Brad reminded her. "You've got to let us do our job, and we will, I promise."

She didn't comment, and it bothered him. However, she did ask a few questions about the interview. "So Mr. Mancheski and Dad knew each other—it was more than just Mancheski asking for directions to Mr. Lenhardt's house," she said. "Did I hear that right?"

"You did," Brad said.

"And Dad thinks that Mr. Mancheski and this Valentino Lombardi hate each other?" she asked.

"It sounds like it," Brad agreed.

"And I'm caught in the middle of their feud?" she asked perceptively.

"That's entirely possible," he said.

Adriana then continued, "You said you have another recording. Let's hear it."

"Okay, if you're ready," he said. "This is an interview I did at the jail with Jerzy. It is disturbing, to say the least." He started it and thought about Jerzy and the jam he was in, one that he didn't know how to change without the help of his colleagues and the prosecutor, help he wasn't likely to get.

The entire interview played without a single interruption by Adriana. A couple of times, Brad had to put his head down close to his phone to see if he could hear Adriana breathing into her phone. He was relieved each time when he was reassured that she was still listening. At the end, her reaction was not unlike her reaction to her father's interview. She said, "Brad, he doesn't mean it. He's been framed, and I bet he's even been threatened like Dad was."

"Unless he changes his mind, this confession is very serious. And if he insists on pleading guilty, there is nothing I can do, or anyone else for that matter," Brad said. "We can only hope that his attorney can talk him out of taking the suicidal route he's on."

"He's been threatened, just like Dad and I have," Adriana emphasized, her voice showing an increase in anger. "I'd like to just strangle whoever is doing this to us."

"Adriana, I wish you'd change your mind and let me meet you somewhere. I'm scared for you," Brad said. "I'm scared out of my wits."

"I'm scared for me too," she admitted, but her voice sounded surprisingly strong. "But I've got to help myself now. You've got to trust me to take care of myself. And I'll trust you to work hard at finding the guys that are doing this. I like you, Brad Osborn. I like you a lot. I need to go now."

"Please, Adriana," Brad begged, but the phone went dead. He dropped his head in his hands, deep in thought. Finally, after offering an intense plea to the Lord for her safety, he put the recorder away and got to his feet. The meeting with the prosecutor and team of officers was about to begin.

Adriana's phone began to ring. Brad pulled it out of his pocket. The number displayed was not one he recognized, but the name was familiar. *Drew.* It took a moment before he remembered that that was the name of the man who had recently dumped her. He ignored the call and put the phone back in his pocket.

***

"What do you mean you can't find her?" Valentino Lombardi screamed into the phone. "She's just a dumb, helpless girl. And I'm tired of excuses."

"But she could be anywhere," Cedric Brewer said.

"Have you checked her home again? She's stupid enough that she might go back there."

"There's another cop out front, and this one is wide awake," Cedric said. "I'm sure she's not there. Her mother is, but she was alone when she drove into the garage."

"Then follow her mother if she leaves. She'll take you to Adriana. And when she does, get the girl and bring her to me. I want to find out what she knows, and then you can get rid of her," Valentino said coldly.

"What if the mother gives me trouble?"

"Whack her if you have to. But bring the girl to me—alive."

"I'll get her, boss."

"You had better."

***

The big house was no longer a friendly place. Krista felt vulnerable there by herself. She'd locked all the doors, knowing it was probably wasted effort. There was an officer out front, but she took no comfort in that.

The one there that morning hadn't protected Adriana. Krista was angry with her ex-husband for getting them all into this dangerous situation, and she was sure it was his fault. She was also worried about her stubborn daughter. She also admitted that she was afraid for herself. Even though she hadn't been threatened, she was sure that Carson's enemies would not hesitate to hurt or even kill her if they wanted to. It was all such a dreadful nightmare.

She went up to her bedroom and began to pack a suitcase. She couldn't stay here another hour. The home phone began to ring. She put the slacks she had in her hand in the suitcase and picked up the extension that sat beside her bed. The display screen read *Drew Parker*. She couldn't imagine why Adriana's former boyfriend was calling. She hesitated but finally answered, and he said, "Mrs. Chambers, I've been trying to reach Adriana. She's not answering her phone."

Krista knew exactly why she wasn't answering; she'd lost her phone. Even if she had it, she wouldn't blame the girl for not answering. Drew had dropped her suddenly and really quite cruelly. She couldn't imagine why he was trying to reach her now.

"I need to talk to her. Is she there?" he asked.

"She's not," Krista said, concentrating on keeping her voice even and unemotional, a difficult thing to do under the current circumstances.

"I'm so disappointed. I really need to talk to her," Drew said. "Will you give her a message when you see her?"

"Of course," Krista said as she prayed she would see her daughter again.

"Good. Have her call me. In the meantime, I'll keep trying her cell," Drew said.

Krista was suddenly concerned. "Drew, what is this about? I hope you're not going to break her heart again."

"Oh no, I won't do that," he promised. Then he dropped the bombshell. At least it was not something Krista wanted to hear. "It will be for keeps this time. I made a terrible mistake breaking up with her. I promise I won't do that again. I love her."

"I don't know if that's such a good idea," Krista said, feeling the anger building in her. "She's over you. You should just move on like she has."

"She'll understand," Drew said confidently. "I'll keep trying her cell phone. Thanks again." He clicked off before she could say anything else.

A few minutes later, still fuming, Krista got in her car, backed it out of the garage, and drove away. She was so upset that it didn't even occur to her to check her mirrors and make sure she wasn't being followed.

The phrase "like mother, like daughter" was true in many ways in the case of Krista and Adriana Chambers. They had their differences, but they were so alike in so many ways that it was spooky. Such was the case now. They both chose the same downtown hotel to hide out in. And neither of them understood how difficult it was to effectively hide from persistent, dangerous, intelligent enemies.

Krista parked her car, got the suitcase from the trunk, and entered the lobby. She approached the registration desk and explained that she didn't have a reservation and asked if there were any vacancies. There were, and she was soon registered and headed for the elevators. A moment later she passed a small souvenir shop. A young woman with blonde, shoulder-length hair and rose-framed glasses was standing in front of a rack of paperback books reading the back cover of one.

Her profile looked familiar to Krista. She took a second look, decided she didn't know her, and hurried on. She was anxious to get in her room and make some phone calls. The first and most urgent one would be to Detective Brad Osborn.

***

Adriana looked up from the book she was perusing as a woman walked by the door of the souvenir shop. She almost dropped the book when she realized that the woman was her mother. She thought about putting the book back and running after her. But before she could make up her mind, she saw a man with slicked-back black hair, tan slacks, and a brown sports coat. There was no doubt who he was, and very little doubt what he was doing. *He was following her mother.* Her knees began to shake and she felt faint. She steadied herself against the bookrack. Then she put the book back and took a couple of deep breaths. She could do this. She slipped from the shop and followed the man who was following her mother.

She hung her purse by its long strap over her shoulder. The knife she'd bought earlier was in her pocket. She swiftly got it out and opened it. Then, holding it close to her side, concealing it under her arm, she picked up her pace and began to gain on the dangerous man who had threatened her father and Jerzy Grabowski and who had broken into her house looking for her. Her heart was thudding dangerously in her chest, but she was more concerned about her mother than herself. And she was totally focused.

CHAPTER THIRTEEN

KRISTA CHAMBERS PUNCHED THE UP button and stood facing the elevator doors. Suddenly, something hard pressed against her back and a cold voice said, "Don't make a peep. You are taking me to your daughter. If you scream or try to attract attention, I will shoot you."

She felt like fainting, but for Adriana's sake she couldn't allow herself to do that. Bracing herself, she slowly turned and caught a glimpse of the blonde girl with the rose-colored glasses just beyond the stranger with the gun. The girl had a grim face. Their eyes met, and stunning recognition came in a flash. Krista started to mouth her daughter's name, but the girl shook her head and stepped closer. Just then the elevator door opened. The black-haired man said, "Get on, or you die now."

Krista looked past him just as her blonde daughter raised her arm and started to bring a knife down at his back. At that exact moment, her captor turned to follow Krista's eyes, and the knife plunged into his neck. Krista twisted out of his way, and the man fell sideways through the door of the elevator. Krista grabbed her daughter, and the two of them watched as the man lay bleeding profusely in the elevator. As the doors closed, Krista looked around them. As near as she could tell, no one had seen them.

"Adriana, we've got to go. My car's outside. Let's—"

"No, Mom, my room is on the main floor," Adriana said urgently, grabbing her mother's arm. "Come on."

The two women hurried down the corridor. "Put the knife away," her mother whispered frantically. "You can't let anyone see it. It's all bloody."

Adriana closed it and shoved it into her pocket. The knife wasn't the only bloody thing. Adriana had blood on her hands. Her mother reached into her suitcase and pulled out a tissue. "Wipe your hands, Adriana."

Adriana did so and stuffed the bloody Kleenex in the same pocket of her jeans as the knife. An elderly couple approached, glanced momentarily at them, smiled, and moved on. "It's room 1090," Adriana said.

They reached it, she pulled her key from her purse, and a moment later they were in her room, hugging each other. Only then did Adriana really think about the enormity of what she'd done. "Mom, I stabbed a man," she said. "But I had to."

Krista said, "You saved my life. But now we've got to do something. Someone will have found that man by now, whoever he was."

"His name is Cedric Brewer," Adriana said. "He threatened Dad and Jerzy Grabowski today. He's the guy who nearly got to me at the house."

"The next person who went to get on that elevator . . ." Krista shuddered. "We need to call someone," she said decisively.

"I'll call Brad," Adriana suggested. "He'll know what we should do."

***

"As if we don't have enough going on," Mike complained when he and Brad were told that they had another homicide at a downtown hotel, the Marriott. "They should put someone else on this. We don't have time."

He'd already made that argument to the sergeant when she first told them to go. She had admitted that they were busy but told them that she'd like them to begin the investigation, and then if it wasn't a clear-cut matter, she would give it to someone else on Monday.

Brad was driving, and they were making good time. "At least the Marriott is a very busy place. Maybe there are plenty of witnesses on this one," Brad suggested. "And if nothing else, there's almost bound to be video of it. I can't imagine any of the big hotels not being covered with cameras."

"Yeah, I suppose, but still, it's a distraction from all the stuff we're doing now." Mike moaned as Brad's phone began to ring.

He pulled it out and answered it without looking at the display screen. "Hello."

"Brad, it's Adriana. I'm in trouble. I need your help," the young woman on the phone said, her voice sounding panicked.

"Where are you?" he asked. "I can't help if I don't know where you are."

"I'm at the Marriott, downtown. Please, can you come?"

Brad's stomach turned. He glanced at his partner. "We're on our way there right now. Are you in a room there?"

"Yes. My mother and I are together. Something terrible happened."

"Stay in your room until Mike and I get there. There's been a murder at the hotel. There should be other cops there by now," he said urgently. "What's your room number?"

"1090. First floor," she said, her voice cracking so badly he could hardly understand her.

"Are you safe right now?"

"Y—yes."

"Then stay put!" he ordered. "I'll be there shortly."

"Brad, is it . . . is it really a murder?" she asked, tears filling her voice.

"That's what we're told. I need to concentrate on my driving right now. Don't let anyone in, anyone at all, until I get there." Brad closed his phone and said to Mike, "That was Adriana. She and her mother are at the Marriott, and she's so upset she can hardly speak. I have a really bad feeling about this."

Several marked units were already at the hotel. Brad had to work his way forward through traffic to get near the front entrance. He threw the car into park, and he and Mike jumped out. "What do we have?" Brad asked when he rushed through the door and spotted Sergeant Deon Golen.

"A dead man in one of the elevators," Deon said. "Stabbed once in the neck. He never had a chance. The man who found him was getting on the elevator at the fourth floor. He about had a heart attack. The elevator, with the body exactly as it was found, is on the first floor now. Come this way."

Brad debated with himself for a moment. He wanted to hurry right then to room 1090, but he knew he should at least take a look at the crime scene first. So he reluctantly followed Sergeant Golen. The floor of the elevator was a bloody mess. "No one has touched the body," Deon said.

"Good. Keep it that way until the lab guys get here," Brad said as he stared at the body. There was something about the guy on the floor that seemed vaguely familiar, causing warning bells to go off in his head. But he couldn't put a finger on it. He turned to Mike. "Get started here while I check on Adriana and her mother."

Mike already had his camera out, and he began taking pictures. Brad hustled as quickly as he could to room 1090. He knocked hard on the door. When it opened, a blonde girl, her eyes red behind glasses with rose-colored frames, her face streaked with mascara, stepped toward him. She said, "Come in quickly," and shut the door behind him.

Brad knew that voice and realized it was a well-disguised Adriana. Beyond her, he saw her mother, also red-eyed and looking quite devastated. "Thanks for coming, Brad," Krista said. "We need advice and help."

"Are you both okay?" he asked, stunned by the way Adriana looked.

"We're okay," Adriana said, turning away from him and walking toward her mother. "Is Cedric Brewer really dead?" she asked as she turned to face him.

"Cedric B . . . Oh my! The guy who broke into your house today. I knew there was something familiar about the dead man," he said, and then, narrowing his eyes, he looked closer at Adriana. "How did you know . . ." He stopped as a terrible dread came over him.

"I stabbed him," Adriana said evenly. "Am I going to jail?"

"She saved my life when she did it," Krista said as she moved protectively toward the younger woman and took Adriana in her motherly arms. "He had a gun poked in my back."

"He thought she could lead her to me," Adriana said. "But she didn't know where I was. Neither of us knew the other was in this hotel until I saw that horrible man following Mom. He said he'd shoot her if she didn't take him to me. I had to do something."

"Okay, let's sit down," he said. "I need to hear everything."

The two women poured out the horrible story for several minutes, every second of it being preserved on Brad's little recorder. He inserted a few questions from time to time. His phone rang and he shut the recorder off long enough to answer it.

"Brad," Mike said angrily. "I could use some help with this case. It's not going to be an easy one. There are no witnesses after all. I need you to get down here right now. Also, the lab guys just found a gun beneath the dead man's body. It was still in the guy's hand."

"I have it solved," Brad said calmly. "It is not a homicide."

"What? How do you know? Aren't you with the Chambers women?"

"Yes, and they are the victims here. I think the dead man had a lot to do with the break-ins, including the one today at Adriana's house. The dead guy has been calling himself Cedric Brewer," Brad said. "Give me a little longer here, and I'll join you."

"Am I safe now?" Adriana asked after the recorded interview was completed.

"No, you're not," Brad said sternly.

"But the guy who was after me is dead," she said, scrunching her eyebrows.

"He's probably nothing but a hired killer. Whoever is behind all this will just hire someone else," Brad explained. "You are in as much danger as ever—maybe even more."

Krista and her mother hugged, and Brad said, "Okay, Adriana, will you let me help keep you safe now?"

"I guess," she said weakly.

He tried to lighten the mood with a grin. "I'll arrest you if I have to," he said.

"You wouldn't," she protested.

"To keep you alive and well, I'll do anything," he said.

"She'll do whatever you say," Krista said. "We both will."

"Good. Right now I'm saying you need to stay right here in this room and not open the door to anybody but me. Is that understood?"

"Yes, sir," Adriana said.

Carrying the knife Adriana had used in the defense of her mother, Brad left them in the room and hurried back to the elevators. Things were proceeding smoothly there. Sergeant Tullock walked in just moments after Brad got back. "Mike called me and explained what's happening, Brad. Where is the girl?" she asked.

"In her room with her mother," Brad said. "I have their statement recorded."

"Good work," she said as she moved past him and peered at the body. Lab personnel were busy processing the scene. "Any witnesses?" she asked.

"Not that I've been able to locate," Detective Silverman said.

"Let's have the hotel pull their surveillance video," Brad suggested as he spotted a camera near the area. It was enclosed in gray glass, but Brad knew what it was.

"You do that, Detective Osborn," she said. "I'll help Mike here."

Brad was anxious to see the video, and he hurried to the hotel's business office. Ten minutes later, he was viewing the footage that proved to back the account given to him by Adriana and her mother one hundred percent. He asked for and received a disk with the entire episode on it. Then he viewed what several other cameras had recorded. He even saw the discovery of the body when the elevator had opened on the fourth floor. There were other relevant bits that he also had burned to a disc. They showed Krista as she came in, registered, and headed for the elevators. Adriana was shown several times, including coming from the souvenir shop and pursuing her mother and the man they were calling

Cedric Brewer. Finally, he had them copy the piece that showed Krista and Adriana hurrying away from the elevator and to Adriana's room.

When he rejoined the other officers, Lydia asked him what he'd gotten. He told her, and she sighed. "That's good. We can wrap this up easily and get back to work on the other matters."

"All of which tie into this one," Brad said. "I'll bet that as soon as we check the surveillance cameras at the jail, we'll see our latest dead man going in to threaten Jerzy Grabowski."

"Are you still hung up on his innocence?" Lydia asked.

"More than ever."

"Unless he is simply another hired killer, like this victim seems to be," she argued.

"Yeah, unless that," Brad said, not wanting to debate the matter with her now. "I think our biggest concern now is what to do about Krista and Adriana Chambers."

***

Carson Chambers had sat in his apartment for several hours, brewing over what to do. He was shamed with guilt and worried about Adriana, knowing that she was in danger because of his sins. He thought about how, in years past, he would have turned to prayer in times of stress, but he had removed himself so far from his faith that he didn't even make an attempt. He just hoped that his daughter was praying and that the Lord would hear her. He still believed in God. He still possessed a shadow of his old religious convictions, but he didn't think he had the right to even ask God for help after all the bad choices he'd made.

He thought about just sitting in his apartment until someone came after him. But as the hours passed, he realized that he didn't want to die. He didn't want to go down without a fight. Finally, he went into his bedroom and began to pack a suitcase. Maybe it was time to go someplace and try to keep out of sight for a while.

He was busy packing his suitcase when his cell phone began to ring. He answered it, not knowing if the lack of a number on the screen meant that his daughter was trying to reach him or if it was Cedric Brewer, Earnest Pyatt, or another of Valentino Lombardi's henchmen. It was with great relief that he heard Adriana say, "Dad, are you okay?"

"I'm fine," he said.

"Dad, you've got to protect yourself. These guys mean business."

"Don't you think I know that?" Carson said. "But I'm more afraid for you than for me."

"I'm okay for now," she said. "Detective Osborn is going to try to help me and Mom."

"So you are not going to try to hide yourself?" he asked. "That's a great relief. You mentioned your mother. Where is she?"

"She's with me," Adriana said. "We are safe for now, but we had a close call, especially Mom."

"What do you mean by that?" Carson asked as a cold chill descended on him.

"Cedric Brewer, or whatever his name is, tried to kidnap her at gunpoint," Adriana said.

"What! Your mother? She has nothing to do with this. Surely they wouldn't bother her too," he protested. He had honestly never considered that Krista might be a target of his enemies' wrath. Valentino knew Carson had left her and that the divorce had not been pretty. Why would they bother her?

"Yes, Mother. They were using her to find me, but regardless of the reason, her life was threatened," Adriana said, accusation in her voice.

"If she's with you, then she must be safe," Carson reasoned. "Tell me what happened. How did she get away from him?"

"I stabbed him," Adriana said bluntly. "I killed him."

Carson's knees buckled, and he found himself on the floor of his bedroom. From that ignominious position, the phone still to his ear, anger began to boil inside of him. His desire to run and hide evaporated. The anger in him became an almost overpowering thing. He wouldn't run. No, he would attack. It was time he took the fight to Valentino and his henchmen. They had gone too far now.

"Dad, are you there?" Adriana asked urgently.

"Yes, I'm here. Tell me exactly what happened," he said as he regained his feet and sat on the side of his bed.

Adriana told him.

When she had finished, his mood was murderous. He spoke a little longer to her before disconnecting.

He thought of his sons. Until now, he hadn't even considered the fact that they too could be targets of Valentino Lombardi. He began to make more calls. He had to check on them, to make sure they were safe, to warn them.

CHAPTER FOURTEEN

AFTER FINISHING HER CALL WITH her father, Adriana felt worse than ever. "Mom, I know how you feel about Dad, and I understand it completely. But I still love him."

"As you should," Krista said. "And just so you know, I don't hate him. I tried to, and maybe for a while I did, but not anymore. How did he react when you told him what happened?"

"You probably won't believe this, but he got terribly angry. I thought he had given up and that he was just going to let them do whatever they wanted with him. But the last thing he said to me just now was, 'Valentino Lombardi will wish he'd never met me.' Mom, they'll kill him if he goes after them, and I think that's what he intends to do."

"We've got to help him or get someone else to help him, to stop him," Krista said urgently.

Adriana looked closely at her mother. Suddenly, it struck her that her mother was a long way from being over her father. She was sitting with her hands folded on her lap, her face pale, her eyes downcast. "Mom, you still love him, don't you?" Adriana asked softly.

Her mother didn't move. But her eyes flickered. She didn't say she did, but she also didn't deny it. "Mom, let's call Brad. He'll know what to do."

"I hope so," Krista said. "We can't let Carson risk his life by doing whatever he is planning. We just can't."

They didn't need to call Brad because just then he knocked on the door. When Adriana let him in, she trembled at the gentle, caring look he gave her. He took her in his arms and held her for a moment. Then he said, "I watched the hotel's surveillance video. I'm so sorry for what you have gone through. You are not only the prettiest and sweetest girl

I have ever known, you are also the bravest." She looked up at him. He smiled. "I am so glad you're safe."

"Why?" she asked, even as she was aware of her mother watching them from across the room where she sat with her arms still folded.

"I told you before, Adriana. Work it out."

"I have," she said shyly. "You've got to be careful too, Brad. I am worried about you too."

"Why?" he asked.

"Figure it out," she said with the slightest of grins.

"I'll do that," he promised. "By the way, I forgot to give you back your phone. I hope I didn't mess something up for you."

"I had this one," she said as she held the cheap one out for him to see.

"That's not what I meant," he said.

She gave him a puzzled look. "Then what do you mean?"

"Someone else has been trying to call you. I hope you'll forgive me, but I finally answered your phone. It was a guy by the name of Drew Parker."

"Drew?" she said weakly.

"Yes, and he wasn't very happy I had your phone."

"Did you tell him who you are?" she asked.

"Not exactly. I just told him that I was a friend of yours, a good friend. I hope that's true."

"You know it is," Adriana said softly. "What did he want?"

"I can tell you that," Krista said as she rose to her feet and approached Brad and Adriana. "He called me too."

"But why would he do that?" she asked.

"He wants you back," her mother said bluntly.

Adriana's eyes popped, and her mouth twitched. But she didn't say anything. Nor did her eyes meet Brad's, but from the corner of her eye she could see that the look on his face was one of dread.

"Adriana, I'll ask you the same question you asked me. Do you still love him?" Krista asked.

Adriana did not look back at her mother, but she lifted her eyes to Brad's and said, "I don't know if I ever really loved him. But one thing's for sure; I have moved on, and I have no intention of even so much as looking back."

"Then you'll need to tell him that," Brad said with a look of relief. "I hinted, but he told me in no uncertain terms that I had better give you back your phone. I have done that now. So when he calls, you can tell him that if you mean it."

"Brad, I mean it. I hope you believe me."

The smile he favored her with was enough to convince her that he believed her. There was a tap on the door. "That will be my partner and sergeant," Brad said. "We have a lot to do."

"Have them come in," Adriana said. "There's something Mom and I need to talk to you about. It has to do with my father."

***

Nervous about why he had been summoned to meet with Brian Bollinger, Earnest Pyatt had weighed his options. He had loyalties to no one but himself. He worshiped money. Whoever was willing to pay him the most was welcome to his services. It was unusual, however, for his type of services to be requested by a prominent law firm. He hadn't been invited to the firm's offices, which was no surprise, but it meant that whatever they wanted him for was not for public knowledge. That meant they must be willing to pay. He'd go and listen. Then he'd decide what to do.

He was still nervous, however. That nervousness was not over the desolation of the meeting place; he was used to such locations and always took precautions. What he was nervous about was what kind of task they might have for him. He couldn't imagine it was one for the kind of services he was most noted for.

He wasn't even sure how they knew about him. He always worked behind the scenes, making sure that only those who absolutely had to know knew of his involvement. And it was not as if he advertised in the yellow pages or the classifieds. He could only assume that a client of theirs knew of his services and had recommended him. Earnest was not a coward—far from it. He was, however, cautious. If he got any negative vibes from the lawyers who had summoned him, he was prepared to bolt. And his escape route was already mapped out.

Mr. Brian Bollinger greeted him that Saturday night as he pulled into a rest area off the interstate over one hundred miles from the law firm's offices. A couple of men in suits stuck closely to Bollinger when he got out of the car. *Protection,* Earnest thought with a private chuckle. They might protect him from some people, but if Earnest had the need or the desire to harm Mr. Bollinger, these two men wouldn't be a problem. Their presence did remind him to be careful, however.

"Mr. Pyatt, thank you for coming. Please, let's walk out back of the little building here," Brian said. The two men in suits were never introduced, and they leaned against their car, a long black Lincoln, as Mr. Bollinger led the way around back of the restroom. Earnest had no doubt that precautions had been taken. He was alert and watchful.

He smiled easily, despite the darkness that prevailed, and said, "I hope this isn't a waste of my time, Mr. Bollinger. I am a very busy man."

"I understand completely," the attorney said. "I will get right to the purpose of our visit."

"It will be good, I'm sure," Earnest said in a tone that no one would mistake as friendly or timid.

"It is a business proposal," Mr. Bollinger said. "I'm sure you have heard of the unfortunate death of our senior partner and my good friend, Garrick Lenhardt."

"It's been on the news," Earnest said evenly.

"Yes, so it has," Brian acknowledged. "I don't know how much you know about the work that we do in this firm." He paused. Earnest said nothing but watched the man's face intently. "We represent criminal defendants, and we have a good track record of clearing folks on the charges that the state or the federal government has brought against them."

Earnest still said nothing. He had nothing to say at this point.

"Well, Mr. Pyatt, it so happens that one of our clients has a lot to lose if we can't help him prevail in the courts and make the charges go away," the attorney said. "The lead counsel in this man's case was my friend and partner. Mr. Lenhardt has worked long and hard in preparing the defense in this particular defendant's case. With him gone, I will be taking over the lead in that case. But the case file seems to have come up missing. We'd like you to find and return it."

Surprised, but not letting it show, Earnest folded his arms across his chest and considered the man and the proposal. When he had tried to anticipate the kind of work he would be asked to do, he had come up with several possible scenarios. This was not one of them. "Why don't you hire a good private investigator to handle this for you? It's not exactly my line of work," Earnest said, his eyes never wavering from the face of Brian Bollinger.

The attorney stroked his large blond moustache for a moment as if weighing his next words. Then he squared his narrow shoulders as if trying to look larger than his small frame permitted. "We have some idea who might have been behind the theft of the file," he said. "And we believe you are familiar with the man and his organization."

Earnest leaned forward. "My services don't come cheap," he said firmly. "And if I have to pry around concerning the affairs of some of my, ah, business associates, my fee goes sharply upward. Whose organization do you have in mind?"

"Valentino Lombardi's," the little attorney said. "We don't know that he is behind the theft, mind you, but as we have considered who might have a reason for our client to go to prison, Mr. Lombardi's name came to mind. He and our client have great enmity for one another."

"Let me make sure I understand you correctly. You want me to find something that was taken from you that would help your client but do damage to Valentino Lombardi?" he said.

"That's about it," Brian said.

"And would your client be Gabriel Mancheski?" he asked.

"Would it make a difference to you if it was?" Mr. Bollinger asked evenly as he once again tugged at his moustache in the shadows.

"It would affect my fee," Earnest said as he thought about what he'd been asked to do. "I have had some business relationships with Mr. Valentino from time to time," he disclosed. "And I am very aware of the enmity between him and your client. This could be awkward."

"So it does make a difference?" Brian asked.

"To you it might," Earnest said. "It will cost you a lot. To be right frank, there's more than just enmity between Mr. Lombardi and Mr. Mancheski; they are bitter enemies."

"I understand that. Let's talk about your price," Brian said.

The attorney didn't bat an eye when Earnest named one. They shook on it, and the little attorney said, "It is important that we have the file back soon—let's say within the next three or four days."

"Half the fee now and the rest when I deliver the file," Earnest said, not bothering to acknowledge the rush. "And of course, cash is the only form of payment I accept."

"Of course. We have it in the car," Brian said, leaving the shadows and leading the way back to the front.

Once the money had been handed over, Earnest said, "Since this matter is just between us, I'll need to have some assurances that you didn't record our conversation," he said.

The two men in the suits stepped away from the car. Mr. Bollinger looked nervous. "We'll go inside where I can conduct a little search of your person, just to make sure you didn't wear a wire," Earnest said, keeping an eye on the two younger men.

"I can assure you I wouldn't do that," Brian said, gesturing his innocence with both hands.

But Earnest was successful in his line of work because he took precautions. He suddenly pulled a 9mm pistol from inside his jacket and pointed it in the direction of Mr. Bollinger's men. "You two, get in the car and drive away. When I'm sure that you haven't pulled a fast one on me, I'll leave your boss here, uninjured, and you can come back and pick him up."

Neither man moved. "Now!" he said fiercely. "You are not acting in a manner that inspires confidence."

"Do as he says," Brian nodded slowly. "We have nothing to hide."

The two men got in the car and pulled away. As soon as their tail-lights had disappeared into the distance, Earnest directed Brian into the restroom. When they emerged three minutes later, Earnest said, "Sorry for the inconvenience, but you understand that I have to be careful. I'll call the number you gave me as soon as I have the file in my possession."

He got in his car and drove off, leaving the little attorney standing by the curb in front of the restroom. Bollinger's nervousness had made Earnest suspicious, but when he found no wire, he chalked the nervousness up to the lawyer's inexperience in retaining people like him. The pay was outstanding. The job would be tricky, but he would get it done, and if done correctly, Mr. Lombardi would never know it was him. He would like to work for the crime boss again in the future, but this payday was too big to pass up.

***

As soon as his men picked him up, Brian got on the phone and called one of his partners. He told him that things had gone well, that they had but to wait. Then, despite the lateness of the hour, he called his client, Gabriel Mancheski. "We have someone working on the problem of your file," he said. "It will be taken care of very soon."

"It had better be," the client said with steel in his voice, and he disconnected the line.

Brian began to sweat. If Mr. Pyatt failed, this was going to be financially devastating to the firm. It was bad enough to lose Garrick, their biggest moneymaker, but Gabriel Mancheski was a powerful, wealthy man who could do the firm a lot of damage if he wasn't appeased. He was guilty of everything he'd been accused of. Brian knew that, but then, they hadn't taken the case because he was innocent. They had taken it for the money, and Garrick had done some excellent work, work that would put doubt in the minds of any jury. Without that file and the information in it, Mancheski was in deep trouble. And if Mancheski was in trouble, so were Brian and his partners. He shivered.

***

"Where will Mom and I stay tonight?" Adriana asked Brad that night in a small conference room at the police station. She and her mother had completed a lengthy recorded interview, had signed written statements, and were both exhausted to the core.

Brad smiled at her. "At your house," he said.

"But we can't!" she protested loudly, hurtling to her feet in sudden anger. "Brad, you said you'd make sure we're safe! Come on, Mom, let's go. We can take care of ourselves if we have to, and I guess we have to."

Brad blocked her path as she headed for the door. He'd tried to interrupt, to explain the measures he'd taken, but he hadn't been able to get a word in. Now he did. "We've made better arrangements," he said. "There will be three officers outside and at least one inside at all times, if you two will agree to that. And believe me, no one will be sleeping on their posts."

Adriana stood stock still at that point, and she thought about what he'd said. "Do you promise, Brad?" she asked, knowing she sounded hard but not sure who to trust now.

"You have my word. And if you'd like, I'll even stay there myself if you didn't mind me sleeping on one of your sofas. And that would be in addition to the on-duty officer that would be constantly patrolling the interior of your house," he said.

Her mother stepped beside Adriana and said, "That is very kind, Brad, but we have a very large house. You can use a bed if you'll stay. One of the spare bedrooms is on the ground floor."

Adriana suddenly felt her mood lighten. Shamed at her outburst, she asked softly, "Will you, Brad? Please?"

"I wouldn't have offered if I didn't mean it," he said, putting an arm around her shoulders and giving her a gentle squeeze.

She shivered, but it was a pleasant shiver. "Will someone accompany us to the house?" she asked.

"You will not be going anywhere alone, either of you, until we have all the guilty parties in custody," Brad said.

"We have church tomorrow," Adriana said.

"I suppose we could stay home this once," Krista reasoned. "I'm sure the Lord will understand."

"No, Mom. I want to go. I need to go," Adriana pleaded.

"I'll take you, both of you," Brad said. "Is that okay?"

It was better than okay as far as Adriana was concerned. "That would be great, but are you sure?" she asked almost wistfully.

CHAPTER FIFTEEN

CARSON TOOK A PAGE FROM Adriana's book the next morning. He shaved his head and bought glasses and new clothes, a type he'd never worn in his life. He even went to a costume shop, watching carefully behind him in case he was being followed. There he purchased a fake beard and moustache. By the time he finished, he hardly recognized himself.

Despite dwindling funds, he purchased an older model Ford F-150 pickup. He also got his pistol, one he had resisted carrying until now. It was a twenty-two caliber Smith and Wesson revolver with a four-inch barrel. He had spent quite a bit of time at the range a few months earlier and was fairly proficient. He placed it in a holster that fit inside the baggy pants he was now wearing. The grip showed until he put on his shirt, also baggy, worn untucked. He also had a hunting knife with a six-inch blade strapped to the calf of his left leg, beneath his pants. He added a pocketknife to his arsenal and felt that there was not much more he could do.

He not only looked vastly different—he also felt that way. He was an angry man, filled with the desire for revenge. It was not a nice feeling, but he held on to it out of necessity. Without it, he wasn't sure he would have the nerve to do what was necessary to protect his daughter—and his ex-wife.

Satisfied with his disguise, Carson began to plan the steps necessary to stop Valentino Lombardi from hurting his daughter.

***

Adriana and Krista, accompanied by Brad, walked into their house on Sunday afternoon after attending church in their ward. There had been lots of raised eyebrows from ward members, but no one had asked any embarrassing questions, for which Adriana was grateful. The ward members had seen Drew there with her a number of times, and many had expected a wedding. She didn't want that happening again. Brad was simply introduced as a friend.

Upon Brad's encouragement, the bishop was privately advised of what was happening with the Chambers family, and he was told who Brad was. Other than that, the ward members were simply left to speculate.

The police presence both inside and outside of their house gave the ladies great comfort. They asked Brad to stay for dinner that afternoon, but he excused himself, saying, "I have to get to the office. We'll be working the rest of the day. I'll be back tonight sometime, but don't wait up for me if I'm late. The officers on duty here will let me in."

Adriana was disappointed on one hand, for she enjoyed Brad's company, but she was supportive on the other hand. She was anxious for those responsible for the terrible crimes to be arrested. And she had confidence that Brad would do everything he could to bring that about.

After Brad had gone, she called her dad's cell phone, but she got no answer. She also tried the phone at his apartment with similar results. She said nothing to her mother, but she was very worried about him.

***

A search warrant was in the hands of Sergeant Tullock by the time Brad arrived at the office. An electronic key had been found in the wallet of the man who had died in the Marriott elevator, along with a driver's license and other items that identified him as Cedric Brewer. The key fit a hotel near the Marriott. The search warrant was for that room.

They entered it a short time later. There was not a lot in the room, just a suitcase and some toiletries. A search of the suitcase did not reveal anything interesting. Brad wasn't sure what they had thought they might find. They already had the man's wallet, pistol, and cell phone. Brad had an idea and expressed it to his partner. "I wonder if he has anything being stored in the hotel's safe."

"I doubt it," Mike said.

"He's been here for three days, so I'd say it's worth looking into," Brad insisted. "The search warrant is broad enough to support us in this."

Mike finally agreed, and the two detectives moved forward. The hotel safe produced a briefcase. The officers simply seized it and took it back to the station, where they opened it. The first item that Brad pulled out was a set of lock picks. Also in the briefcase was another cell phone, a large amount of cash in large bills in a brown envelope, and miscellaneous papers, none of which seemed to have any bearing on the case. However, over half of the space in the briefcase was taken up by a find that Mike described as a gold mine. The missing Gabriel Mancheski defense file had been located.

The cell phone was taken to the lab, where the one Cedric had at the time of his death had already been taken. It was the officers' hopes that there would be phone numbers and contacts that would lead them to Valentino Lombardi or anyone else who was behind the violence of the past few days. The file brought about some debate. Sergeant Tullock made the decision that it would simply be placed in evidence and that, for now, nothing would be said outside the chain of command about its recovery. The chain of command included the lieutenant, the captain, the police chief, and the prosecutor, Ross Harris. No one else was told, not even the law firm of Brian Bollinger. It was considered evidence in the burglaries of the Chambers and Lenhardt residencies. In addition, Ross Harris wanted time on Monday to analyze the file, and the commanding officers wanted to search it for clues as to the whereabouts of Valentino Lombardi.

Late in the afternoon, Brad got a call from the jail. Once again, he was told that he was wanted by the murder suspect, Jerzy Grabowski. Sergeant Tullock sighed and told him that he better go and see what he wanted. "Maybe it would be better if you go this time, Sergeant," Brad said.

"No, you have his confidence," she said. "I'll still be here when you get back, and I'll expect a report."

"All right," Brad said with resignation. "I can't imagine it will take too long."

***

To say that Valentino Lombardi was in a rage would have been an understatement. Cedric Brewer had not checked in with him for nearly twenty-four hours. That was unacceptable. Now, after hours of making fruitless attempts to reach him on either of his two cell phones, the crime boss was mad.

He didn't think the man would be so foolish as to run out on him, but Valentino was beginning to wonder if that might be the case. He knew that his former associate, now archenemy, Gabriel Mancheski, had bribed his employees before—just one of the things that made Valentino's hatred for Gabriel so strong. Cedric Brewer had, he thought, been totally loyal, but now the crime boss was beginning to doubt it. Cedric claimed to have successfully stolen the defense attorney's file on Mancheski, a move which Valentino hoped would lead to Mancheski's conviction and imprisonment. That would open the way for Valentino to move his operations into his enemy's territory.

Much of his current anger was caused by the fact that Cedric had not yet delivered the file to him. He'd been assured that it was safe, but now, since Cedric had vanished from the radar, he wasn't so sure about that. If that file found its way back to Mancheski or his attorneys, it could be a disaster.

He once again tried both of Cedric's cell phones with the same discouraging results. He then dialed another number. When Max Barclay answered, he instructed, "Max, I need you to go back and find Cedric Brewer."

"Find Cedric?" Max asked. "I thought you considered him your best man."

"Not anymore," Valentino said. "He has failed to keep communications open with me. You are to find him, force him to turn over the Mancheski file, and then get rid of him."

"But I don't know if it is safe for me to go back," Max said, sounding just a bit desperate.

Valentino was in no mood to listen to any of his men question him. Angrily, he said, "Max, if you'd gotten the file when you were supposed to instead of killing a man who I had not ordered you to dispose of, we wouldn't be in this situation now. Don't let me down! A single anonymous phone call would clear an innocent man who is sitting in jail and put you there instead."

"I'll take care of Cedric," Max promised.

"I also need you to remove the girl and her father," Valentino added. "They are a serious liability. Make sure it's done soon."

"You got it, boss," the tall, thin man said, but Valentino wasn't sure he sounded committed. He would need to begin looking for replacements for both Max and Cedric.

"Hurry it up. And stay in touch," Valentino said and clicked off the call. Heads would roll if Mancheski wasn't removed from the scene. Valentino wasn't satisfied with having to use Max, but it would take longer to get new men oriented and in place to finish the job. He dialed another number and barked out more orders. Finally, his anger slightly abated knowing that he had men coming who would get the job done if Max failed, he grabbed a bottle of expensive scotch.

***

The prisoner sitting across the table looked like he hadn't been sleeping well. Not that Brad blamed him. He couldn't think of anything much worse than sitting in jail facing charges for a murder one didn't commit. He couldn't help but feel sorry for Jerzy Grabowski. "Thanks for coming," the suspect said, peering tiredly through the thick lenses of his glasses. "I'm sorry I'm such a bother."

"It's not a bother," Brad said, although it really was. "What can I do for you today?"

"I would like to make another statement," Jerzy said. "Do you have your recorder?"

Nodding, Brad pulled it out and placed it on the table. "What is this about?"

"The murder, what else?" Jerzy asked, his shoulders slumping.

Once he was set up and ready to take Jerzy's latest statement, Brad said, "Okay, go ahead, Jerzy. What do you have to say now that you haven't covered in our previous interviews?"

Jerzy lifted his head. "I lied the last time I spoke to you. I didn't do it. I didn't kill anybody." He fell silent.

Brad looked at him, but Jerzy dropped his eyes. "Listen, if you lied the last time you spoke to me, would you like to at least explain why you lied?" Brad asked.

"I was threatened."

"By whom?" Brad asked.

"I don't know who he was. Some guy came in to visit me. It was just before I called and asked you to come in. He told the officers that he was a friend, but I'd never seen him before," Jerzy said, his shiny head hanging low, his shoulders hunched. "And he certainly was not a friend."

"Describe him to me," Brad said.

"He was probably somewhere between thirty and forty," Jerzy began. "He looked like he was probably about my height, but not fat like me. His hair was black. He had it combed straight back."

"What was he wearing?"

"Brown sports coat, I think," Jerzy said. "He had a mean look about him, in his eyes. He said that if I didn't plead guilty something would happen to Adriana Chambers—you know, the young woman who stopped to help me."

"Did he also threaten you?" Brad asked.

"Oh yeah, he said I'd die if I didn't take the rap. And I suppose I will, but I didn't do it. Miss Chambers came and talked to me," he said.

Brad rocked back in surprise. "She did?" he asked. "When?"

"Just a few hours after you were here. She knew that I had changed my story. She told me to tell the truth," Jerzy said, finally lifting his head and meeting Brad's eyes. "She said she'd be safe, that I had to tell the truth. She's a brave girl, far braver than I am. You have no idea what a brave, good girl she is. I've been thinking about what she said, and I can't go against it. I just can't."

"Actually, Mr. Grabowski, I have a very good idea how brave she is. She is truly amazing," Brad said. He couldn't tell Jerzy what Adriana had done or even that Cedric Brewer was no longer a threat. They were keeping the man's identity under wraps for now. The press knew only that an unidentified woman had stabbed and killed the victim, also unidentified, and that the investigation was ongoing.

"You've got to keep her safe, Detective," Jerzy implored.

"We're doing our best," Brad responded. "Does your attorney know that you confessed and that you're now withdrawing that confession?"

"I haven't talked to her since I talked to you last time," he said. "Do you have any idea who did the murder?"

"We're working on it," Brad said.

They talked for a little longer, then Brad ended the interview and left. He could just about imagine what Lydia and Mike would say when he got back to the station. He was right. Lydia was furious. "How could you let him do that?" she asked.

"I didn't let him do anything," Brad shot back. "If you'll remember, I offered to let you go instead of me. You should have gone. Would you like to hear the recording?"

"Not really. I prefer the last one," she said. "We'll find a way to use it in court yet."

"Whatever," Brad said. "So what now? Are we any closer to finding Valentino Lombardi?"

"Not much, but we'll get there," she promised. "We believe he has a residence somewhere in the state now."

***

Carson ignored his phone. He couldn't tell Adriana what he was planning to do. She would try to talk him out of it, and he was in no mood for that. He had to act now. He had a number for the man who was blackmailing him. He would start there. He made the call from his newly acquired, battered old pickup truck.

He wasn't sure that Earnest Pyatt would answer his call, but he was wrong. "You have a lot of nerve calling me," Earnest said when Carson identified himself. "It had better be good."

"We need to meet," Carson said. "There's something you need to know."

"I know what I need to," the blackmailer countered. "I'm calling the shots, not you. All you need to do is send me the money and keep your mouth shut."

"That's all changed," Carson said darkly. "Valentino Lombardi shouldn't have made threats against my daughter."

"I don't know what you're talking about, but nothing has changed," Earnest said. "So don't go getting flaky. You have nothing to gain and everything to lose."

"That's where you're wrong," Carson said angrily. "The balance of power has shifted. The ball's in my court now. That's why we need to meet. I'll explain it all, and I think you'll see it my way when we do."

"I doubt that," the blackmailer responded ominously.

"Listen, if I knew where to find him, I'd talk to Valentino directly. But I don't have a way to contact him anymore. So I am going to have you do it for me. We need to meet tonight."

Carson named a place and a time and then hung up. He thought he'd gotten the interest of Mr. Pyatt. He would know soon enough. Now he needed to get in place and be ready for the meeting if Pyatt took the bait. He'd debated between naming a public place or a private one. He'd settled on a private one; he'd asked Pyatt to come to his apartment. That was risky. He hadn't intended to return there until after it was all finished, if he even survived. But at the last minute, he'd decided it would be best.

CHAPTER SIXTEEN

A STORM HAD BEEN BUILDING during the evening, and shortly before his meeting with Earnest Pyatt, Carson could see thunder and lightning beginning in the distance. He was nervous, but his anger kept his mind sharp and alert. He was as ready as he'd ever be.

When there was a tap on his door, Carson calmed his shaking hands, one of them holding his .22 caliber pistol. If that was Pyatt it was too late to turn back. Keeping the gun out of sight, he opened the door. The look on Earnest's face was deadly. He wasn't sure how his own looked, but he tried to control the trembling in his voice as he spoke. "Thanks for coming, Mr. Pyatt," he said. "I appreciate it a great deal."

"Not for long you won't," Earnest said darkly as he passed Carson and then turned to face him.

The look on his face turned to surprise when he saw the pistol that Carson was holding steadily, pointed at his chest. "Sit down over there," Carson said as a calm determination overrode the nervousness. With his free hand he pointed into his small living room.

Earnest held his ground, the surprise fading and anger taking its place on his face. "Don't be a fool, Carson. The fact that you can point a gun doesn't change anything."

"Sit down," Carson said again, his eyes narrow, his hand steady.

"And if I don't?" Earnest asked, taking a threatening step forward.

"Then I'll do to you what my daughter did to Cedric Brewer," Carson said, taking a step back, not in retreat but to keep the distance between them.

Earnest laughed, an ugly, evil sound. "No one did anything to Mr. Brewer."

"That's where you're wrong," Carson said with a laugh of his own. "I take it you haven't heard. And I suppose that means that Mr. Lombardi hasn't heard either. Doesn't make it any less of a fact."

"Enough of your games, Carson. You have no idea how much trouble you're in," Pyatt said in a low, threatening tone. "Now, give me the gun."

"I told you to sit down. We're going to talk," Carson said, surprising himself with his own determination.

"Like I asked before, what will you do if I don't?"

Carson paused before answering as lightning lit the room and a loud clap of thunder shook his apartment. "I already told you, only I'll be using a gun instead of a knife, like my daughter did, and the first shot will simply take out your knee, not kill you outright," Carson said.

A momentary look of doubt crossed Earnest's hard, angry face, but he didn't hesitate long before speaking again. "I think I'll go now. Twenty-two caliber pistols don't frighten me, especially in the hands of a loser like you. You and I have nothing to talk about. I'll expect your next payment on time."

He leaned forward, indicating that he was about to take a step. "Last chance, Mr. Pyatt. Sit down," Carson ordered sharply.

Earnest shook his head as the thunder and lightning outside increased in intensity. He took another step forward. Carson lowered the gun and calmly pulled the trigger. Another thunderclap filled the apartment with so much noise that the sound of the shot was totally masked. Pyatt's eyes opened wide and he howled in pain. His knee was fine—Carson didn't blow it out. His right foot, however, didn't fare so well. The bullet entered his foot but apparently didn't go clear through. At least, it didn't go through the sole of the shoe because when Earnest began hopping around in pain, there was no hole in the rug that covered the hardwood floor where he'd been standing, nor was there any blood. "Next one is in your knee," Carson said, waving the gun in the direction of the sofa. "So sit down."

Carson was relieved that the bullet hadn't gone into the floor. He especially had not wanted a bullet to find its way into a neighboring apartment. He was glad at the moment that his pistol was only a small caliber.

"You're crazy!" Earnest shouted. "I gotta find a doctor."

"Not until you sit down and give me the information I need from you," Carson said.

"I'll kill you," Earnest threatened as he backed toward the door onto a large throw rug. Blood began to seep out of his shoe onto the rug.

It appeared that he wasn't going to sit down, and Carson didn't want to shoot him in the knee, so he simply asked his question. "Where does Valentino Lombardi live?"

Earnest, who was going quite pale and steadying himself against the wall, said through gritted teeth, "I can't tell you that."

"You don't have a choice." Carson maintained his composure although he was anything but calm inside. "Give me his address, now!"

"Can't do that," Earnest insisted, taking another stumbling step toward the door, which was also a step toward Carson because Carson had stepped in front of the door. "I'm leaving now."

Carson, thinking quickly, stepped aside as if to let Earnest pass. But as soon as Earnest was a half of a step past him, he raised the gun high and brought it down on the back of the thug's head. Earnest crumpled to the floor, unconscious. Carson quickly retrieved a roll of duct tape from a storage room in the hallway near his bathroom. In five minutes, he had Earnest bound so tightly he was sure the captive would be unable to move when he regained consciousness. Then Carson thoroughly searched him. He removed a pistol from a shoulder holster, along with a cell phone, wallet, and pocketknife.

There was now quite a bit of blood from the injured man's foot. Carson retrieved a first-aid kit from his bathroom and turned his attention to the damaged foot. He was able to stop the bleeding by removing Earnest's shoe, wrapping the foot with a thick bandage, and taping it tightly. He also tended to the blackmailer's head, where blood was oozing from the small cut created by the barrel of Carson's pistol.

After the wounds had been tended to, Earnest began to regain consciousness. He groaned in pain as Carson dragged him into the kitchen and propped him in a corner. Without a word, Carson left him and began cleaning up the blood on his floor. The rug that covered the hardwood floor in front of the door was ruined. He cleaned it the best he could then worked on the hardwood beneath it. When he'd finished, it didn't look too bad.

As he worked, his mind was busy. He couldn't believe what his short-sighted selfishness had led to. Not only had he lost his family, his small fortune, and even his self-respect, he had now shot a man. He felt terrible. He promised himself that if he got out of this mess alive, he would do what he could to make amends and straighten out his miserable life.

He wished he could turn back the clock and do things differently, but since that wasn't possible, he decided to move ahead with his plans.

He had to do what he could to stop the evil swirling around him and his family. He finished his cleaning, threw the rags in the trash can beneath his kitchen sink, knelt down in front of the blackmailer, and said, "Now, you will give me the information I want."

Earnest lifted his head from where it had been resting on his chest. His eyes were glazed, his tongue was thick, and his complexion had become very pale. "If you don't want to sit right here and die, you will tell me where to find Mr. Lombardi."

The lightning and thunder had moved into the distance, but the rain was pouring hard. Carson listened for a response, but all he heard was labored breathing and the pounding of the rain. "You are not going anywhere until I get my answer," Carson said. "So start talking."

The injured man stubbornly said nothing. Carson stood and walked over to his kitchen table, where he had laid the blackmailer's wallet, cell phone, and 9mm semiautomatic next to his own gun. He thought for a moment then picked up the 9mm and stepped back in front of Earnest. "I appreciate the use of your pistol," he said darkly. "It's bigger than mine. It should do a lot more damage to your knee."

"I'll kill you," Earnest threatened.

"I think not," Carson said. "I seem to have all the weapons. Start talking."

Earnest maintained his stubborn silence, but his cell phone didn't. It began vibrating. Carson stepped over and picked it up. When he looked at the display he was surprised to find that the name of his late neighbor's law partner, Brian Bollinger, listed. On an impulse he answered the phone with a simple, "Hello."

The blackmailer voiced a protest, but Carson simply backed out of the room as he listened to the voice on the other end. "Mr. Pyatt, have you found the Mancheski file yet?" the voice asked.

Carson was rocked. *What is going on?* he wondered even as he decided it was Brian Bollinger's voice. He'd only spoken to him once or twice; Garrick Lenhardt had been his friend, but that friendship hadn't extended to the other lawyers in his firm. Trying to make his voice sound like Earnest Pyatt's, he said, "Not yet. I need time."

"Are you working on it?" he asked.

"Of course," Carson said.

"Well, get it done—soon! We can't let Valentino use it. I'm paying you good money, so hurry it up. I'll call you for a report in the morning.

I expect results." The attorney disconnected. Carson stood there looking at the phone in his hand, relieved that Mr. Bollinger apparently hadn't suspected that he was talking to anyone other than Mr. Pyatt.

"Get that phone back in here!" he heard the blackmailer demand weakly. "I swear, you'll regret you ever messed with me."

Carson smiled. It seemed that Mr. Pyatt was working for the other side—against Valentino Lombardi's interests if what he'd just heard was any indication, and he was sure it was. He went back to his kitchen. "That was Brian Bollinger. He wondered if you had found the Mancheski file yet. I told him you were working on it. I lied because you clearly aren't, all bound up and bleeding like you are. He wants you to get it right away." Carson chuckled. "That won't be happening, now will it? Okay, now I need that information."

Earnest stubbornly shook his head as he struggled in vain against the tape wrapped thoroughly around him.

Carson looked at the phone he still held in his hand. It inspired an idea. Within a minute he had found the number that Earnest had listed for Valentino Lombardi in his phone. He pulled the number up and then held the phone out so the blackmailer could read the digital screen. "You don't dare," he hissed.

"Actually, I do," Carson said. "I need to talk to Mr. Lombardi. And since you won't give me his address, this will have to do. I'll just call him—on your phone. That ought to make Valentino happy."

Earnest was clearly in a lot of pain; it showed on his face. But when he spoke again, it was still in a threatening tone. "You don't want to talk to Mr. Lombardi," he said. "Believe me, you don't."

"Actually, I do," Carson countered. "I understand that you don't want me to, but since I don't want to have to shoot your knee, I'll just use your phone and pretend you told me."

"Don't!" the injured man screamed as Carson hit the call button and waited while it began ringing.

Carson stepped back into the living room. The pounding rain diminished the blackmailer's screams from the kitchen. Despite himself, Carson couldn't seem to keep his hands from trembling while the phone rang. But when he heard Valentino's voice on the other end, his anger and hatred calmed him once more.

"What do you need, Pyatt?" Valentino asked angrily. Apparently he wasn't pleased to be getting a call from the guy right now.

"This isn't Pyatt—it's Carson Chambers. Mr. Pyatt was good enough to let me borrow his phone."

There was a growl then some deep breathing on the other end of the line but no words. Carson went on quickly. "Earnest gives his regards. He's a little tied up at the moment or he'd talk to you himself. It seems you don't pay him enough."

This time, the growl was followed by Valentino's response, "I pay him plenty. And you, Mr. Chambers, are a slow learner. I know he delivered my message because he's been bringing me your money quite regularly. You should have just kept paying. You know what I have to do now."

"You won't do anything. And you should have left my daughter out of this," Carson said. "You crossed the line."

"I don't cross lines," the crime boss countered. "I draw lines."

"Not anymore," Carson said. "Mr. Pyatt and I have decided to team up. It seems that he is willing to work for the highest bidder, and that is no longer you. We own the lines now, and you have crossed one of them."

There was more growling and deep breathing. Then Valentino said, "He knows better than to team up with you, so I know you're lying. You just made it worse for yourself."

"Well, we've both teamed up with your friend Gabriel Mancheski," Carson told him as his mind worked feverishly. "I will be helping Earnest find the file you had stolen from the home of Garrick Lenhardt by, if I'm not mistaken, Cedric Brewer. Earnest asked me to help him after he was hired by Brian Bollinger, the new senior partner of the firm, to get it back. They want it more than you do. At least, they're willing to pay more."

"You're lying, you scum," Valentino said.

"Actually, I'm quite serious. I just spoke with Mr. Bollinger myself. Let me give you his number and you can call him yourself and ask him. He'll probably get a kick out of talking to you."

"It better not be—"

Carson cut off Valentino's angry retort with the number. Then he added, "That's Bollinger's personal number. Call it, and then call me back on Earnest's phone. I'd be happy to talk to you again."

"Don't you move, Carson," Valentino said, and Carson could just visualize the man working his mouth angrily. "You stay right where you are while I make the call."

"I'll be here," Carson said.

"And where is that?" Valentino asked.

"As if I'd tell you that," Carson said and cut off the phone call.

He walked back into the kitchen, where Earnest Pyatt was still struggling in vain against the tape. "Mr. Valentino is calling Mr. Bollinger to confirm who you are working for now. He'll call us back in a minute," Carson said.

When the blackmailer's eyes met his, Carson could see something new there. It was fear, just what he wanted. "Give me his address, and I'll make sure that Valentino doesn't bother you over this little misunderstanding," Carson said.

The gangster had become a believer. He gave Carson an address in another city. Then Earnest said, "Now, get me a doctor."

"That'll have to wait. I've got to make sure this address is correct first." Hoping he had a minute or two more before Valentino called back, he shoved the phone in his pocket, picked up his roll of duct tape, and taped the blackmailer's mouth shut.

The phone began to vibrate in his pocket. He pulled it out and looked at the digital display screen. Assured that it was Valentino, he took the call. "Tell Pyatt he's a dead man," Valentino said and immediately terminated the call.

"That was Mr. Lombardi. He said to tell you that you're a dead man," Carson said. "I have to run now. I have some things to do. Be patient, Mr. Pyatt. And enjoy yourself."

With the tape on his mouth, all Earnest could do was struggle and mumble. Carson left, taking both the twenty-two and the 9mm with him. A minute later he pulled the old Ford pickup onto the street in the pounding rain. Then he looked at his watch, saw that it was after ten, and made another call with his own phone as he left the area of his apartment.

***

Fatigue was setting in. Brad had slept very little for the past few days. He was sitting now on a sofa in the Chambers' house. A female officer was sitting across the room, Krista was in her bedroom nursing a pounding headache, and Adriana sat on the sofa near Brad. The TV was on, but Brad's mind was on the case when his phone began to vibrate.

He pulled it out, saw that it was Carson Chambers, and answered it hopefully.

"Detective Osborn, this is Carson Chambers. I need you to do something for me."

158   CLAIR M. POULSON

"Where are you?" Brad asked as his eyes met Adriana's.

"I can't tell you that. But I will tell you where I've been—at my apartment," Carson said. "I had a visitor there who needs to see you."

"Okay, who is it?" Brad asked suspiciously.

Adriana, leaning forward with a question in her eyes, mouthed, "Who is that?"

Brad raised his empty hand and signaled for her to wait. She settled back against the sofa but didn't take her eyes from his face. Brad listened as Carson explained, "His name is Earnest Pyatt. He is the man who has been blackmailing me for Valentino Lombardi. However, it seems that he is willing to work for whoever will pay the most. He was recently retained by Brian Bollinger, Garrick Lenhardt's partner, to find a file you're probably looking for, one that belonged to Garrick. And, oh, by the way, have you kept Cedric Brewer's death quiet?"

"Yes," Brad said. "The press knows a man was killed in the hotel, but they don't know his identity or anything about who killed him or why."

"Thank you. I thought that was the case. That's good. Go get Mr. Pyatt now. But be careful. He's a killer, so don't take him lightly. Of course, right now he's sitting silently on my kitchen floor. He'll need medical attention; he's been shot. The door's not locked, so just go in when you get there."

Before Brad could respond, Carson terminated the call. Brad thought about trying to call him back, but he was quite certain the man wouldn't answer. "Who was that?" Adriana asked again.

Brad took a deep breath. "It was your father," he said. "I need to go over to his place right now."

"I'll go with you," she said anxiously.

"No, you need to stay here. Anyway, your dad won't be there by the time I get there," Brad said. "But someone else will be. And don't ask who because I can't tell you."

Adriana was disappointed, but Brad was firm. He called and asked his partner to meet him at Carson's address. Mike grumbled but agreed. "Don't leave here, Adriana," Brad said as he shrugged into his jacket and headed for the door. He smiled at her. "Stay tough," he said. "I'll tell you what's going on when I can."

She smiled back at him, but she couldn't hide the worry and the disappointment in her eyes. Brad added, "I'll see you later," and then left the house. He wasn't sure what had happened at her father's apartment, but he had a feeling it wasn't good.

CHAPTER SEVENTEEN

WHEN EARNEST PYATT'S PHONE BEGAN to vibrate, Carson looked at the screen. Seeing it was Brian Bollinger, he took the call. "Mr. Pyatt, I just had a call that makes me very angry. I paid you a lot of money to do a job, and to do it discreetly, and you have the nerve to tell Valentino Lombardi. What do you think you're doing?"

Carson considered his answer then, trying to sound casual, he said, "This is not actually Pyatt. If you are interested in his whereabouts, call Detective Brad Osborn. I'm afraid your little secret is out." With that, he ended the call. The phone rang again, but he simply let it ring.

He had an address, but he didn't have a plan. He had a goal, but he didn't have a clue how to achieve it. All he had considered, up to this point, was convincing Valentino to agree to leave his daughter alone and to leave him alone as well. He'd considered threatening Valentino, but he didn't know how to go about it. Now that he was driving toward the address where Pyatt told him Lombardi was staying, fifty or sixty miles away, he felt his palms begin to sweat.

Carson thought about the time and decided that if he was simply going to barge into Valentino's house, it would be best to do it in the deepest part of the night. Three or four o'clock in the morning seemed to make more sense than eleven or twelve. So he decided to wait, as hard as that was. He was mentally geared up for action right now, but he wanted to succeed. He wouldn't have any chance unless he stopped and formed some kind of plan. Once he knew what he was going to do, he would proceed to the guy's home.

He pulled into the parking lot of a grocery store, parked the truck, and sat there for a few minutes, deep in thought. He finally decided that it would be best to locate Valentino's house, sort of scope it out, before he made firm plans. Then he would go somewhere and decide what to do next. With the beginnings of a plan, he got out of the truck and went into the store. He was nervous, and that made him hungry. He bought some bread and salami, a bag of potato chips, a fruit pie, several candy bars, and a couple of bottles of water before he returned to the truck.

Munching on the potato chips, Carson drove slowly south toward the address Earnest Pyatt had given him. He knew that he had a drive of close to an hour ahead of him, but he didn't mind. He needed to think and he could think while he drove. The challenge of his life lay ahead of him. For his daughter's sake he had to succeed. Failure was not an option.

***

While waiting outside the apartment for Mike, Brad scouted the complex by driving slowly past a couple of times. He finally parked, wishing Mike would hurry. He couldn't understand how the man could always manage to arrive late, no matter how urgent the case was, and Brad felt it was urgent that they get inside that apartment. If Carson had been telling the truth, there was an injured man inside. He was nearly busting out of his skin with agitation when Mike finally pulled up and parked behind him.

Brad had to bite his tongue when Mike said, "Been waiting long?"

He wanted to lash out, but instead he started walking toward the building. "Let's go see what's happening in there."

They entered with weapons drawn. It only took a minute to find the injured man in the kitchen. Brad tore the tape from the man's mouth and asked him if he was okay. Earnest swore and told him in vivid terms that he was not okay, that he'd been shot and that they had better get him some help right then.

"Looks like you bit off more than you could chew here, Mr. Pyatt," Brad said, unable to suppress a grin as he showed him his ID and introduced himself and his partner.

"Get me an ambulance," Earnest demanded. "Carson Chambers tried to kill me."

"Looks to me like he did just the opposite," Brad said as he began to free him of the duct tape. "It looks like he administered first aid, maybe saved your life."

"I've been shot," Earnest complained weakly. "Carson shot me in the foot. And he tried to bash my head in."

"I guess you better call an ambulance," Brad said to Mike. "I'll see how his foot looks." He began to cut the bandage away before he had completely freed Earnest from the tape on his arms.

It was a nasty wound, but there was nothing more Brad could do that Carson hadn't already done. The bleeding was controlled, and that, he thought, was the most important thing. All he could do was wait for the ambulance to arrive. While they waited, Brad pressed Earnest for some answers. "Where was Carson going?" Brad asked. "Surely he told you."

"Yeah, he told me all right, the fool. He is going after Valentino Lombardi. Lombardi will have him killed, and then he'll have me killed," Earnest said and then shuddered. He was very pale, but it wasn't just from the pain. He was clearly scared to death. "You gotta protect me," he begged.

"Why would we do that?" Brad asked. "We aren't exactly on the same side. Anyway, I don't know what we could do."

"You could put Valentino in jail and keep him there," Earnest pleaded, his face creased in pain.

"We'd love to, but we need evidence," Brad suggested as he wondered where the injured gangster was headed with this.

He soon found out. Earnest said, "I'll help you. I swear. I can give you enough to put him away for the rest of his life. But you gotta keep me safe and keep me out of jail. He could even have someone kill me in there."

"What kind of information or evidence can you give us?" Mike asked, moving over beside Brad.

"Something big, that's for sure. He ordered the hit on Garrick Lenhardt," he said. "When is that ambulance coming? I'm dying here."

"You're not dying, and it will get here when it gets here," Brad said coldly. "How do you know that Lombardi did that?"

"I just do," Earnest said. "Someone who knows told me."

"Someone you think knows, you mean?"

"Oh, he knows all right."

"Then tell us who he sent to kill Lenhardt?"

"You already know. You arrested him. Jerzy Grabowski," he said.

Mike gave Brad an *I told you so* look. Then to Earnest he said, "We'll need something to back up what you've said."

Just then, paramedics entered the apartment and the conversation was cut short. The paramedics soon had the injured man loaded in the ambulance. The officers locked up the apartment and followed the ambulance to the hospital. They watched Earnest being rolled toward surgery and disappearing through a door that they were told they couldn't go through. But within a few minutes, a nurse summoned the officers, saying that the patient was refusing anesthesia until he talked to them. They followed her through the forbidden door.

When Brad and Mike reached his side, the blackmailer had wide, fear-filled eyes. Earnest focused those eyes on Brad's face and begged, "Please, you've got to protect me. There's got to be an officer outside whatever room I'm in as long as I'm in the hospital."

"We'll see what we can do, but first we need some specific information from you. And we have to wait for that until your surgery is completed and you are out of the recovery room," Brad said firmly.

"No, please, you guys have to stay while they operate. Afterward, I'll tell you more."

"Mr. Pyatt, we have a lot of work to do. One or both of us will be back to talk to you after you're awake," Brad promised. "But we've got to go now."

"That's not good enough. Valentino will be checking every hospital around or having someone else check them. They'll find me. You've got to help me," he begged pitifully.

"He doesn't know you've been shot, does he?" Brad asked. "How could he possibly know?"

"Mr. Lombardi knows things. He finds things out. People tell him things. You've got to help me," Earnest said, his eyes wide with fright.

Brad just shook his head and Mike turned toward the door. "Don't go yet!" Earnest exclaimed. "I'll tell you more now. You've got to find Max Barclay. He'll tell you that Valentino ordered Jerzy to kill the lawyer. He works for the boss. He's the one that told me."

"Where do we find him?" Brad asked.

"I don't know. But he's around somewhere, I'm sure. He might even be looking for me right now. He could be coming into this hospital any minute now. Please . . ."

"Describe him," Brad said.

"He's about thirty, tall and skinny. He has short black hair," Earnest said as rapidly as his pain would allow.

"What color are his eyes?" Brad asked.

"Gray."

"How is his hair combed?"

"He wears it short. It always looks neat."

"Is there anything else about him that would help us recognize him—a tattoo or something."

Earnest thought for a moment, winced in pain, then said, "I don't remember any tattoos, but look at his fingers. They are very long. I never saw such long fingers."

"Does he wear glasses?" Mike asked.

"No, but he wears a gold watch, an expensive one. That's all I can think of. I'm hurting bad. I've given you something, now you gotta stay here and keep me safe," Earnest said plaintively.

"First, give us Lombardi's address, the one you gave Carson."

He wrote down the address Earnest rattled off, and then he said, "Okay, we'll take care of you. And we'll talk to you again when you're out of surgery."

"In case you check, that house is not in Valentino's name. He's too cautious for that. He actually has several addresses, but I'm sure that's the one he's at now," the injured man said, his face ashen and his voice growng weak.

"Give me his other addresses," Brad demanded.

"I can't. I don't know them," Pyatt insisted.

"If he's not at this address, we'll be back," Mike said angrily. "You better not be lying."

"I'm not, but you've got to protect me. You promised," he whined weakly.

"We'll see that you aren't touched," Brad said as he and Mike headed for the door.

As soon as he and his partner had returned to the waiting area, Brad said, "One of us needs to stay here. The other one needs to find Carson Chambers and stop him before he gets himself killed."

"You are the one who knows Chambers. You go. I'll wait here and watch for Barclay, the so-called tall, thin man," Mike said. "If he exists," he added with a grin. "Oh, and you probably better call Lydia. She might want to accompany you."

Knowing that Mike was right, Brad phoned his sergeant, despite the lateness of the hour. After explaining what was happening, excluding the bit about Max Barclay, he told her that he was going to try to stop Carson from making a bad mistake.

She agreed with him but did not offer to go with him. Instead, she reminded him to contact the local authorities when he reached their city and accept whatever help they offered. Yawning, fighting fatigue, Brad said, "I'll do that."

As soon as that conversation was over, Brad dialed Adriana's cell phone, knowing she was probably asleep in bed, but he felt that he owed her a call. She answered very quickly. "Hi, Brad, is everything okay?" she asked anxiously.

"Adriana, I hated to bother you, but I knew you'd want to know what I found out. Were you asleep?"

"I wish," she said. "I was earlier, but I had a nightmare, a horrible thing. I woke up screaming. Mom rushed in along with the officer. I was so embarrassed."

"What kind of nightmare was it?" Brad asked with concern.

"Oh, Brad, it was terrible. I dreamed that someone was after me with a knife, a great big knife. He was stabbing at me, yelling that I was going to get what I deserved for stabbing that man. I woke up just as he was thrusting the knife at me."

"I'm sorry, Adriana. Are you okay now?"

"I'm afraid to go to sleep again," she said. "It was horrible."

Brad didn't know what to say. It broke his heart that she was suffering this way, but it wasn't a surprise. She had been through an extremely trying experience, a horrible one. "After we finish talking, why don't you drink some warm milk and try to sleep again," he suggested.

"I hate warm milk," she said. "But thanks for the suggestion."

"Maybe you could try reading something uplifting, the Book of Mormon, maybe, or the New Testament. Get your mind on something else," he suggested.

"Thanks, Brad. That's a good idea. I'll try that," she said.

"I won't call you again tonight," he said. "I don't want to disturb you if you do fall asleep again. On the other hand, if you need to, call me at any time. Okay?"

"Okay," she agreed. "Now tell me what happened at Dad's place."

He told her. She began to cry. "I killed a man, and now Dad has shot one. When is this ever going to end?" she said. "Where is Dad now? Have you talked to him?"

Brad briefly explained.

"You've got to stop him," Adriana cried. "He'll get himself killed."

Brad feared that he'd only made things worse for her. "Please, Adriana," he said. "Try not to worry. I'll see what I can do about your father. You read the scriptures, pray, eat some ice cream, and then try to get some sleep."

"I'll try," she promised.

***

Max Barclay had just received new orders. Those orders had been given in person. Valentino's words were still echoing in his head as he drove away. "Find and eliminate Earnest Pyatt," had been the order.

First Cedric and then Pyatt? he'd wondered. "You want me to wipe out two of your best men?" Max had asked, wondering then if he might be next.

"I have more help coming from New York," Valentino said. "They should be here soon. In the meantime, go after Pyatt first. Finding him should be simple. Contact an attorney by the name of Brian Bollinger. He's the former partner of Garrick Lenhardt. Pyatt has apparently been working for him behind my back. Make Mr. Bollinger help you find him. Do whatever you have to do to get his cooperation."

"Do you have a phone number for Bollinger or, better yet, his address?" Max asked.

Valentino had both. He recited them to Max and then said, "After you've taken care of Pyatt, go after Brewer. Don't quit until they are both out of my hair. Do you understand me?"

Max understood only too well—he was next if he didn't get to Pyatt and Brewer soon. He tried both of their cell phones as he pulled onto the street in front of the mansion and turned east. He hadn't expected either one of them to answer, and so he was surprised when Earnest did.

***

A dark, older model sedan was slowly driving past him after leaving the mansion that Pyatt had told him was Valentino's current residence. Carson was slumped down in the seat of the old pickup, peeking over the top of the dash when the cell phone he'd taken from Earnest Pyatt began to ring. The driver of the car who was passing him had a cell phone to his ear. Carson pulled the ringing phone from his pocket but didn't recognize the number on the digital display. Taking a chance, he answered the call anyway.

"Hello," he said, trying to keep his voice about the same pitch as Earnest's.

"That you, Pyatt?" he was asked.

"Who else would it be?" he answered, trying to sound as much like the blackmailer as he could.

"You need to meet me right away," the voice said.

"Who is this?" Carson asked, thinking that Earnest probably would have known but not knowing what else to say.

"It's Max, you idiot. I need to meet with you."

Carson had a good idea why Max, whoever he was, wanted to meet with him. If it was Max that had just passed him, then he'd been talking to Valentino, and he'd probably been told to get rid of Pyatt for betraying him. He smiled grimly to himself and began to speak again, but he kept his voice muffled as he said, "I can't hear you. I think I'm losing the connection." Then he ended the call.

Just then his phone began to ring. He put down Pyatt's, picked his own up, and looked at the screen. He recognized Detective Osborn's number. He hesitated then took the call. "Hello, Detective," he said. "Did you find Mr. Pyatt?"

"Yes, thanks, Carson. He's in surgery right now. He's not too happy with you,"

"I'm not too happy with him," Carson countered. "He wants me dead."

"I don't know if that's true, Carson," Brad said. "He told me that he gave you the address where Mr. Lombardi may be staying and that you were going after him. If he wanted you dead, he wouldn't have told me that, would he?"

"I don't know," Carson said, suddenly not so sure of himself. He hadn't expected that, especially considering the threats Pyatt had made after Carson put the bullet in his foot.

"Don't do whatever it is you're planning to do," Detective Osborn said, urgency in his voice.

"I've got to," Carson said. "I owe it to my girl. I've caused her so much trouble. I've got to get Lombardi to leave her alone."

"Listen, Carson," Brad said, "Mr. Pyatt gave us some information on Valentino. We plan to arrest him as soon as we can get a little more information when Pyatt gets out of surgery. Meet me somewhere, and we'll talk this out."

"You'll just arrest me for shooting Earnest," Carson said and that's exactly what he believed.

"No, that's not what I plan at all," Brad said. "He was blackmailing you. You can claim self-defense. Let's meet someplace and we'll work things out. Leave Valentino up to us."

"I can't do that, Detective. I'm sorry. Tell Adriana I love her," Carson said and abruptly terminated the call. He shut his phone off, shoved it in a pocket, and turned his full attention back to his surveillance of the huge home where he was now quite sure Valentino was staying.

***

The only option now was to continue driving south as rapidly as possible and try to intercept Carson before he got himself killed. Brad had hoped that Carson would listen to reason. It was clear now that this was not going to happen. He didn't want to have to arrest Carson, but that might be the only way to save his life. What he had told Carson on the phone about his actions being self-defense wasn't entirely accurate. He needed to do what seemed most likely to calm things down. Arresting Carson might be the best solution.

As he drove, Brad thought about the information Earnest Pyatt had given them. His claim that Valentino had hired Jerzy to murder Garrick Lenhardt was going to be very damaging to any defense Jerzy's attorney might mount. And it was going to make it almost impossible for Brad to convince his colleagues that they should drop the charges against Jerzy. If he could find time the next day, he felt like he should once again visit Jerzy at the jail.

***

After circling the block for a third time, Carson was no closer to coming up with a concrete plan. The place was huge, it was fenced, and there would very likely be armed guards on the grounds and in the house. He had to find and get past all of them in order to get inside and confront Valentino. His stomach was churning and his determination was fading.

He parked once more almost a block up the street from the mansion and stared at the gate. Suddenly, lights lit up the gate, then it slowly swung open, and a large black limo pulled out. The gate closed behind it, and the car turned toward Carson onto the street. He hunkered down in the seat and watched, his eyes barely clearing the bottom of the window. The limo's glass was so dark that there wasn't a chance of seeing inside it. Carson wondered if Valentino was in there, if he had decided to leave in order to avoid a confrontation of some kind.

He waited, watching the receding taillights in the light drizzle of rain that had just begun. Then, on a sudden impulse, he started the pickup, made a hard turn, and drove in the direction of the limo. He closed the gap a little bit then stayed a constant distance back following it, his windshield wipers beating the ever-increasing rain away. If Valentino was in that vehicle, perhaps Carson would get a chance to confront him after all. That would be dangerous but not nearly as risky as trying to break into the mansion. As he drove, he decided on a plan. Once again, he became firmly committed.

***

The address was easy to find, even though storminess had once again returned, obstructing visibility and making the roads dangerous. Thunder and lightning picked up; the rain began to fall harder. Brad turned onto the street he'd been looking for, and shortly he was driving past a gated estate matching the address Earnest Pyatt had given him. He drove slowly past the mansion, watching for any cars parked along the street. He had no idea what Carson was driving. But if he saw anything that looked out of place he would stop and check it out.

He'd called the local police, and they had promised to send some backup if he needed it. In the meantime, they would simply be standing by. This was a very upscale area and he didn't see any cars parked on the street. He circled the entire block, and then he drove around neighboring blocks. If Carson Chambers was in the area, he was well hidden.

Brad called the local officer he'd spoken most recently with. He described the mansion and the tall fence surrounding it, and the officer confirmed that it was the correct place. When Brad told him there was no sign of Carson, he suggested that Brad come into the police station for a while and then drive back there later. He agreed and headed toward the city center. On the way, he tried Carson's phone again, but it was clear that the man had no intention of answering it.

CHAPTER EIGHTEEN

THE EVER-INCREASING STORM COULD be an advantage for Carson. Traffic was almost nonexistent. The old truck's windshield wipers couldn't even come close to keeping up with the deluge. He closed the distance between himself and the black limo. They approached a traffic light just as it turned red. The limo slowly came to a stop. Carson pulled up behind it. With Earnest Pyatt's 9mm in his right hand, he opened his door with his left and stepped into the downpour.

Shielded by the pickup door, he took aim and fired at the driver's side rearview mirror. It was a good shot. The glass shattered, and the limo leaped forward into the intersection just as a car came from the right. The limo driver swerved to avoid a collision, but in doing so, he lost control and spun across the intersection, sliding on the rain-soaked pavement. The limo crashed into the pole that held the traffic light. The other car sped away, slipping for a moment on the slick pavement before gaining control.

Carson leapt back into his truck and backed up a few yards. The driver of the limo got out and stepped toward the front of the vehicle. He gazed at the car's smashed grill, kicked the buckled bumper, shook his fist, and then turned and walked to the back of the limo, where he opened the back door.

Even at a distance and through the pounding rain, Carson recognized Valentino Lombardi when he stepped from the limo and looked at the front of the car, which his driver was angrily pointing to. Then he pointed first to the ruined mirror then the street to where Carson was sitting in his truck. Valentino reached inside his jacket and out came a pistol. He raised it and fired it toward Carson's truck. Luckily for Carson, the bullet went somewhere other than where Valentino had intended.

Carson shoved the truck into gear, stomping hard on the gas and ducking as low as he could. The truck spun on the wet road for a moment then shot forward with the rear end fishtailing dangerously. Valentino shot again. Carson's windshield shattered, but he kept his foot down hard and held the steering wheel steady. One more bullet struck the truck just before he reached the back end of the limo. He braced himself against the steering wheel as his pickup crashed.

Carson's head snapped forward, but he wasn't hurt badly. He dropped to the seat, squirming across to the far side before he opened the door and scrambled out, the 9mm in his hand. He raised it as he peered over the front of his truck. It was smashed badly against the larger limo. The impact had shoved the limo forward just enough that the pole with the traffic light was now leaning at about a forty-five-degree angle. The driver was lying on the pavement a few feet from the vehicles. Valentino was stumbling toward the back of the big vehicle, but as he slipped and fell, his pistol flew from his hand and landed several feet away from him, out in the street. Carson quickly sprinted around the back of his truck and then cautiously moved toward Valentino, his eyes focused mostly on his target but darting quickly to the inert limo driver and then back.

The driver still wasn't moving. Carson ignored him and cautiously moved on. Valentino struggled to his feet, looked around wildly, spotted his pistol, and began stumbling quickly toward it. Carson stopped and, after another good shot, watched the other gun slide clear across the intersection. Then he surged forward as Valentino turned to face him.

"You'll die for this, Carson," the crime boss screamed wildly.

Carson stopped a yard from Valentino and raised the gun until it was pointed squarely at his enemy's face. "I shot Pyatt. And now, unless you do exactly what I say, I'll shoot you."

Valentino eyed him angrily, the water running down his face. "Put down the gun, Chambers," he said. "You are way out of your league."

A car approached them from behind. It slowed down, and the passenger window rolled down. The driver leaned across and said, "Do you guys need any help?"

He spotted the gun when Carson moved the barrel toward him. "Just drive," he said.

The guy drove, splashing dirty water over both men. In a moment, the car was out of sight. "Now, Valentino, step over to your car," Carson ordered. The crime boss hesitated, but when Carson shook the gun, he did as he was told. Carson stepped backward several steps. He reached into his truck and picked up the roll of duct tape, the same one he'd used on the blackmailer, never once taking his eyes from Valentino. "Face the limo and put your hands behind you," he ordered when Valentino started to move.

Valentino stubbornly refused. Carson raised the gun. He didn't figure it would be long before cops showed up. He didn't want to be here when they did. "Do it now," he shouted over the sound of the pounding rain. Valentino didn't move. Carson hesitated just a moment, thinking that he'd already shot one man; surely he wouldn't get a lot more time in prison for shooting one more. He lowered the pistol and fired, intentionally missing Valentino's foot by only an inch or two. The big man's eyes grew wide. "Do it now," Carson shouted.

Valentino turned, put his hands behind his back, and threatened, "I'll get you for this."

Carson ignored the comment as he approached Valentino. Then he took a huge chance and stuck the gun loosely in a pocket before he grabbed Valentino's hands. Valentino shook loose. Carson grabbed his gun and rammed it against Valentino's head. He didn't hit him hard enough to knock him out, but it was hard enough to make the man slump forward against the limo, struggling to stay upright.

Carson swiftly put the gun back in his pocket, grabbed the man's arms, and securely bound them behind Valentino's back. He glanced at the driver. He was stirring now. Keeping an eye on him, Carson opened the back door of the limo, shoved Valentino in, and slammed the door shut.

Sirens sounded in the distance. Carson looked up the street and could see flashing blue lights through the rain. He glanced once more at the driver then ran and jumped into the front of the limo. He turned the key; the big engine started. He shoved the gear lever into reverse and gunned it. The tires spun for a moment, and then the car began moving backward, shoving Carson's pickup back with it. As soon as he was clear of the pole, Carson shoved the gear lever into drive and gunned the engine. The limo shot away from the damaged truck, narrowly missing the damaged pole, striking the bottom of the traffic light where it was hanging low over the street then shooting away from the intersection. Carson turned left at the next intersection and increased his speed. He raced through a red light and drove one more block before slowing down and turning right. Two blocks later, he turned left again and sped straight up that street.

Even though the rain was letting up, it was hard to see because one of the limo's headlights had been broken. He slowed a little. He wasn't sure where to go, so he just kept driving straight.

***

The cell phone began to ring. Brad, who had been dozing in a small conference room of the police station, jerked awake. It took him a moment to realize where he was. Finally oriented, he grabbed his phone and looked at the display screen. "Carson, where are you?" he asked urgently.

"Don't worry about me. Do you want Mr. Lombardi?"

"Yes," Brad said. "Do you know where he is?"

"He's with me for now," Carson said. "But he won't be for long."

"Is he okay?"

"He's fine, just angry," Carson said. "And I'm okay too. And in case you're wondering, I didn't shoot him."

"Good. Tell me where you are, and I'll meet you," Brad offered as he slid back from the conference table and rose to his feet.

"I'll call you back shortly," Carson said, and the call was terminated.

Brad shook his head and hurried out of the squad room. A minute later, he was back in his car driving toward the mansion where they believed Valentino Lombardi was staying. He had a gut feeling that Carson wasn't there, but he felt the need to go somewhere and didn't know where else to go.

His phone rang again, and he grabbed it quickly, expecting it to be Carson. He was wrong; it was a local officer. He gave a short, terse message to Brad and then ended the call. There had been an accident several miles from the mansion. There was a wrecked Ford F-150 pickup there and a man who claimed to be Valentino's limo driver.

The rain had let up, but there was still water flowing in some of the intersections, and the street surface was dangerously slick. After fishtailing a couple of times, Brad slowed down. He finally reached the intersection he'd been asked to go to. There were several patrol cars there and an ambulance with lights flashing. There was also a tow truck backing up to an older model Ford pickup. One traffic light was hanging dangerously low over the right-hand side of the intersection because the pole it was attached to was badly bent. Brad parked his car to the right and walked back to the accident scene.

The man who claimed to have been driving the limo was just being loaded into an ambulance. Upon inquiry, Brad learned that after the limo had hit the power pole, the man had been standing next to it when the pickup struck from the rear. The impact had thrown him onto the pavement, where he'd struck his head hard, the impact knocking him unconscious. He claimed that he was driving businessman Valentino Lombardi around the city, trying to help him relax. He claimed that Valentino was having a hard time sleeping, and whenever that happened, a nice ride in his limo relaxed him.

Brad didn't believe a word of it, knowing about the earlier events of the night, but he kept his thoughts to himself. The limo driver apparently didn't have any idea who the driver of the truck was. Brad looked the truck over. The windshield was shattered and there was a lot of damage to the front end. In addition to that, he discovered something the local officers had missed. He pointed out a bullet hole in the front right fender. Before the ambulance left, Brad spoke to the limo driver, asking him specifically about the bullet hole. The man claimed no knowledge of what had caused the incident, saying that it must have happened sometime in the past.

Brad's phone rang again, and he answered it.

"Brad, it's Mike. Pyatt made it through surgery okay, but he's still scared to death that someone is coming after him."

"Keep an eye on him," Brad suggested. Then he explained where he was. "I think that Carson Chambers is driving Valentino around in the damaged limo."

"I'll see if I can get someone to relieve me here and I'll come down," Mike said.

"I have the car," Brad reminded him. "You'll need to get a different one. But there's no hurry. Until I get a lead on where Carson and Valentino have gone, there's not much I can do."

Brad's call waiting beeped. "I'm getting another call, Mike. I better take it," he said. A moment later he was listening to Carson.

"If you want Mr. Valentino, you can have him now," Carson said. He gave Brad an address and abruptly terminated the call.

***

The rain had stopped. Carson was standing at the corner of a closed service station, soaking wet, watching the limo where he had parked it—across the street in the abandoned parking area of a dry cleaning business. He'd left Valentino in the backseat, taped tightly enough that he wouldn't be going anywhere without help.

Shivering from the wetness, he simply stood and watched, hoping that someone would come and get Valentino soon. He didn't have to wait long. He recognized Detective Osborn when he pulled up in a plain blue car about ten minutes later. The young officer stood for a moment and surveyed the area; then he cautiously approached the banged-up limo. As soon as Carson saw the officer open the back door, he slipped away. Ten minutes later he was in a cab, headed to a cheap motel several miles from the city. He needed rest and he needed to unwind.

***

Shortly after ten on Monday morning, after a long night of troubled sleep, Adriana got a call from her father. "Dad, you're okay!" she exclaimed when she heard his voice.

"Physically, yes," he said. "But I'm probably in a whole lot of trouble with the law."

"What did you do, Dad?" she asked apprehensively, hoping he hadn't hurt anyone else.

"Earnest Pyatt, the man who delivered the blackmail notes and picked up the money, is in the hospital. And he shouldn't be a problem anymore. Your detective got him to open up about Valentino Lombardi," he said.

"My detective?" Adriana said. "If you're talking about Detective Osborn, he's just a friend."

"You're not fooling anybody, Adriana," Carson said. "He's a fine young man. Whatever you do, don't let him get away."

"Dad!" she said as she felt the blood rush to her face, glad that there was no one in her room to see her embarrassment.

Carson chuckled. "Anyway, Detective Osborn told me on the phone last night that Valentino was behind the murder of Garrick Lenhardt."

"That awful man," she said with a shudder. "I hope they catch him and lock him up forever."

"So do I," Carson agreed. "Actually, he was taken into custody last night, thanks to me, but you never know what will happen now. If you hear anything about what Detective Osborn has done with him, would you let me know? I expect he'll tell you, hopefully today."

"Okay, Dad, I will," she promised, wondering what her father had done and how he knew Valentino was in custody. But she let it slide. Maybe Brad would tell her. "Where are you, Dad?" she asked.

"For now, I better not say. Not everything I did to try to stop Valentino was legal. I could be in a lot of trouble. For now, I want to stay out of jail so that I can help more if I need to."

"Okay, Dad," she said. "I won't ask you again, but please, please be careful. I don't want you to go to jail, but I also don't want you to get hurt."

"I'll be careful, I promise," he said.

An hour later, the doorbell rang. The female officer who was on duty in the house answered it as Adriana stood back, hoping it was Brad. Her heart fluttered as he walked in. "Hi," he said to both the officer and Adriana. "How are things here?"

Things were fine but boring, it seemed. Boring for her, Brad explained, was good. His night had not been boring, and that was good too. He'd made progress.

"You look exhausted," Adriana said after she finally got Brad alone in the kitchen. "And you're probably hungry."

"It was a long night," Brad agreed with a yawn. "I haven't even been to my apartment yet. I wanted to make sure you were okay first. By the way, where's your mother?"

"She's at her office. An officer escorted her there. She says there are some things she simply has to get done."

"Can we talk for a bit?" Brad asked. "I need to bring you up to date."

"I'll fix you some breakfast," she said.

"I'm starved, and thanks, that would be nice. Your dad is a gutsy man," Brad began.

"He told me that he is in trouble with you guys, the law, for helping you catch Valentino," Adriana said.

"Probably not as much trouble as he might think. Personally, I don't blame him for what he did last night," Brad said. "Let me tell you about it."

Adriana busied herself preparing bacon, eggs, hash browns, and toast as Brad talked. When he'd finished the account of her father's activities, as far as he knew them, she had the food prepared. She set two places at the table, poured some juice, and served up their breakfast. "I haven't been able to eat this morning for worrying," she said as she sat down next to him.

Brad offered a blessing on the food, and they began to eat. "So, did you arrest Valentino?" she asked between bites. "Dad told me that you did."

"Thanks to your father, he's in jail, yes. But our case against him is weak, I'm afraid. Earnest Pyatt says that Valentino hired Jerzy to murder Garrick Lenhardt, but you and I both know that can't be true because Jerzy didn't do it. I went to the jail this morning and talked to Jerzy. He says he doesn't understand what's happening. He's scared, the poor guy."

"Didn't Valentino admit anything to you?" Adriana asked.

Brad laughed. "He's a tough old nut, that guy. He lawyered up so fast my head was spinning. He denies doing anything illegal, anything at all. His attorney was at the jail almost before I got Valentino there. His lawyer claims that Valentino doesn't know anything about your father being blackmailed. He also told me that Valentino doesn't know anyone by the name of Earnest Pyatt. He says his client told him that Pyatt, whoever he is, must be one of Mancheski's thugs. These guys are all a bunch of liars."

"So what charges are you holding him on?" Adriana asked fearfully.

Brad chewed thoughtfully for a moment, and then he swallowed and said, "He had a gun. He fired it at your Dad's truck—at him. He hit the truck at least twice. He is being charged with attempted murder. His lawyer denies everything. Of course, that isn't our jurisdiction. It's even a different county, so he's not in our jail."

Adriana laid her fork down. She had lost her appetite again. "I'm still not safe, am I?" she said, trembling slightly.

"That's right. We can't relax yet," Brad said. "Two of the men are out of the way, but who knows who else Valentino has out there."

"What happens next?" Adriana asked.

"I've got to keep trying to solve the homicide of Mr. Lenhardt, find out who really did it. Everyone but me thinks that what Earnest Pyatt is saying is the nail in the coffin for Jerzy Grabowski. You'll still have to testify, I'm afraid," he said.

"When will the trial be?" she asked.

"The date hasn't been set, but Ross Harris, the assistant DA prosecuting the case, is pushing to have it held soon. And I understand that Jerzy's attorney, a woman by the name of Gloria Metz, agrees with him on that. You'll get to know her. She's an excellent attorney, one of the best court-appointed defense attorneys in the state. She is now Jerzy's best chance of getting off. You're still his second best chance," he added with a smile.

***

When Max Barclay heard the news of the arrest of Earnest Pyatt and the death of Cedric Brewer, he became uneasy. Max was a cold-blooded killer, but that didn't make him a brave man. He had spent much of the night diligently searching for the two of them but with no success.

It was on the TV in his hotel room that he heard the news of the two men. The cops announced the identity of the man killed in the Marriott hotel on the evening news. The news broadcast informed the public that Brewer was killed when attempting to kidnap a woman. Max listened closely, but no other names were released. That story was followed by one stating that an unidentified man had shot Mr. Pyatt during a break-in at an apartment, that Pyatt had been treated at a local hospital and arrested on a variety of felony charges.

Max had followed Valentino's order and tried to find Brian Bollinger, the attorney. Recently divorced, Brian lived alone. Under cover of darkness and storm, Max had even broken into his condominium, but he wasn't there. He suspected that Brian had left town. Max smiled at the thought that the attorney was probably running scared—as he should be. Max called his cell phone over and over, but Brian didn't ever answer it. A call that morning to his law office also netted negative results. The woman who answered the phone stubbornly refused to give out any information, and he was not allowed to speak to any of the other attorneys in the firm.

He shut off the TV and rubbed his eyes. How could this have happened? Regardless of what the media reported—or failed to report—Max knew that what had happened to the two men was directly related to Valentino and the events he was orchestrating. Max wondered if he could be next. Not if he could help it, he vowed. He picked up his cell phone and punched in Valentino's number. It went immediately to voice mail. He clicked off and dialed the number at the Lombardi mansion.

It was eventually answered, but the woman on the phone said that Valentino had left the evening before in his limo with his driver. She wasn't sure where he was going, but he hadn't come back. She was at a loss regarding what the crime lord was up to but told Max not to worry, that Valentino was capable of taking care of himself.

Max came to the conclusion that someone was gunning for Valentino's people. The question was who and why. Then Max had a most disturbing thought. Could Gabriel Mancheski be behind whatever was happening to Valentino's people? If so, it was probably time to get out of town. But he was tired, very tired. He'd worked all night and then all day long. It was now Monday night, and he had checked into this room so he could get some rest, make some calls, and decide what to do next. Well, there would be no more calls. And as for what to do tomorrow, he knew exactly what that would be. He would drive east first thing in the morning. He placed little value on the lives of others, but he didn't want to die.

CHAPTER NINETEEN

THE DAYS PASSED IN A sort of haze for Adriana Chambers. She was able to attend most of her classes, and her mother went to work most days. But they never went anywhere alone—cops were near them day and night. Adriana's life was not her own, and she desperately wanted it back. The only bright spots she found during the passing days were those times when Detective Brad Osborn made himself the officer who kept her safe while keeping her company.

Most of those hours spent with him were, in fact, dates. They went out to dinner, attended movies, and even went to a couple of sporting events. Even though she enjoyed every minute she spent with him, he was constantly distracted. He was regularly looking over his shoulder, in the rearview mirror, and everywhere someone could launch an ambush. It put a strain on their budding relationship, and she wished it would all end and she could really get to know Brad as a person, as a man, instead of as a police officer.

Valentino Lombardi was free on bond. Brad explained that he wouldn't be surprised if the case against him fell apart. The trial of Lombardi's competitor and sworn enemy was back on track in federal court. Brian Bollinger, having returned from wherever he had disappeared to, was given the file the police had recovered. He was moving ahead on the complicated defense of strongman Gabriel Mancheski.

More importantly to Adriana Chambers was the upcoming trial of Jerzy Grabowski. Ross Harris and Gloria Metz had convinced the judge that it was in everybody's best interest to set Jerzy Grabowski's trial early. The judge adjusted his calendar, and the trial was scheduled to begin on a Monday morning in the middle of July.

The closer that day got, the more Adriana and Brad worried. No one else shared their opinion that Jerzy was innocent. A key witness for the prosecution was the man with the damaged foot. Earnest Pyatt, sitting in jail, was clinging stubbornly to his claim that Cedric Brewer had told him Jerzy had been hired to do the foul deed. He had a big incentive to do so, charges against him being reduced if he testified. Hearsay rules could sometimes be bent. Ordinarily a witness could not testify to what another person told him, but that didn't necessarily apply if the person being quoted was deceased. So the fact that Cedric was dead gave Ross hope that he could get Earnest's testimony to the jury. If he did, Jerzy would be convicted, despite the testimony that Adriana would be giving.

***

Tall, thin Max Barclay hadn't heard from Valentino since the night the boss was arrested. That changed one night on the tenth of July. He was relaxing in a bar in New Jersey when his cell phone rang. He nearly choked on his beer when he looked at the digital display on his phone. It was Valentino. Hesitantly, he answered.

"Hey, Max, haven't heard from you for a while. I need for you to get back here. Jerzy Grabowski is going to trial next week."

"So soon?" Max asked. "I didn't think it would happen until after the first of the year."

"Yeah, well, it got moved up. And you still have a job to do."

"Are you sure you—" Max began.

"That girl of Carson's has to be silenced," Valentino cut in angrily. "Remember who gives the orders."

Max remembered. This was not a matter of money. This was a matter of staying alive.

"I could send someone else, but it's your job to finish. So get it done. And I want you to shut Pyatt up as well," Valentino added. "He messed up big time when he turned against me. No one turns on Valentino Lombardi. He's in jail, but I'll see to it that someone posts his bond. You be here and take care of him."

"I'll get it done," Max stuttered. He'd honestly thought he wasn't going to have to finish this job. He'd been wrong.

"Get back here right away. There's nothing for you to do in New Jersey."

Max winced. He hadn't talked to Valentino or anyone from the organization since Valentino's arrest. And yet Valentino knew where he was. He was lucky to be alive. He couldn't take any more chances. "I'll get right on it," he promised.

"Good. And in case you wonder, all the charges against me have been dropped, no thanks to Carson Chambers. He's next," Valentino said, and the call was abruptly ended.

***

The morning of the trial arrived. No more threats had been sent to Adriana, and even though Cedric Brewer was dead and Earnest Pyatt was cooperating with the police, she was tense and worried that morning as she observed the beginning of the trial. She glanced around the large courtroom. Her father had been a friend of Mr. Lenhardt, the man Jerzy was accused of killing. He should be here. But she didn't see him. Not that it came as a surprise. She hadn't seen him since the night he had picked her up in front of her home. He called her from time to time, assuring her that he was okay and asking about her well-being. He promised that at some point he would return. He refused to tell her what he was doing or even where he was. It was safest for them both that way, he'd explained.

The prospective jurors were already in the courtroom when Jerzy Grabowski was brought in. He had aged and lost weight during the weeks he'd been in jail. He sat with his head bent; the eyes behind his thick, gold-framed glasses stared at the table top in front of him. Surely he wouldn't be found guilty. It would be so unfair. Adriana silently prayed for him.

During a recess at noon, Brad met Adriana in the courthouse and offered to take her to lunch. As they were eating, she asked, "Why is Mike sitting at the prosecutor's table instead of you? And where have you been all morning?"

He smiled wanly and said, "Think about it, Adriana. Mike is convinced of Jerzy's guilt. I'm not. It's that simple. Ross wants help from someone who is totally behind him in this prosecution. From what I've been told, I won't be here much, just to testify about the part of the investigation that I was involved in and Mike wasn't. Sergeant Tullock is keeping me busy on other cases." He shrugged his shoulders. "That's just the way it is."

"Will you be here when I testify?" she asked. "I need you to be here."

"It's not likely," Brad said. "I'm sorry. Anyway, I don't think you will be called until Gloria, the defense attorney, presents her case."

"That's crazy," Adriana said angrily.

"You'll get your chance, and you will do well, with or without me." He changed the topic. "Have you heard from your father today?" he asked.

"Yeah, he called me early this morning. He was just wishing me well. I am worried about him. I just wish I knew what he was doing."

***

Carson's paycheck had been electronically deposited in his account. Since he wasn't going to be paying any more blackmail, he had a few dollars to spend. He'd needed to buy a car. Probably the most common car color was white. At least, that was what Carson figured. If a man drove a white car that was neither too old nor too new, he was not likely to attract attention. Based on that assumption, he had bought a ten-year-old midsized Ford just a few days after his little run-in with Valentino.

He had always kept his hair short and neatly combed. He changed that—his hair was over his ears, hung close to his eyes, and covered his collar. He kept it black with hair dye. He had also grown a beard, which he kept dyed, in an attempt to hide his cleft chin and make his square face less obvious. He had a moustache, long sideburns, and even wore glasses. With the kind of clothes he now wore, he hardly recognized himself anymore.

The question was would anyone else recognize him? So far, his radical new look had served him well. If anyone did demand identification, his out-of-state driver's license would show his new picture and an alias. The registration was also in his assumed name. He didn't have a single thing with him or on him that had his true name on it. He was now known as Harry Porteras, to what few people he had to have an identity for. It had taken him a couple of weeks to get the identity change made, and he'd done it far from his home, in a different state.

He was a changed man, and for all he knew, a wanted one. His change went far beyond his radically altered appearance. He had given up coffee, alcohol, and a few other bad habits he had acquired since dumping his wife. And he had even begun praying again. He hoped that someday he could start over, get back in the Church, and be the kind of man he'd once been. There was only one thing he hadn't been able to change very much: his voice. But he did work hard at using a Southern accent, and he was getting fairly good at it, he hoped.

For now, his main purpose in life was watching out for his beloved daughter and his ex-wife. He occasionally spoke to his sons. They weren't real proud of him. They had always blamed Krista for the breakup, but he had set them both straight and begged them to mend their relationships with their mother and sister. He thought they were trying to do that, but his own relationship with them had gone sour. He hoped to someday win them back again, but not at anyone else's expense.

He had done one other thing to make his disguise complete. He had listed himself, or rather Harry Porteras, with an online dating service. He was seeing a woman now, one ten years younger than himself and one who knew nothing about his true past. He enjoyed her company, but his thoughts, of late, were never far from the woman he had hurt so badly. He knew that the chance of ever getting her to forgive him and take him back was so remote as to be basically nonexistent. But despite that, he still loved her.

The woman he was dating, Wendy Cline, was a moderately attractive woman but not someone who was flashy and would attract a lot of attention. With short brown hair and blue eyes, Wendy was a short woman of about forty who was slightly overweight. She seemed to like Carson, but she didn't ask a lot of questions about him and he didn't volunteer much. She had been married, was divorced, and had a son who was a sophomore in college.

Carson had called his employer and asked for a leave of absence. Knowing the trouble his family had been going through, they told him to take some time. All that they asked was that he do some work for them by phone and on the computer from time to time, and if he would, they would continue to pay him. They didn't want to lose him, he'd been told, but they did ask that he not drag it out for more than two or three months. He agreed, and so he'd been free to keep an eye on Adriana without her even knowing he was around.

That blistering Monday afternoon, he was going to put his new identity and disguise to the test. It was almost as frightening as confronting Earnest Pyatt and Valentino Lombardi. To make it easier, he had persuaded Wendy to take time off her job as a waitress and accompany him to the Jerzy Grabowski trial.

A local woman, Wendy knew only what she'd seen on the news about the murder of Garrick Lenhardt. Without making up a lot of details, Carson explained to her that he'd known Lenhardt's family and that he was curious about the trial. She was excited about it. "I'd love to go," she'd told him. "I've never been in a courtroom except for my divorce."

He parked the white Ford in the courthouse parking lot shortly before one o'clock, and he and Wendy went inside the imposing structure. He found the courtroom where the trial was being held, and taking a deep breath, he led Wendy in. They selected a seat near the back of the gallery just before most of the spectators began to return from lunch.

He kept peering toward the door and finally saw his daughter come in. Detective Osborn was with her, but after he helped her find a seat across the room from where he and Wendy were seated, the officer did not take a seat. Adriana held his hand as she sat down. She looked up at the young officer with a pleading look in her eyes, a look that almost broke Carson's heart. She said something, her eyes misty. The detective said something in return, tenderly touched her cheek, then turned and hurried out. She watched him until he was out of the door. He was a good man, one worthy of his daughter's affection.

Wendy leaned close to him and said, "Here comes the murderer." He drew his eyes away from his daughter and looked toward the front of the courthouse. The accused man was being escorted from a side door. He wore a loose-fitting suit. He looked haggard and worn, barely looking at his defense attorney. Carson would hate to be in that man's place. A tremor shook him. For all he knew, someday he might be. Not that he'd ever killed anyone, but he had committed serious crimes that night when he shot his blackmailer in the foot—that, and Valentino had evidence that would almost guarantee Carson would go away for an unsolved hit and run.

After the defendant was seated, a tall, impressive, well-dressed man in his early forties entered the room and sat down at the prosecution table. Carson knew about Ross Harris. He was one of the best prosecutors in the district attorney's office. A moment later, a much less neatly dressed man sat beside him. He knew that was Brad Osborn's partner, Detective Mike Silverman. The two talked for a moment, and then they both looked forward when the bailiff stood and called the court to order, instructing everyone to stand.

A moment later, the Honorable Darnell Shuda came to the bench with a swirl of robes and asked everyone to sit as he did the same. Wendy and Carson both sat. Carson studied the judge as he began to speak. He was a silver-haired man of about seventy, just under six feet tall and weighing a respectable one seventy or so. He said, "We will continue with jury selection," and proceeded to conduct that activity.

The doors at the back of the courtroom opened, drawing Carson's eyes. He was watching everyone who came in, keeping an eye out for anyone who might, in his opinion, pose any kind of threat to his daughter. The young man standing back there now, looking around the room, was not someone Carson had expected to see. He was glad for his beard when he felt his face grow red from the anger that filled him. The fellow might not be a threat to Adriana, but he shouldn't be here. Carson watched when the man spotted Adriana and moved quickly toward her. Carson held his breath to keep from saying something to Wendy that would give away his feelings.

***

Adriana was aware of the people nearest her shifting in their seats. She looked toward the aisle and couldn't believe what she saw. Drew Parker, looking as attractive as ever, was working his way toward her. He slipped between her and the man to her left and sat down. He turned to her and, with that big, handsome smile of his, he said, laying a hand on hers, "I thought you might like a little moral support."

She couldn't help but feel the attraction she had felt when they were dating, but when her face grew red, it was not a blush; it was anger. The last thing she needed right now was Drew complicating her life. She pulled her hand away and whispered, "You shouldn't be here, Drew."

"Why not? It's a public trial," he said, smiling at her. "And I was hoping that afterward, we might go someplace and have a bite to eat. I really, really want to talk to you, Adriana. I miss you more than you can imagine. You won't return my calls, and as you know, I've made lots of them. Adriana, I made a mistake, and I am going to make it right. I promise."

Short of creating a scene, she couldn't do anything but put up with him being here. She wished that Brad had been able to stay and sit by her. She needed him now more than ever, especially considering the attraction she felt, despite her anger, for Drew. She folded her hands on her lap and looked forward, vowing to ignore Drew if she possibly could. However, he made that very hard to do. When he put an arm around her shoulders, she wanted to make him move it, but she didn't want to attract attention, so she just sat there, trying to think about Detective Brad Osborn and wishing it was his arm around her.

Of course, she knew that once this case was over, she might not see Brad again. He might not have the same feelings for her that she had for him.

***

Carson bristled when he saw Drew put his arm around his daughter's shoulders. Why didn't she shake it off? She was too good for him. Anyway, he'd had his chance . . . That thought turned and stabbed Carson right in the chest. He'd had his chance with Krista, and he'd blown it. The woman at his side leaned against him and said, "Are you okay, Harry?"

"Yeah, I'm fine," he said, embarrassed that he'd apparently let his feelings show.

The selection of the jurors took quite a bit of time, but the jury was finally seated shortly before eight that evening. Judge Shuda announced that opening statements would begin at nine o'clock the next morning. He rapped his gavel sharply and closed court for the day. The bailiff told everyone to rise, and the judge swept out.

The gallery emptied quickly. "Are you coming again tomorrow?" Wendy asked as they worked their way to the aisle.

"I think I will," he said, his eyes meeting hers for a moment before looking toward where Drew was possessively ushering his daughter out.

As they exited the courtroom, Drew had his arm around Adriana's waist. Carson followed Wendy through the door and then stopped, watching his daughter closely. He was close enough to hear them speak. Adriana said, "I can't go to dinner with you, Drew. I'm not supposed to go anywhere without a police escort."

"Hey, sweetheart," he said. "I'll take care of you. I have a gun in my car. Come on, let's go."

Adriana didn't answer immediately, and Carson thought for a moment that she was going to give in. But then he saw her eyes focus on something some distance away, and she said, "Here comes the policeman I'm supposed to go with."

"I'll explain to him that you are with me tonight," Drew said. "I'll make him understand."

Carson also spotted the officer. It was Detective Osborn, and he was hurrying toward her, looking around in the crowd, clearly making sure there was no threat to her. For a moment, he looked right at Carson. Carson felt himself stiffen, but the detective's eyes moved on without any sign of recognition. A moment later he was next to Adriana. "Let's get out of this crowd," Brad said to Adriana.

"Sorry, Officer, she's going with me tonight," Drew said.

"I don't know who you are, but she is not going with anyone but me," Brad said firmly. He took her by the hand.

"This is my fiancée," Drew said as he stepped in front of Brad. "And she's going with me. I'll see that she's safe."

Carson watched as Adriana looked from one young man to the other. He had to fight the urge to step over and argue for the officer, but he couldn't do that without giving away his facade. It wasn't necessary anyway. Adriana took the situation firmly in hand. "Drew, I am not your fiancée. You broke up with me, and it's over. I'm going with Detective Osborn. And please, Drew, don't come here again like this. I don't want to see you."

"Adriana, I'm not giving up on you," Drew said stubbornly.

"Nor am I," Brad said. His words gave Adriana a warm feeling. "Come on. We can't be standing around here like this. It's not safe." He took her by the hand and, cutting around Drew, he started away. For a moment, Drew bristled and even bunched his fists. Carson moved toward them, Wendy in tow.

Detective Osborn looked at him again, and once more the officer's eyes lingered. He even squinted suspiciously. Carson looked away and began to walk off just as Adriana also looked at him. He froze but then sighed in relief when she gave no sign of recognition. A minute later, Brad and Adriana were walking briskly up the large hallway, threading their way through the rapidly diminishing crowd.

"Who is that girl?" Wendy asked as she took hold of his hand.

"What girl?" Carson asked.

"The one you've been watching. Do you know her?"

Carson shook his head. "Let's get out of here," he said.

"She's pretty, Harry, but she's way too young for you."

"That's for sure," Carson replied impatiently.

"Do I need to be jealous?" Wendy asked with a little whine.

"Don't be silly," he responded. "Would you like to go somewhere for dinner?"

"I'd love to," she said. "May I choose the place?"

"Of course," he said.

"I love Chinese food," she said. "And I know just the perfect restaurant."

CHAPTER TWENTY

BRAD HAD TAKEN ADRIANA WITH him to the station, where he had to take care of a small matter on another case he was working. Then they decided to go get some dinner. "Do you feel like Chinese tonight?" Brad asked when they reached his car again.

"That would be great," she said. "I haven't eaten there for a long time. Maybe your friends will be there."

"Ling and Chang?" he said. "They probably will be."

When they entered the restaurant a few minutes later, Chang met them inside, a big grin on his face. "Hi, Brad," he said. "And hi to you too, Adriana."

"You remembered my name," she said, pleasantly surprised.

"I always remember the names of pretty girls," he said. Then he grinned. "Brad mentions you when I see him at church." He nodded his head briskly. "You are a very handsome couple. Let me show you to a seat."

"Thanks, Chang," Brad said.

They followed him, and when he showed them to a table, he said, "My sister is waiting on this table tonight," he said. "She will take good care of you two special people."

Brad hesitated. His eyes were on someone who looked familiar. Just a couple of tables away sat a bearded man in a flowered shirt. He was with a woman who also looked familiar. She had short blonde hair, was a slightly heavyset, attractive woman, and was wearing a light blue blouse. She looked his way at that exact moment. He was sure her eyes lit up in recognition. Then it struck Brad as he looked away. They had been at the courthouse, had been standing nearby when he had sent Drew packing. He tensed. Adriana was pulling back a chair. Brad took her hand and pulled gently. "Let me sit on that side," he said.

She looked at him blankly. "Okay," she said. "I guess it doesn't matter to me."

"Thanks," he said. When he was seated, Adriana's back was to the man in the flowered shirt and the woman with the blue blouse. He, on the other hand, was facing them. It was just a precaution, but he was slightly uneasy about them.

"Ling will be with you two in just a minute," Chang said with a smile and moved smoothly away to help more customers.

Adriana leaned forward and asked, "What was that about? Did you see something that made you nervous?"

He nodded. "There's a couple behind you. They were at the courthouse. I just don't want to take any chances. I'm sure it's nothing, but I feel better having them where I can see them."

***

Carson couldn't believe it. His disguise was good, but was it good enough? It was about to be tested more than he cared to have it tested. He wished he'd made the decision of where to go for dinner instead of allowing Wendy to. But it was too late now.

The move the young detective had made when he and Adriana were getting ready to sit down was not lost on Carson. It put Adriana with her back to him, and that was probably best since she was the one most likely to recognize him. But he didn't like the way Detective Osborn kept glancing at him. He shivered and went back to eating his dinner.

***

Another call from Valentino that afternoon had Max Barclay scrambling to finish his job. One third of his contract was done. Pyatt wouldn't be testifying. It had turned out to be much easier than he had thought it would. Pyatt wouldn't be saying anything about Valentino at Jerzy's trial. Now all Max had to do was take care of the girl and whatever cop she was with when he got the chance. The last thing he had to do to satisfy Valentino was find Carson Chambers. When he was finished with those things, he could head back to New Jersey.

He knew where the Chambers girl was most of the time, but security around her was tight. Valentino had made it easier for him today when he told him not to try to catch her without a cop. "Just get rid of the cop, too," he had ordered. Max was simply going to have to make the hit and then take off. He had a spare car and another disguise ready to go. He would lay low until the girl's funeral. That was when he'd get Carson Chambers because he was sure the man would come back from wherever he was hiding in order to attend his daughter's funeral.

He shifted uneasily in the seat of his pickup. He was parked just a few spaces from that pesky detective's car. He had followed him and the Chambers girl from the courthouse to the police station and then to the Chinese restaurant. He had kept his distance at the police station. It was too risky to do anything there. But this place was acceptable. The sun was down and it was getting dark. The parking area was poorly lit, and it wasn't too busy tonight. He would wait until they came out of the restaurant, shoot the girl and the detective as they were getting into the car, and then he was out of here.

He looked at the exit and glanced back at the detective's car, considering how to do it and do it quickly. He pictured the exact spot he would allow them to reach before he took action. He would take out the officer first, and then he would shoot the girl. He didn't want the cop to have time to go for a weapon. The girl, he was quite certain, would not be armed. With his plan firmly fixed in his mind, he relaxed in his seat and kept a close eye on the exit.

***

Carson and Wendy finished their meal. He was anxious to get out of the restaurant. Detective Osborn was making him nervous, and Wendy, quite frankly, was driving him nuts. She wouldn't quit talking. Of course that meant he didn't have to speak very much, and even though he was talking low and working hard to sound like a Southerner, he was still afraid Adriana or Detective Osborn might hear him and recognize his voice.

As they left the table, Carson intentionally looked the other way as they passed his daughter. He was relieved when they were outside. He hurried Wendy toward his car as much as he could. They walked past an old green Chevy pickup. There was a man sitting in it, slumped down in the seat, appearing to doze. Wendy noticed him too. "What is that guy sitting in his truck for?" she asked. "I wonder if his family is inside. He must not like Chinese food."

"Probably not," Carson agreed as he hustled her to his car. His gut was churning. Something about that guy bothered Carson. He looked at the luminous clock on his dash when he started his car. Adriana and the officer had come in twenty minutes after he and Wendy. He made a hasty decision—he was going to be here when they came out.

He took Wendy straight home, declining her offer to come in for a little while. "I'm really tired," he said. "I need to get home and get to bed."

"You can take a nap in my place," she said. "We can watch TV together for a while."

She was getting pushy and it was irritating him something awful. "Sorry, Wendy. Another night, maybe. But I really do want to go home now."

"Your loss," she said seductively. He kissed her briefly, subconsciously comparing her kiss to Krista's. Her kiss came up way short in the comparison. He opened the door for her, held it until she was inside, then closed it and rushed back to his car.

To his relief, the detective's car was still parked where it had been earlier. So was the green truck with the man slumped down in the seat. He passed by and parked at the far end of the parking lot. Then he reached in his jockey box, retrieved Earnest Pyatt's 9mm semiautomatic pistol, shoved it in his pocket, and got out of the truck.

He worked his way around the outer edge of the parking lot, keeping in the shadows. He wanted to get as close to the suspicious man in the green pickup as he could without being spotted. But he wasn't anywhere near where he wanted to be when the exit door opened. Adriana and Detective Osborn came out, hand in hand, and headed straight for their car. The detective was looking around, his eyes taking in everything, right hand inside his jacket.

Carson stopped and pulled out the 9mm. The man in the car suddenly brought his gun up and aimed through the window. Carson shouted loudly, "Adriana, run!" At that exact moment Detective Osborn reacted to the threat by shoving Adrianna aside. Carson fired his pistol at the gunman a fraction of a second later.

It seemed like everything after that occurred in slow motion. The officer was still pulling Adriana down low, and then he moved toward the old truck, firing his pistol once, keeping in front of Adriana to provide her some protection. Carson's shot missed the gunman, but he saw sparks fly where it hit the door, low and to the front. Detective Osborn's shot had also missed, and the officer was falling backward like he'd been struck with a bullet. But he was still holding his pistol, and a flame shot from the barrel a second time. The gunman's windshield shattered. Glass splattered onto the gunman while he was in the act of pointing his gun at Adriana. The shattering glass apparently did some damage because the gunman jerked his hand back, dropping his pistol beside him. Carson fired again as the gunman began to pull his pickup out of the parking space. Once again, sparks flew as his bullet struck the steel body of the truck. He was shooting from far too long of a distance to be accurate. He turned back and saw that Adriana had stopped crawling forward and was rushing back toward Detective Osborn, who was now on his back on the pavement, the gun still in his hand.

Carson ran toward them even as he could hear Adriana crying Brad's name in panic. When he reached them, Brad's eyes were open, and he raised his gun at Carson. "Drop it," he said.

He hadn't even thought about the fact that he was still holding the pistol. It was down at his side, but he dropped it to the pavement. "Are you hurt badly, Detective?" he asked.

Adriana came to her feet in a single bound. "Dad, is that you?" she cried.

"Look out, Adriana," Detective Osborn shouted as she stopped and looked at the strange character in front of her. "Step away from her," he commanded.

"Brad, it's my father," Adriana said.

"Doesn't look like him to me," he argued anxiously.

"She's right. It's me," Carson said as he backed away from her with his hands out, clearly visible to the wounded detective. "I've been trying to watch out for you the best I could, Adriana. Detective, that gun I just dropped belongs to Earnest Pyatt. I took it when I left him in my apartment."

Brad squinted in the dim light of the parking lot. "It really is you," he said. "You're lucky I didn't shoot you."

"And I thank you for that," Carson replied, a grin crossing his bearded face.

"Oh, Daddy," Adrianna said like a little girl. "I've been so worried about you."

He held out his arms and she stepped forward and into his embrace. A moment later, they both turned their attention to Brad and knelt beside him. "Brad, do you need an ambulance?" she asked.

Carson had been looking for blood, but he couldn't see any. The detective was sitting up now, fumbling with his phone instead of his pistol. "I'm fine," he said. "I've been wearing a bulletproof vest lately. It saved me."

He put the phone to his ear. A moment later, he spoke. "Mike, someone just tried to kill Miss Chambers and me. Get a call out for the shooter. I'm giving the phone to a witness. He can describe the vehicle better than I can."

He held the phone out to Carson, who took it and began to speak. He described the pickup the best he could and then told the officer what he could about the shooter. He concluded with, "The windshield is shattered, there are bullet holes in the truck, and the shooter may be injured." He handed the phone back to Brad, who was now on his feet, looking just fine.

"Thanks," Brad said to Carson. "You may have just saved both of our lives."

"You were shooting too," Carson reminded him. "Am I under arrest?"

"Not hardly," Detective Osborn said. "And by the way, that's a good disguise. I'm sure glad I didn't shoot you."

"So am I. Now, if you two can keep it to yourselves, I'd like to keep this disguise. And I'll still be around," he promised.

"Thanks, Dad," Adriana said. "I won't say a word."

"Your secret is safe with us. Now go," Brad said with a feeble grin, "before I change my mind."

Carson picked up the 9mm. When Brad didn't object, he carried it back to his old Ford sedan and drove off.

***

The shooter's old green pickup was found several blocks away. The shooter was not found. However, he did leave blood behind. Detective Osborn assumed that he'd taken shards of glass and perhaps a bullet, either his or Carson's. Of course, as he'd promised, he didn't mention anything about Carson's identity. He and Adriana simply said that someone else with a gun opened fire when the shooter shot at them. "He left," Brad said to his colleagues, "on foot. We didn't see his car. Whoever it was, he was a huge help."

When pressed to describe their armed benefactor, they gave a vague description of Carson as he would have appeared without his disguise. There were no other witnesses, so their description was the official one.

Because of the attempt on Adriana's life, security was beefed up. She wasn't allowed to go anywhere without a minimum of two officers. Having no way of knowing how seriously the shooter was injured, the assumption was made that he would likely try again. Security at the courthouse was also beefed up.

The next morning, when Brad arrived, Adriana was already seated in the gallery. There was no sign of Drew Parker trying to muscle his way in to sit beside her again. Not that he would have had any success since she sat between two officers. Brad slipped in, spoke to her quietly, and promised that he'd check in with her at lunchtime.

As he slipped out of the courtroom, a bearded man in a flowered shirt entered. He nodded almost imperceptibly to Brad. Brad smiled at him as they passed and nodded in return, saying softly, "Take care, sir."

***

It wasn't hard to see why Ross Harris had a great record as a prosecutor. When he gave his opening statement, he laid out his case to the jury in a most convincing fashion. "In conclusion," he summed up, "the evidence will show that Mr. Grabowski entered the house of the well-known attorney, Garrick Lenhardt, with the intent to take his life and make it look like it was a bungled robbery. After you have heard the evidence and viewed the exhibits, you will no doubt find the defendant guilty of murder."

If Adriana didn't know better, she would have concluded that Jerzy was guilty, and it depressed her. She lowered her head and offered a quiet prayer.

However, when the defense attorney, Gloria Metz, spoke, all one hundred pounds of her, Adriana felt somewhat better. Ms. Metz was not much over five feet, but she bristled with energy, and she promised to poke holes in Assistant District Attorney Harris's case. "Your duty as jurors," she summed up to the twelve jurors, "is to listen to all of the evidence, and only then should you begin to form your opinions as to my client's guilt or innocence. And remember, the state must prove to you beyond a reasonable doubt that the defendant, Jerzy Grabowski, murdered the victim, Garrick Lenhardt. I am certain that you will find the defendant not guilty at the end of the trial. Thank you for your service."

Then the trial began in earnest. The first witness, Detective Mike Silverman, was called. Adriana knew that Brad was going to be testifying later but not until after the bulk of the evidence had been laid out for the jury—in a manner that would make it hard for Brad to undercut it in any way.

After Mike had finished, he was cross-examined by Ms. Metz, but she didn't spend a lot of time trying to attack his testimony. She planned to make her case when she called her own witnesses.

A couple of lab technicians also testified that morning, and following short cross-examinations, the noon recess was called.

As Adriana was escorted from the courtroom, she caught her father's eyes briefly. He smiled at her, and she smiled back. He was alone that day, and she was glad. She hadn't liked seeing him with the woman he'd been with the day before. Adriana hoped that she wasn't a serious girlfriend, but she had no way of discovering anything until the trial was over.

Brad was waiting for her just outside the courtroom; however, she did not have a quiet lunch alone with him. Her assigned bodyguards accompanied them. They were, however, seated at a separate table, giving Brad and her some limited privacy. But because of the danger of being overheard, they did not talk about the events of the night before except in general terms.

CHAPTER TWENTY-ONE

BECAUSE OF THE DANGER OF discovery if he went to an emergency room to treat his wounds, none of which were terribly serious, Max Barclay had spent a fair amount of time in the bathroom of a cheap motel room thirty miles from where he'd attempted to ambush the couple. He'd picked a bunch of small pieces of glass from his face, scalp, and arms. He'd put some alcohol and salve on the side of his neck where a bullet had grazed him, and added a crude bandage.

It had been a close call. He didn't know yet where all the bullets had come from. There must have been another cop he'd failed to see hidden somewhere. He couldn't imagine how that had happened because he had been cautious and watchful. But it was that other cop, wherever he was hidden, that had forced him to leave before finishing the job. He knew he'd hit the officer with the girl, because he saw him go down, but he didn't know how badly hurt the bodyguard was. Max supposed he might have killed the man, but somehow he had the feeling that was not the case.

As he answered his phone now, he wasn't sure how he was going to explain his failure to the boss.

"Did you get them?" Valentino asked without preamble.

"I got the cop," he hedged.

"He's dead?" Valentino asked.

"I'm not sure. He went down," Max said lamely.

"That's not good enough," Valentino growled. "Did you get the girl?"

"Well, not exactly," Max answered evasively. "There were other cops. I got shot. I was lucky to get away alive."

The breathing on the other end of the phone call sounded threatening. The words Valentino spoke next were exactly that. "You must not be hurt too bad or you wouldn't be talking to me now. I'm losing patience with you, Max. Have you lost your touch, or have you lost your nerve? I won't tolerate any more failures."

"I'll get her," Max said, doing his best not to stammer.

"Then I was right. You're not seriously injured?"

"I've patched myself up. I'll be okay," Max answered.

"Only if you get the job done," Valentino answered sharply before he clicked off.

Max put his phone down. He was shaking badly. He hated to admit it, but he actually feared that Valentino was right. Perhaps he was losing his nerve *and* his touch. He needed to find a bar and put down a few drinks to get his nerve back. Then he had to go in search of the girl again. But first he needed a car. The one he'd stolen the night before, after abandoning the bullet-ridden pickup, was still parked behind the motel. It had to go and he had to come up with one that wasn't hot. He needed to buy a cheap vehicle, and he needed to do it soon.

When Max left his shabby room a few minutes later, he had rearranged his priorities. He would drive the stolen car somewhere within reasonable walking distance of a used car lot. Then he would buy a car. After that came a bar. Finally, when his nerves were sufficiently restored, he would go in search of the witness again.

***

At the end of court that day, Brad wasn't taking any chances with Adriana's safety. He had persuaded the brass in his department that she needed to be kept somewhere she couldn't possibly be found. That meant she couldn't be kept at home any longer. Someone still didn't want her to testify and would do anything possible to stop her. Ms. Metz was counting on her testimony to create reasonable doubt in the minds of the jurors. Her testimony placed her clearly in the area of the murder. The prosecution had to use her, but they didn't intend to ask her anything about what she saw after she came back from her house to deliver a screwdriver to the defendant.

If she got that testimony in, Ross Harris was prepared to do everything he could to discredit it. Someone else, for whatever reason, apparently wasn't taking any chances. Neither was Brad. This particular witness was becoming increasingly important to Brad on a personal basis. He was still angry at himself for allowing her to come so close to disaster the night before. He wasn't going to let that happen again. He was taking every precaution he could think of. Beyond that, the only thing he could do was pray, and he was doing plenty of that.

Once Adriana was placed in a safe house across town for the night, he returned to his own apartment. His cell phone rang. "Detective, this is Carson Chambers," he heard. "What have you done with my girl?"

"She's safe, Carson, I promise you."

"She better be. Will you tell me where she is?"

"I think it would be better not to do that," Brad said. "You will be of the most help if you will simply be another set of ears and eyes at the courthouse tomorrow. She'll be testifying in the morning."

"I'll be there," Carson reaffirmed. "But I'm also counting on you making sure she's safe. I may have made a mess of my marriage, but I love my daughter."

"I know you do. So do I," Brad said before he even realized that he had just spoken aloud what before he'd only been thinking. He felt like a fool.

"I think she feels the same," Carson said.

***

Adriana was exhausted when she walked into the courtroom the next morning. She had fallen asleep a few times, but each time, she awoke screaming. The nightmares were the worst she'd ever had. Finally she was so shaken that she got up and joined the police officer in the living room of the safe house and watched television for the rest of the night. She knew that she couldn't go on much longer like this.

Her father was dressed differently, and the hair, beard, sideburns, eyebrows, and moustache were now blond. He wore different glasses, too, but Adriana still recognized him when he came into the courtroom. Her mother looked over at him as he began to work his way into a seat across the courtroom. Her eyes lingered for a moment, and then she looked at Adriana. "That goofy-looking guy seems vaguely familiar," she said. Then she chuckled. "I can't imagine why. I don't hang out with people like that. I never have."

Krista took another look in the man's direction. He was staring right at them but quickly turned away. Adriana looked forward again, trying to block her mother's view. Her mother nudged her. "This is a little unsettling. It's almost like that guy recognizes me."

"He just thinks you're attractive, Mom," Adriana said. "You are a very good-looking woman, you know. A lot more guys look at you than you realize."

Krista shook her head, glanced once more at the bearded man, and then spoke to Adriana again. "I'm sure I know him from somewhere," she insisted.

Adriana scrambled for a way to divert her mother's attention. The presence of the two plainclothes officers on either side of them gave her an idea. "I think I know," Adriana said.

"He looks familiar to you too?" Krista asked.

"Yeah. He's probably an undercover guy," Adriana said. "I know that Brad said there would be cops undercover until the trial is over." She had intentionally not called her father an undercover *cop* because then she could, without betraying her father's trust, tell the truth.

"Yes, that must be it. There have been a lot of cops around the house the past few days. I'll bet he's one of them," Krista said. That seemed to satisfy her because she didn't look in that direction again.

A minute or two later the judge took the bench, and the trial was resumed. The first witness that Ross Harris called that morning was Adriana. She shivered in apprehension. Her mother placed her hand on her arm and spoke quietly. "You and I have been through a lot the past few weeks. This is nothing in comparison. You'll do fine," she said reassuringly.

"Thanks, Mom. I'm glad you're here today. Brad was going to try to get here before court started, but I don't see him yet," she observed. Then she got to her feet and worked her way to the aisle and walked forward, her head held high. As she passed beside the defendant's table, Jerzy looked up at her. She caught his eye and winked. He turned red and smiled in return.

Once she had sworn to tell the truth, she took her seat in the witness chair and faced bravely forward. She glanced again at Jerzy. He was watching her intently and hopefully. She caught her father's eye, and he made a slight nod of his head and smiled. Then she looked at her mother, who also smiled her encouragement. She also looked at the door, willing Brad to come in, but he didn't appear. Finally, she looked at the jurors. Twelve somber faces stared back at her.

Finally, the prosecutor spoke. "Please state your name and address for the record," he said.

"Adriana Chambers," she said, fighting to keep her voice from trembling. This was a truly frightening experience, made worse, she was sure, by the previous night's nightmares and lack of sleep. She added her address and waited for the next question.

Ross Harris had been sitting at the prosecutor's table, but he got up now and, carrying a legal pad and pen, strolled to the podium between his table and the witness stand. She pulled her eyes off of him and quickly looked around the gallery. Despite all the security, she feared that an assassin could find a way in here. Of course, Brad had assured her that no one would get in here with a gun, but she still worried.

"Miss Chambers, did you know the decedent, Garrick Lenhardt?" Ross asked.

"Yes," she said, remembering the instructions she had received to not say anything beyond a truthful answer to each question.

"Would you explain to the jury how you knew him?"

"He lived in the same neighborhood as I do," she said. "And he was a friend of my father's. He had come to our house a few times in the past, and he often spoke to me when I jogged past his house in the mornings."

"You say he came to your house a few times. That was a ways in the past, was it not?" Ross asked. "Your father left your mother some time back, did he not?"

Her eyes flickered toward her father. He looked down. Then she looked toward her mother. She rubbed her eyes. Finally she fixed her eyes in the direction of the jury and said, "It's true that he and my mother are divorced."

Harris asked her how long ago that was and she told him. Then he asked, "Do you recognize the defendant, Jerzy Grabowski?" he asked.

Adriana nodded as her eyes met Jerzy's. "Miss Chambers, a nod is not sufficient. I need a verbal answer," he said, his voice slightly irritated.

"Sorry," she said and felt her face flush. She took a breath and then said, "Yes."

"Would you point him out to the jury please?"

She pointed toward Jerzy and said, "That's Mr. Grabowski, seated beside Ms. Metz."

"Thank you. Have you known him for a long time?" he asked.

"No, sir, I haven't," she said.

"How many times have you spoken to him since you first met him?" Ross asked.

She sat for a moment before answering. She said, "Twice."

"Was the first time the day that you met him?"

"Yes."

"And what day was that?"

"June 2 of this year."

"Was that the day Mr. Lenhardt was murdered?"

"Yes."

"Thank you, Miss Chambers," he said, smiling at her. "Can you tell us where you first met him?"

"Yes," she said.

Ross looked at her impatiently. "Would you share that information with us?" he asked with a touch of sarcasm in his voice.

"Yes," she said. She gave the name of the street and the approximate address where she had stopped to help him.

"Is that near your own home?"

"Yes."

Again, he looked at her impatiently. "How far was it from your home?"

"About four blocks," she said.

"Thank you, Miss Chambers. Do you remember about what time . . ." He stopped, smiled at her, and said, "Strike that. What time did you first see the defendant?"

She smiled back, shifting her eyes to the jury. A woman dressed in a bright yellow blouse in the front row met her eyes, and she nodded sympathetically at Adriana. This was not easy, and that woman seemed to be trying to reassure her that she understood how difficult it must be.

Adriana spoke without looking at Mr. Harris, keeping her eyes on the woman in yellow. She said, "It was around ten in the morning."

"And can you tell us what you were . . . Strike that," he said again. "What were you doing when you first saw the defendant?"

The woman in yellow shook her head as did a couple of other jurors.

"I was driving west on the street."

"Please tell the jury what the defendant was doing when you saw him?"

"He was standing at the side of the street beside his car."

"Now, in the interest of time, Miss Chambers, would you simply recite briefly what you did and what the defendant did over the next five minutes or so?"

"I stopped my car at the side of the road across the street from Mr. Grabowski," she said. She wasn't about to call him *the defendant*. Her sympathies were entirely with him. "He had a flat tire, and I walked across the street and asked him if he needed help. He said he did, and I began to help him. I got the spare tire out of the trunk of his car, and then I jacked up the front right end of his car. The flat was on the right side, near the curb. But when I tried to take the hubcap off, I couldn't do it without a flathead screwdriver."

"Excuse me, Miss Chambers. Before you go on, would you describe the defendant's car for us?" Ross Harris asked.

"It was quite an old Buick, light blue, four door, rust spots along the bottom, and even a few dings," she said. "It had out-of-state license plates. I remember thinking it was a state from the east, but I can't remember which one."

"Thank you, Miss Chambers," Ross said. "So what happened next?"

"I asked Mr. Grabowski if he had a screwdriver. He said he didn't think he did."

"Did he search in the car for one?" Ross asked.

"Yes."

"Did you look in the car too?"

"Only in the trunk," she said. Adriana knew where this was leading, but there wasn't a thing she could do about it.

"So you didn't find one in the trunk?" he asked.

"That's right. There wasn't one in there."

"Did Mr. Grabowski find one?"

"No."

"Where exactly did he look?"

"In the front and backseats," she said.

"Can you be more specific?"

"No."

"Why not?"

"I didn't see exactly where he looked. I mean, you know, he leaned in the back and in the front, but he didn't come up with one. He told me he was sure he didn't have one."

"Okay, Miss Chambers, what did you do at that point?" Ross asked.

"I told him that I didn't have one in my car either but that I lived close by and that I'd go get one from home and come back and finish changing the tire," she said.

"And did you do that?"

"Sort of. I mean, I went home to get the screwdriver."

"How long were you gone?" he asked.

"Probably ten minutes or so," she said.

"Why did it take you so long? Did you have trouble finding a screwdriver?"

"That only took me a couple of minutes, but I received a phone call while I was there."

"So, Miss Chambers, did you use the screwdriver to help the defendant?"

"No."

"Why not?"

"When I got back, he was driving away. He—"

The prosecutor cut her off sharply. "That's all Miss Chambers. Thank you very much." He turned and walked quickly back to his seat.

"Ms. Metz, you may cross-examine the witness," Judge Shuda said.

The defense attorney stood up and approached the podium. Like Ross Harris, Gloria carried a legal pad and a pen. He hadn't used his one time during his questioning. She wondered what Ms. Metz would do. She also wondered what had happened to Brad. He'd promised he'd be here if he could. But he still had not appeared.

She noticed that Detective Silverman kept looking back toward the door. She wondered if he was also expecting Brad to return. She didn't think about it long, for Ms. Metz said, "Good morning, Miss Chambers. I have a few questions to ask you."

Adriana nodded at her, and the defense attorney said, "You testified that when you came back to finish helping Mr. Grabowski with his flat tire, he was driving away. What direction was he going?"

"West," she said.

"You also testified that he was going on the opposite side of the street when you first stopped to help, is that right?"

"Yes."

"What direction was he facing?" Gloria asked.

"East."

"Your home is east of that location, is that right?"

"Yes."

"And what direction is Mr. Lenhardt's home from where Mr. Grabowski had the flat tire?"

"It's east too."

Ms. Metz turned toward the jury and then asked, very distinctly, "So are you telling the jury, Miss Chambers, that the defendant was facing the direction that would take him toward the victim's house, not away from it?"

"Yes, that's right. I know he was driving that way because I could see the tire smudges on the curb. They were west of where his car stopped after his tire blew."

"So did it appear to you that he was driving east, toward the victim's house?"

"Yes."

"That's interesting. Wouldn't it seem more logical, if someone had just killed a man, that he would be driving away from the scene of the crime, not toward it?" Gloria asked, again glancing at the jury.

"Objection, Your Honor," Ross Harris thundered, rising to his feet. "The question calls for a conclusion the witness isn't qualified to give."

"Sustained," Judge Shuda said. But the point had already been made. Adriana hoped that the jury would see the significance of the direction the car was facing.

Gloria smiled at the jury. Adriana also looked at them. The woman in the yellow blouse gave Adriana a knowing smile when they locked eyes. And the big question was yet to come.

Gloria Metz turned back to Adriana, looked down at the podium, picked up her pen, appeared to make some check marks, then set the pen down again and looked up. "Miss Chambers, when you saw the light blue Buick driving away as you pulled up, was there just one person in the car?"

Before Adriana could answer, the back door opened, and an officer rushed in, going directly to the prosecution table. Ross said, "Your Honor, could we have a moment, please?"

"Miss Chambers, please wait on your answer. Make it quick, counselor," the judge said.

There was a frantic conversation, and then Ross Harris stood up. "Your Honor, a critical matter has just come to my attention. We need a recess, please."

The judge looked at Gloria. She shrugged her shoulders and said, "I can take up my cross-examination when we come back into session. I have no objection as long as it's short."

The judge looked at his watch. "You have fifteen minutes," he said and rapped his gavel sharply.

"All rise," the bailiff called out. The judge left the bench, the jury was escorted out, and even the defendant was taken out of the courtroom.

Ross Harris and Detective Silverman rushed out the door, both with concerned looks on their faces.

A minute later, Adriana, when signaled by Ms. Metz, stepped down from the stand. "What's happening?" she asked when she had reached the defense table.

"I have no idea," Gloria said. "But I can't help but think that whatever it is could be damaging to Ross Harris's case. He looked very worried. I'm sorry to let you be interrupted right at such a crucial time, but I intend to make the recess work in our favor." She grinned at Adriana. "We'll back up a ways on my cross-examination. I hope to get our point in again on the direction the car was facing, and if Mr. Harris objects, it will only draw even more attention to a flaw in his case. After that, I'll lead you back into the matter of there being someone in the car with Mr. Grabowski."

"Are the police going to be allowed to testify about Jerzy saying there was someone else in the car?" Adriana asked.

"Probably not, but I'll put Jerzy on when we do our defense. His testimony in that regard, coupled with yours, should put some reasonable doubt in some jurors' minds," Gloria explained. "If we succeed, that will be all it takes. The jury must find guilt beyond a reasonable doubt, and it must be unanimous."

As they were visiting, the officers assigned to protect Adriana stepped close, and Gloria said nothing further about her strategy. Adriana turned to one of the officers and asked, "Where is Detective Osborn? He was going to be here during my testimony."

It seemed that Brad had been sent to investigate another murder. That was all the officer knew. Adriana fought back tears. She had so badly wanted him in the courtroom. She moved back and sat beside her mother while the recess wore on. She explained what little she knew about what was happening. "You are doing very well," Krista said after she'd told her about Brad's situation. "You're a great witness."

"Thanks, Mom," she said. She looked over at her father. Their eyes met, a flicker of a smile crossed his bearded face, and he nodded ever so slightly. He seemed to think she was doing okay as well.

She turned back and closed her eyes. She didn't ever remember a time when she had been so exhausted. She prayed that she could make it through the rest of her testimony.

CHAPTER TWENTY-TWO

WHEN MIKE AND THE PROSECUTOR reentered the courtroom, they had long faces, but they said nothing to Ms. Metz. The judge came in a moment later, and after everyone was seated, Ross Harris stood up. "May we approach the bench?" he asked.

The judge simply signaled the attorneys forward. "What is going on, Mr. Harris?" the judge asked sternly.

"We've had a difficulty with a witness. I am going to have to reconsider how to present the rest of my case. I'd like to ask for a postponement so that I can do some planning," Ross said.

"What?" Gloria exclaimed. "I'm right in the middle of cross-examination of one of your witnesses. I object strongly to a delay for any reason."

"I'd be okay if we go ahead with the rest of her testimony. But then I'd like a week or preferably two," Ross said.

The judge's eyes narrowed, and he leaned closer to the two lawyers. "Mr. Harris, you pushed me to schedule an early trial. It took a lot of juggling of the court's calendar to do that. Now you want me to juggle some more?"

"It's very important to the state's case," he pleaded.

"I strongly object," Gloria whispered fiercely. "I'd like to know exactly what the problem is. I have the right to know."

"Ms. Metz is correct. What has happened that is causing you to ask for this continuance?" Judge Shuda asked.

Ross hesitated, but then he said, "We have a problem with a witness—it's a serious problem. One week, Your Honor. Please, give me one week."

"What kind of problem?" Gloria asked stubbornly.

Adriana was probably the only person in the courtroom besides the clerk, who was seated fairly close to the judge's bench, who could hear the whispered conversation. She had returned to the witness stand on the opposite side of the judge's bench from the clerk's station. She was listening intently. The last thing she wanted was for this thing to be stretched out longer. She wished she could say something. She lived in fear every day and the nightmares were taking their toll on her. She wanted this trial to be over, hoping that some of the danger would pass when it was finished and that she could begin to sleep normally again.

The judge spoke again when the prosecutor hesitated following Gloria's question. "Who is the witness and what is the problem?" he asked.

"I've had officers looking for a key witness to my case," Ross answered. He looked at Gloria. "The witness is Earnest Pyatt."

Adriana stiffened. That was the blackmailer.

"And they can't find him?" Judge Shuda prompted.

"Well, that was the problem, but he turned up," he said. "The trouble is he's dead. He's been shot."

Adriana felt like she'd been slapped. So that was the murder Brad was working on. Someone had killed the man who was going to say that Valentino Lombardi had hired Jerzy to murder Mr. Lenhardt.

"A delay won't bring him back to life," Judge Shuda said coldly. "You are out of luck. We are going to proceed with this trial. Take your seats."

"Judge, please," Ross begged.

"Take your seats," the judge said more sternly.

They took their seats. The judge spoke again, "Ms. Metz, you may continue your cross-examination of Miss Chambers."

Gloria approached the podium, looked down at her legal pad, made a note with her pen, and then, lifting her head, she said, "Miss Chambers, since we were interrupted the jury might have lost some of the flow of what you were testifying to. So, I'd like to back up a moment and review your testimony of the direction the defendant's car was facing when you stopped to help him."

Sure enough, Ross jumped to his feet and said, "Objection. Such a review is a waste of the court's time. It's a delay tactic."

"Overruled," Judge Shuda said quickly. He lowered his eyebrows. "You are not one to be talking about delay tactics. Go ahead, Counselor," he said, nodding at Gloria.

Gloria took her time leading Adriana through the repeated testimony. Ross started to stand a couple of other times, but a stern look from the judge stopped him both times. Then they were back to the question she'd asked Adriana just before the recess. Gloria looked down at her notes then looked up again and asked, "Miss Chambers, when you saw the light blue Buick driving away as you pulled up, was there just one person in the car?"

"I'm sure there was someone else in the car," Adriana said.

"Seated where?"

"In the passenger side, next to Mr. Grabowski."

"Could you tell if it was a man, a woman, or a child?"

"No, I just thought there was a passenger in the vehicle."

"So that could explain how Mr. Grabowski was able to finish changing the tire. Is that what you thought?"

"Objection!" Ross thundered. "Counsel is leading the witness."

"I'm going to allow it," the judge ruled.

"But, Your Honor—" Ross began again.

"Overruled. Sit down," the judge said with a touch of impatience. "You may answer the question, Miss Chambers."

"Yes, that's what I thought. I figured that someone had come along with a screwdriver and helped him."

"Objection," Ross shouted again.

"It is essentially the same objection," Judge Shuda said. "But Ms. Metz, let's move on now."

"I think that's all I have," she said.

"You may step down, Miss Chambers," the judge said.

As she stood up, Adriana looked toward the jury. The woman in the yellow blouse smiled at her. She smiled back and left the witness stand.

***

"I think we should compare the bullet that killed Mr. Pyatt with the one I took out of my vest," Brad said to Lydia.

The sergeant looked at him thoughtfully, and then she said, "That's a good idea. See that it's done."

Brad had a feeling that whoever killed Earnest Pyatt was the same person who had tried to kill him and Adriana. And unless he missed his guess, Valentino Lombardi was behind it. He wished he could somehow find something that they could charge Lombardi with that would stick. He was convinced that the crime boss hadn't ordered Jerzy to kill Mr. Lenhardt, but Brad was certain he had ordered someone else to do so.

He was also convinced that Lombardi was behind more killings than one. Brad believed that all the trouble of the past few weeks was the fault of Valentino Lombardi. He just wished he could prove it and take Valentino permanently out of circulation.

***

Detective Osborn wasn't the only one who wanted Mr. Lombardi stopped. Valentino Lombardi and Gabriel Mancheski had been enemies for most of their lives. The very fact that Gabriel was facing federal racketeering charges was, Gabriel felt, the fault of Valentino. He felt like his chances of beating those charges were fairly good, but they would not have been if Valentino had gotten Mr. Lenhardt's file before the police did. He'd been lucky and he knew it. However, he was not as confident as he would have been had Lenhardt been lead counsel in his case instead of Brian Bollinger.

Gabriel was bent on revenge. He was well aware that two of Valentino's top hired killers were now dead. He knew he had others, and some of them were pretty good. If Valentino were removed, Gabriel felt like he would have a good chance of luring those men into his organization. He called in one of his best men and gave some specific orders. "Find Valentino. Get rid of him. Then leave the country until I tell you to come back," Mancheski said.

When his man asked if it was to be made to look like an accident, Gabriel replied, "That won't be necessary. Just get him out of my hair."

***

Max Barclay had, in his own opinion, done his best, but the cops had kept such tight security around the girl that he simply couldn't get another chance at her. A call from the boss let Max know that he was not pleased. "You have failed me, Max," Valentino said. "You know what that means."

Max knew exactly, and he fled. The least he could do was make it harder for Valentino's new men to find him. By Thursday morning he was in Mexico.

***

Brad was not surprised that the bullets matched. The problem now was finding whoever had fired them. Thursday morning, he couldn't work on the Earnest Pyatt case because he was called to testify for the state in the trial of Jerzy Grabowski.

His involvement in the case had taken days of work, and his testimony took all morning. He simply laid out the work that he had done, that which had not already been covered by his partner's testimony. He identified pictures, discussed documents, and testified of interviews he'd conducted and other matters that Ross Harris felt would further his case. His opinion as to the guilt or innocence of the defendant was not asked for, nor was it given.

Gloria Metz, however, did ask for his opinion, but an objection by the prosecutor stopped him from giving it. By the end of the day on Thursday, Ross Harris rested his case. Gloria was to begin presenting her case for the defense on Friday morning, and she was reasonably optimistic.

The first thing she did when she rose to her feet that morning was make a motion to the court. She asked that the jury be taken out. When they were gone, she said, "Your Honor, I'd like to move for dismissal of the charge against my client. The burden of proof has not been met by the state." This was quite standard procedure, and it was no surprise when her motion was denied. When the jury returned she announced, "I call the defendant, Jerzy Grabowski, to the stand."

Earlier that morning, Gloria had spoken briefly to Adriana. "It's always risky calling the defendant to testify in his own behalf. Sometimes it backfires. That usually happens in cases where the defendant is actually guilty. Since we know that Mr. Grabowski is innocent, I don't feel like it's too much of a risk, and frankly, other than him and what you testified to on cross-examination earlier, we don't have a lot more to offer."

That was discouraging to Adriana. She hated the thought of Jerzy going to jail for the rest of his life for something he was innocent of. He appeared nervous, as nervous as she felt watching him. She prayed for him and looked over at her father, who nodded an almost imperceptible acknowledgement to her.

Ms. Metz expertly led Jerzy through his version of events as they had occurred on that fateful day. His story never varied a bit from what he'd initially told the officers when he was arrested. His bald head glistened with sweat, and he nervously removed and replaced his thick, gold-rimmed glasses every few minutes.

He testified of the help he'd received from Adriana and then from the tall, thin man. He looked right at the jury box as he vehemently denied killing Mr. Lenhardt. He even denied any knowledge that a murder had been committed prior to being confronted by the police. He made it clear that the screwdriver, which was already admitted into evidence, was not his and that it had been produced by the tall, thin man to pop the hubcap off.

Gloria looked at her notes for a long time after Jerzy's story had been recited. Finally, she seemed to reach a decision. She looked up and asked, "Mr. Grabowski, while you were in jail, just a few days after your arrest, did you give a statement to Detective Brad Osborn that was radically different from what you have told us today?"

Adriana could see shock on the faces of the members of the jury when he said, "Yes, I did."

"And what did you tell the officer at that time?" she asked.

"I told him that I had killed Mr. Lenhardt with the screwdriver. I told him that I'd tried to rob the lawyer and when he resisted I stabbed him."

"Did you ever recant that statement?"

"Yes," he said.

"And why did you do that?"

"Because it wasn't true. I didn't kill anybody. I've never killed anybody."

"When you recanted that statement, did you tell Detective Osborn why you had confessed in the first place?"

"Yes."

"Please tell the jury what led you to make a false statement," Gloria asked.

Ross quickly objected but was overruled by the judge.

"A guy I didn't know came to visit me. I couldn't imagine why anyone would come to see me. I don't know anybody from around here. I'm from New Jersey," he said. "That's kind of how I got my name, even if my old ma spelled it wrong."

That brought a nervous chuckle from the spectators in the court-room and even members of the jury. "Anyway," he continued, "this guy, he said that I had to confess, that if I didn't something terrible would happen to Miss Chambers. She is the sweetest, prettiest girl I ever did meet. I couldn't let her get hurt. I thought it would be better if I went to prison for the rest of my life than for her life to be in jeopardy."

"But then you changed your mind?" Gloria asked.

"Yes."

"What made you change your mind?"

"Miss Chambers came to see me at the jail," he said, and a murmur rolled around the courtroom. Gloria had not asked Adriana about that visit, nor did Ross mention it following Gloria's cross-examination. Jerzy went on. "She told me that she couldn't let me take the blame for something I didn't do, that she'd be safe. I didn't want to change what I'd said to the detective, but she was so adamant that I finally promised that I would do it. So I did. I told the truth again to Detective Osborn like I did before."

"Can you describe for the jury what the man looked like who made the threat to you?"

"Yes," he said. "He was probably between thirty and forty. He had black hair and wore it slicked back. He had on tan slacks and a brown sports coat."

Adriana shuddered. Brad's hand closed tightly on hers, and she leaned her head against his shoulder. The very mention of Cedric Brewer made her ill. The nightmares returned every night. She didn't know if she'd ever get over what she'd done, even though she knew she'd only done what she had to in order to save her mother's life.

Gloria touched on a few more points with Jerzy and then sat down. Ross Harris attacked the defendant with venom in the cross-examination, but nothing that Ross asked him caused Jerzy's testimony to change in even the slightest degree. Ross finally gave up and sat down.

Gloria Metz again stood up. She looked over the gallery, and for a moment her eyes met Adriana's. She mouthed something to her which looked to Adriana like, "I need you again." Then she said, "The defense calls Adriana Chambers."

"What does she want?" Adriana asked Brad.

"Probably just to confirm what Jerzy said," Brad guessed. "It'll be fine. I think I'm going to get called too. She told me to be here just in case."

Adriana again made her way to the stand. She was reminded that she was still under oath. Then she waited as Gloria checked her notes. Finally Gloria said, "Earlier in your testimony, you said that you had talked to the defendant twice. You said that the first time was when you stopped to help him change his tire. We didn't ever get to the second time. Is it true that you visited Mr. Grabowski at the jail, that that visit was the second time you had spoken to him?"

"Yes," Adriana said.

"And why did you do that?"

"Because Detective Osborn told me that Mr. Grabowski had decided to plead guilty. I knew he was innocent. I was sure he'd been threatened or that he had been told that I'd be killed if he didn't do what he was told. I asked him not to lie and he agreed to tell the truth."

"Miss Chambers, were you threatened at any time during the course of the investigation of the murder of Mr. Lenhardt?" Ms. Metz asked.

Adriana struggled with her emotions and finally managed to respond, "Yes, I was." She looked into the gallery at Brad for support. He smiled and gave her a thumbs-up.

"Would you tell the jury about those threats?"

Adriana looked at the jury. The lady in the yellow blouse was in blue today. She smiled encouragingly at Adriana. Adriana took a deep breath then let it out and said, "The first one was at my home. Someone broke in and wrote a message on my mirror in lipstick and another one was typed on a sheet of paper."

Gloria walked over to the defense table and picked up a piece of paper. Then she said, "Your Honor, may I approach the witness."

"Yes," the judge said.

"Adriana, have you ever seen this before?" Gloria said holding up the threatening note.

She gasped, and her hand flew to her mouth. That paper brought the nightmare back. "It's okay, Miss Chambers. Take your time."

She soon composed herself and said, "Yes, that's the threatening note that was left on my dressing table."

"Would you read it to the jury? I know this is hard, but please try."

"Objection, Your Honor. This is inflammatory. It has nothing to do with the matter at hand."

"Approach the bench," Judge Shuda said. When Gloria and Ross were there, the judge added, "I think that it has a great deal to do with the case, Mr. Harris."

"The fact that the witness was threatened is not a defense of what the defendant did," Ross argued.

"Your Honor," Gloria countered, "the threats were left there the same day that Mr. Lenhardt's house was burglarized during his funeral. There is a tie."

"I disagree," Ross argued. "I still think it's inflammatory."

"I'm not so sure of that. I want to hear what the threat was. Your objection is overruled," Judge Shuda said sternly. Then he turned to

Gloria. "Ms. Metz, the witness has identified the document. Rather than have her read it, I would like you to do so, then she can tell us if you read it correctly."

"Thank you, Your Honor," Gloria said. The attorneys returned to their respective tables, and she then read the note, causing a hush to come over the gallery. The jury seemed shocked. She handed the note to Adriana. "Did I read it correctly?"

"Yes," Adriana said, her face pale and her hands shaking.

"Thank you. I move to have this document admitted as defense exhibit number one, Your Honor."

"No objection," Ross said glumly.

"It is admitted," the judge said.

"Miss Chambers, what was the other threat?" Gloria asked.

Adriana discussed the lipstick message on her mirror and the doll that had been hanged in her bathroom. The jury continued to show expressions of shock.

"Now, Miss Chambers, you are a brave woman. Would you tell the court and the jury now if the threats made against you were ever acted on?" Gloria asked.

"Yes, Ms. Metz." She said.

"Just once?"

"No," she said. "Three times."

"Starting with the first time, would you tell us what happened?"

"Your Honor," Ross Harris said, "I strongly object. This is all theatrics. The jury doesn't need to hear what may or may not have happened to Miss Chambers."

"Can you tie it in, Ms. Metz?" Judge Shuda asked.

"Yes, I can," she answered.

"Then you may proceed, Miss Chambers."

Adriana then described the events that had occurred the day Cedric Brewer broke into her home. She described how she escaped through the backyard and over the fence, then turned and peering through a crack in the fence, watched him enter the house.

"Miss Chambers, would you describe this man for the court, please?" Gloria asked.

"He was not a big man. He had black hair. He wore it slicked back. He had on tan pants and a brown jacket." She dropped her head in her hands and sobbed quietly as a collective gasp went through the gallery.

"Did you ever see this man after that day?"

"Do I have to say?" Adriana asked as her courage faltered.

"Please, yes. I know it's hard, but the jury needs to hear it."

"Objection!" Ross shouted.

"Overruled," Judge Shuda said, never taking his eyes off of Adriana. "Go ahead, Miss Chambers. And would someone please give her a Kleenex?"

"I have one right here," Gloria said.

Adriana wiped her eyes and said, "I was in a hotel. I didn't dare go home." She then described seeing the same man following her mother and then grabbing her at gunpoint and trying to shove her into the elevator.

"And what did you do when you saw that happening to your mother? Did you try to help her?"

For a moment, Adriana lost control. She fought to summon the courage she had had that fateful day. She finally managed to say, "I had a knife. I snuck up behind him. I tried to hit him in the back with it so Mom could get away. But he heard me, I guess, and he turned."

"What happened when he turned?"

"My knife cut his thr . . . neck," she said. She sought Brad's eyes. He again gave her a smile and nodded encouragingly.

"What happened then?"

"He fell into the elevator. Mom and I ran. We hid in my room and called the police," she said.

"Thank you, Miss Chambers. Were there any other occasions in which an attempt was made on your life?"

"Yes."

"You don't have to tell us about it. I'll have another witness testify to that." Gloria returned to her seat.

"Mr. Harris?" Judge Shuda said.

"No questions," he said soberly.

CHAPTER TWENTY-THREE

"THE DEFENSE CALLS DETECTIVE BRAD Osborn."

He was also reminded that he was still under oath. After he was seated, the defense attorney asked him if it was true that he'd been summoned to the jail by Mr. Grabowski and that the defendant had then confessed.

"Yes, it's true," Brad said.

"Is it also true that he summoned you a second time?"

"Yes, it's true."

"And what did he say to you on that occasion?"

Brad then testified to what Jerzy had already told the court.

"Did you check to see if he'd had another visitor that day?"

"Yes, I did."

"How did you do that?"

"I checked the visitor log at the jail."

"What did you find when you checked it?"

"Mr. Grabowski had had a visitor that day prior to my visit."

"Did you learn who that visitor was?"

He told them there was a name written there and what that name was. She then said, "Your Honor, may we approach?" The judge gave his permission, and Gloria and Ross walked up. She said, "I can call the officer that was at the jail that day. Or if we'd like to save time, I can have Detective Osborn give some hearsay and give the description of the man who visited the defendant."

"Mr. Harris, it's up to you," the judge whispered.

"I won't object. I assume that we are going to hear the same description already given by the defendant and Miss Chambers. I already know about all that, of course."

"Very well, you may proceed, Counselor," the judge said.

Brad was then asked to give the description that the jailer had given him of Jerzy's visitor. He did so, and then Ms. Metz asked him, "Did you respond to the hotel the night the incident with Miss Chambers and her mother and an assailant occurred?"

"Detective Silverman and I were called on a dead body in an elevator," Brad said.

"A dead body, Detective? Did you identify that body?"

"It was a man by the name of Cedric Brewer. He was dead from a knife wound to the throat."

"Can you describe the body, how it was dressed, and so on?"

By now, the description of slicked-back black hair, tan pants, and brown coat was becoming quite familiar to the jury. There were a few more questions before Ms. Metz addressed the next deadly attempt on Adriana's life. In response to a question, Brad said, "Miss Chambers and I had eaten at a restaurant in town. As we were leaving, I spotted a man in an older model, green pickup. He raised a gun and I shoved Miss Chambers as I told her to get down. We both fired. I was hit in the chest, right in my bulletproof vest. As I went down, I shoved Adriana out of the way. More shots were fired."

Carson stood up in the back of the gallery and signaled with his hand to Brad. Brad watched him as he pointed to himself and then nodded. At the same time he was mouthing, "You can tell about me." Or at least it looked that way to Brad.

He said, "We might both have been killed that evening if it had not been for someone else, someone who also fired at the assailant. Between the two of us, several shots were fired. The assailant fled after his windshield was shattered and several bullets struck his truck. I don't know if a bullet hit him or not, but he might have been shot."

"Detective Osborn," Gloria said as Mike Silverman and Ross Harris both looked at him with wide eyes. "Who was the other shooter, the one who helped you?"

"That man right there," he said, pointing to the back of the room where Carson again stood up.

Adriana and Krista both looked over at him. He smiled in their direction.

"Who is that man?" Gloria asked.

"That is Carson Chambers, the father of Miss Adriana Chambers," Brad said as Carson sat down.

There were a number of people in the room who were acquatinted with both Carson as well as the murder victim, Garrick Lenhardt. They were all shaking their heads in doubt as they stared at Carson.

"Did you ever identify who the shooter was?" Gloria asked.

"No, but I have reason to believe he has killed someone else," Brad said.

"Objection," Harris said. "This has nothing to do with the present case."

"Is that true, Ms. Metz?"

She shook her head and said, "It does, actually. May Mr. Harris and I approach the bench again?"

Permission was granted. "What is the connection?" Judge Shula asked.

"Detective Osborn can testify, or if you'd like, I can call a lab technician who can testify regarding ballistics. At any rate, we just learned this morning that the bullet that struck Detective Osborn was fired from the same weapon that was used in the murder of Mr. Harris's missing witness, Earnest Pyatt," Gloria revealed. "I would have thought that you knew this already, Ross."

He shook his head and then said, "I suppose it would be okay if we let Brad make the connection, but I can't see where it's important."

"Go ahead, then, Ms. Metz," Judge Shuda said.

So Brad explained to the jury what Gloria had just told the judge and prosecutor. After Brad finished with his testimony and a short cross-examination, Gloria called Carson Chambers to testify briefly concerning the attack in the parking lot of the Chinese restaurant. Gloria finished her defense late that afternoon.

"Counsel," Judge Shuda said to the two attorneys after the jury had been led from the courtroom, "meet with me in chambers. I want the jury instructions ready tonight. Then we will hear your arguments in the morning."

"Carson, wait," Krista called out after she and Adriana and their escort of officers had made it to the large hallway.

Carson was just turning the corner. He stopped and looked back. Krista ran toward him as he made a few steps in her direction. "Hello, Krista," he said when they both stopped.

"Hi, Carson. I didn't recognize you," she said.

"That was the idea."

"Ah, I, ah . . . I just wanted to thank you for saving our daughter. What you did took a lot of courage," she stammered.

"I've been a fool, Krista," he said, not apparently caring who heard him. "I'm so sorry for what I've done to you. I wish there was some way that I could make it up, but I know that's not possible."

"You never know," she said softly. "I've missed you."

"And I you," he said. "I better go now. I'm not safe yet."

"Take care of yourself," she said. "And thanks for watching out for Adriana."

"It's the least I can do," he said, tugging at his heavy beard. "I'll be here in the morning. Will I see you then?"

"I'll be here," she said with a little smile tugging at the corners of her mouth. He reached up, touched her cheek, then turned and hurried away. She was still watching him when Adriana stepped beside her. "What a fool that man is," Krista said. "But I guess he's a brave fool. I still, ah . . ." She stopped, rubbed at her eyes, and said, "Let's get out of here."

***

One of the spectators in court that day was Brian Bollinger, the former law partner of the late Garrick Lenhardt. He was a nervous wreck. Getting the file back had not been as helpful as he'd hoped. It didn't contain nearly as much information as he'd expected. Lenhardt had gone to his grave with information that would probably have helped in defending the case against his client, Gabriel Mancheski. As it was, Brian didn't see any way he could win. Back at his office, he had a meeting with his client. He dreaded it. He had nothing but bad news for a man who didn't take bad news well.

One of the other partners was going to be in the meeting with him, but Brian knew that the focus of Gabriel's anger would be on him. He was right. "You didn't get the entire file back?" Gabriel accused him.

"I'm quite sure we did," Brian argued. "But there were things that Garrett knew that he didn't write down."

"You need to figure it out. Lenhardt had things well in hand," Gabriel countered angrily. "You had better put together a defense and quickly. I will not go to prison because of your incompetence."

No, just because of your criminal activities, Brian thought but wisely didn't say. What he did say, however, provoked the crime boss into a rage. "We better see if we can make a deal with the US attorney," he said.

"There will be no deals!" Mancheski raged, rising to his feet and violently kicking a chair, slamming it against the wall of Brian's office.

He pointed a finger at Brian, his hand shaking, and added, "You either keep me out of prison or you will get what Valentino did."

"What are you talking about?" Brian asked, visibly shaken by the man's outburst.

He didn't find out. The seventy-five-year-old gangster turned white, began to shake, and collapsed on the floor.

***

Brad and Adriana were again having dinner, but this time it was at her house, with her mother, and it was home-cooked food. Brad's cell phone rang. "Sorry to disturb you, Brad," his sergeant, Lydia Tullock said. "But I thought you'd be interested in hearing what I just learned."

"What's that?" he asked as his stomach began to churn, afraid that he was about to hear more bad news.

"Gabriel Mancheski has had a stroke, a severe one, right in Brian Bollinger's office. According to the responding officers, Brian told him that he should make a plea deal with the US attorney, that they couldn't win in court. He began to rage and then collapsed. He probably isn't going to make it."

"That breaks my heart," Brad said facetiously.

"So will this," Lydia said. "Mancheski threatened Brian just before he collapsed. He told him that if he didn't keep him out of prison, the same thing would happen to him that happened to Valentino Lombardi."

"What does that mean?" Brad asked.

"We don't know, but we can speculate."

"Has anyone checked Lombardi's mansion?"

"Yes, and he hasn't been there for several days. Of course, he has other residences, but it will be a while before we can figure out where they all are. We can't let up on Adriana's protection, but there is at least a chance that Mancheski had him eliminated," she said.

"Maybe Mancheski will tell us something more," Brad said.

"Not likely. He's in a coma and not expected to regain consciousness," she said.

***

Ross Harris did an outstanding job in his argument on Friday morning. Adriana began to fear for Jerzy. However, Gloria did a good job too. The jury was out for only a few hours. When they came back in, the announcement of the jury created a stir through the courtroom. The man accused of taking the life of a prominent citizen of the community was declared not guilty by the jury.

Adriana squealed in delight and hugged her mother. The now beardless man sitting beside her, Carson Chambers, hugged them both, and then looked embarrassed. Brad also got a hug from Adriana, a very tender one.

Jerzy was ordered released, and he too got a hug from the young woman he had described as the prettiest and sweetest girl he'd ever known. Ross Harris congratulated Gloria Metz and then, in the presence of several officers, spoke to Sergeant Lydia Tullock. "Sergeant, I hope that you and I have both learned a lesson here. Detective Osborn was right all along. Next time, if you come to me with a case and he feels differently than the rest, I'll seriously consider what he has to say. In the meantime, whoever did kill Garrick Lenhardt is still at large. We need to find that person and make an arrest. But the next time, it had better be the right person."

Mike muttered something to Lydia as the little group broke up in the hallway, "Who's he kidding? We gave him the right guy, and he didn't do his job."

Lydia gave the detective a scathing look and said, "Actually, Detective, we messed this one up. We should have kept digging. We got the wrong man. Gloria didn't just win today; she convinced both me and the prosecutor that her client was innocent. We're fortunate that we didn't send an innocent man to prison for the rest of his life."

CHAPTER TWENTY-FOUR

DETECTIVE BRAD OSBORN WAS SITTING at his desk, deep in thought, when his partner came in, glanced at him, and said, "What's eating you, Brad? Did Adriana dump you now that the case is over?"

Brad looked up. "Not hardly. We're getting along great. She's amazing," he said. "But I have to miss a date that we had set for tomorrow night. I was going to ask her to marry me."

"Brad, don't put something like that off," Mike said sternly.

"But I have to. Something's come up."

"Believe me, that doesn't seem like a good idea." Detective Silverman shook his head.

"It's not, and I hate the thought, but I think I have to," Brad said with a frown. "I just got a crazy phone call."

"We get lots of those. Why is that bothering you, and why should it make you break a date with someone you obviously care for deeply and want to marry? Don't be a fool, man. If you let that girl get away because of some crazy phone call, you are an idiot."

"She loves me, and hopefully she'll forgive me. But this is critical. You see, it has to do with who the call was from and what it was about. I need to go talk to the sergeant," Brad said.

"Okay, tell me about it first, Brad. After all, we are both partners and friends."

"You're right," Brad said, and he told him. Then together, they told the sergeant. Mike saw why Brad felt the way he did.

With a heavy heart, Brad postponed the important, life-changing date with the girl he had come to love.

***

After a long, hot drive in his old Buick, one with no air conditioning, Jerzy Grabowski finally reached his home state. He grinned as he crossed the state line. It would be a long time before he made a fool's trip like the one he was just completing.

He entered a restaurant in Atlantic City about eight that evening. He was meeting a man there that he hadn't seen in many weeks. He had mixed emotions about the meeting. He would sooner have avoided it. His summer had not exactly been an enjoyable or a profitable one. But he'd learned some things the past few weeks. He wasn't the same man he'd been before being framed for murder.

He was shown to a table. He sat down and looked at his watch. He was a little early. The other man would probably be late—he wasn't exactly known for his punctuality. The other man had arranged the meeting with Jerzy on his way back across the country. Maybe he would be stood up. That thought made him break out in a sweat, and he pulled a handkerchief out and wiped his face and his bald head.

As he stuffed the handkerchief back in his pocket he spotted the man he was waiting for. He was tall and thin with gray eyes, short black hair, and very long fingers. Jerzy stood nervously as Max Barclay approached. "Hey, old friend," the tall, thin man said with a grin. "It's been a long time."

"Longer for me than for you, I daresay," Jerzy said.

"Hey, don't look so glum. It all worked out pretty well," Max said easily as he took a seat opposite of Jerzy.

"I almost went to prison for something you did," Jerzy said, trembling slightly.

"That couldn't be helped. Valentino thought it best. After all, I was more important to him than you."

"I guessed that. I thought all you were going to do was steal a file," Jerzy said. "Nobody said anything about killing anybody. You didn't even tell me you had."

"Couldn't be helped. The guy proved to be a problem."

"You got paid, but I didn't," Jerzy said.

"Not my fault. Something happened to Valentino. He's vanished. No one seems to know what happened to him."

"Somebody owes me."

"All you were to do was drive me to the neighborhood and then drive me away," Max said with a chuckle. "That ain't worth much."

"Sitting in jail for nearly eight weeks is. I think you owe me. I know you got paid well."

"Not for that deal, I didn't," Max said. Then he grinned. "But I got paid well for taking care of Earnest Pyatt."

"You killed Earnest, too?" Jerzy asked, nervously taking his glasses off and putting them back on again.

"Yep," he said. "Made Valentino happy, that one did. Earnest turned on him and was working for Mancheski."

"That's crazy. Nobody turns on Valentino," Jerzy said.

"So Pyatt learned," Max said with a chuckle. A waiter finally showed up. They gave him their order, and after he was out of earshot, Max said, "I suppose I could give you a little something for your trouble although, with Valentino gone, I gotta find someone else to work for. And that's not very easy."

"Who else did you kill?"

"Nobody," Max said.

"But you tried," Jerzy argued, looking about nervously. "And the girl you were going to kill just happens to be the sweetest person I've ever met."

"Are you nuts, old friend?" Max asked as Jerzy again pulled out his handkerchief. It was so saturated that it did little more than spread the sweat around his head. "I wouldn't kill a girl."

"But you would kill a cop," Jerzy said, looking around again.

Max suddenly grew sober. His face grew red. "Don't be a fool," he said with clenched fists. "I never killed no cop."

"But you tried," Jerzy said.

"Who told you that?" Max asked.

"No one told him that. He figured it out," a voice from behind Max said.

The tall, thin man jumped to his feet, and his hand went inside his jacket. But that was as far as it got before Detective Brad Osborn tackled him and another officer slapped a pair of cuffs on his wrists.

"You are under arrest for the murders of Garrick Lenhardt and Earnest Pyatt and for the attempted murder of myself and Adriana Chambers," Brad said darkly as he and the New Jersey officer jerked Max to his feet.

"I didn't do anything," the hit man protested.

"That's not what you just told Jerzy," Brad said. Then he turned to Jerzy. "You did well, Jerzy. You can give me that mike now."

Jerzy opened his shirt, and Brad helped him remove the tape that held a small microphone in place. The tall, thin man lost every bit of color in his face. He also lost the pistol from beneath his coat. "I expect this will match the bullets I took out of my bulletproof vest and Earnest Pyatt's body," Brad said as he dropped it into an evidence bag.

EPILOGUE

SOMETIMES IT'S A LONG ROAD back when someone stumbles in life. But if one is persistent, the road can be traversed. Carson Chambers was on that long road. He prayed that someday he would find the end of it and that when he did, Krista would be waiting there.

Jerzy Grabowski was also working his way back onto the road of his life. He had disappointed Adriana, but she had forgiven him when she saw that the change she had helped make was sincere. He assisted Ross Harris in convicting Max Barclay of murder. For his assistance, and with the weeks he'd spent in jail on false charges, he was given no more jail time for the crime of assisting Max in committing burglary. He was even allowed to return to New Jersey, where he was to serve out his probation.

Valentino Lombardi, as far as anyone could tell, had come to the end of his road. And it was assumed that it was not a happy ending. Gabriel Mancheski lived for a while, but his road also came to an abrupt end a few weeks after his stroke. His road did not include a trial. He never came out of his coma before his death.

Drew Parker gave up on the road back to the girl he had jilted. He'd been forced to find an alternate road to travel on.

Brad Osborn, on the other hand, didn't have to start over again. He forged ahead on the road that led to marriage to the woman of his dreams. And despite a short delay in putting a ring on her finger, she was ecstatic when he got back from New Jersey and offered it to her.

ABOUT THE AUTHOR

CLAIR M. POULSON RETIRED AFTER twenty years in law enforcement. During his career he served in the US Army Military Police, the Utah Highway Patrol, and the Duchesne County Sheriff's Department, where he was first a deputy and then the county sheriff. He currently serves as a justice court judge for Duchesne County, a position he has held for over twenty years. His more than forty years working in the criminal justice system has provided a wealth of material from which he draws in writing his books.

Clair has served on numerous boards and committees over the years. Among them are the Utah Judicial Council, an FBI advisory board, the Peace Officers Standards and Training Council, the Utah Justice Court Board of Judges, president of the Utah Sheriff's Association, and the Utah Commission on Criminal and Juvenile Justice.

Other interests include activity in the LDS Church, assisting his oldest son in operating their grocery store, ranching with his oldest son and other family members, growing hay and pastures, and raising horses, cattle, llamas, goats, and fallow deer.

Clair and his wife, Ruth, live in Duchesne and are the parents of five married children. They have twenty-five grandchildren and one great-granddaughter.

If you would like to contact Clair, you may do so by going to his website at *clairmpoulson.com*.